BENEDICT BROWN

A CORPSE AT A SCHOOL REUNION

Copyright

This is a work of fiction. Names, characters, places, and incidents are either the product of the author's imagination or are used fictitiously. Any resemblance to actual persons, living or dead, events, or locales is entirely coincidental.

Copyright © 2023 by Benedict Brown

All rights reserved. No part of this book may be reproduced or used in any manner without written permission of the copyright owner except for the use of quotations in a book review.

First edition May 2023

Cover design by **info@amapopico.com**

To my wife Marion,
my children Amelie and Osian,
and my accomplice Lucy.

Reader's Note

I try to write my books in such a way that anyone can dip into the series and enjoy a twisty mystery filled with fun and humour. That is still true with this book, but let's be honest, this is the ninth novel out of ten, and I imagine that reading it first would be like watching the penultimate Star Wars film before seeing any of the others. You'll still enjoy all the quirky characters and get the main plot, but I've no doubt that you'll find yourself asking, "Wait, what's an Ewok?" at some point before the end.

Though it offers a spoiler-free, self-contained mystery to thrill and delight you, this book has a lot (too many?) call-back jokes and references to the rest of the series. But if you absolutely love books about high school reunions and think this is just your cup of tea, then go for it.

Oh, and by the way, no, there are no Ewoks in this book.

Chapter One

"Our little girl is all grown up." Mum was in a state of wide-eyed shock.

"I never thought this day would come." Dad was just as bad, and my stepfather could do nothing but stand looking dazed.

Practically everyone I know was squashed into the front porch of my childhood home. There were several suspects from the past cases of my surprisingly successful detective agency, an old schoolfriend and even a distant cousin or two. Stranger still was the fact that they were staring at me as though I was supposed to say something inspiring.

My ex-boyfriend Danny had no words for me. He held his hands out, sized up my outfit for some reason, then pulled me in for an excessively long hug. If I hadn't already been feeling awkward, this certainly did the trick.

"I just... If only... I can't believe you're actually..." This was as much as my best friend Ramesh managed before the tears came. Our favourite millionaire put an arm around his shoulder to comfort him.

"There, there, buddy." Dean spoke as though his words held some profound yet unfathomable meaning. "There, there."

I felt it was time that someone put a stop to all the moping. "I'm only moving house, you know. Not dying."

"Yes, but it's been a long time coming, Izzy," a voice from the back of the group called. From the hesitant tone, I was fairly certain that it was my primary school teacher who I hadn't seen since I was eleven years old. "Such an event doesn't come around every day." I suppose this went some way to explaining why my mother had invited so many people to our house to mark the occasion.

The time to depart had finally arrived. Just like everything else these days, I would have to be a grown-up about it. After all, I had a real grown-up business now, not to mention a mortgage with my name on. I'd even had a grown-up haircut from a fancy salon – instead of just asking Mum to hack away with a pair of kitchen scissors when I couldn't see past my fringe anymore.

You're Izzy Palmer, you're thirty-two years old, and you're a private detective. You've got your life under control!

This had been my mantra for months now but, at some point, my brain had begun to repeat it in a particularly sarcastic tone.

I took a deep breath and picked up the last box of my possessions from the garden wall. With a heartfelt wave to my cheerleaders, I opened the door to my car. Yep, that's right. *I* have a car. And not only that, I have a driving licence to go with it as (I don't know if I've mentioned this) I am a grown-up!

I'm so mature, in fact, that I didn't betray the emotion that was running through me as I took one last look at the house that I'd lived in for the past three decades. My loved ones spilled out of the porch to see me off and, because I'm only human, there was a lump in my throat as I got into the driver's seat of Mum's old yellow Corsa. Ramesh rushed forward, but the car was already moving. He ran alongside me, wailing, until the pace was too much, and he fell to his knees in sorrow.

So began the journey to my new house, three doors down on the other side of the road.

When I stopped the car, I could hear Ramesh beating the pavement in despair with his fists. "It came too soon!" he lamented. "I thought I was ready, but this day came too soon."

I waited for him to calm down before calling over. "I could do with a hand unpacking if you're interested?"

He looked up, shrugged and crossed the road.

"We'll join you too, Izzy?" Mum hollered from number thirty-four. "Have you got any tea bags?"

"Of course she's got tea bags, Rosemarie." My stepfather was often the first to defend me. He shook his head in disapproval at his wife's patronising question. "She is a grown-up."

I waited until he looked away before gesturing to my mother that, no, I didn't have any tea bags.

Rather than hanging around to organise the unpacking, I pulled out my keys and, with no little excitement, scampered up the garden path to my very own house. It was a tiny, mid-terrace box with a pebbledash façade and a miniature front garden that had more weeds than blades of grass, but it was mine. I was finally a homeowner, and I can't tell you how excited that made me.

As I unlocked the door, I felt like one of the Pevensie children stepping into Narnia. I'd already been inside several times, but that was when the old owners lived there, and it was still their house. Having navigated the narrow hall, I noticed all sorts of things that I hadn't seen before. There was a moulded dado rail that led visitors along the entrance towards the lounge. Taking that turn off the corridor, I realised that the mantlepiece above the bricked-in chimney had curly ends, like on a posh bath. Through the front window, I could see all the way to the school on the other side of the road and, on the ceiling, there was a truly massive crack in the plaster that I should have spotted before committing myself to a lifetime of debt to pay for the place.

So, no. Not everything was perfect, but that didn't matter because I finally had a sanctuary from the outside world; I had a house of my own! This was the building where I would grow old and, who knows, maybe I'd even find someone special to share the place.

My quiet introspection didn't last long as my ex-ex-boyfriend's chatty Welsh aunt had arrived. She was babbling away to Detective Inspector Irons from the Croydon branch of the Metropolitan Police about the secret to baking a good scone. Ramesh's uncle had brought a stereo with him to, in his words, "crank out the Abba", and, perhaps inevitably, Ramesh himself soon broke into a singalong of 'Waterloo', before my mother – the star of stage and… well, other stages – realised she was being outshone and added a lilting harmony to his efforts.

Before I could break the bad news that I didn't have any biscuits to go with the tea I also didn't have, Dean had opened a bottle of champagne to christen my new abode. All of a sudden, we had a party on our hands. It was eleven o'clock on a Wednesday morning, and this certainly didn't fit with my plans to be a responsible grown-up. The cheery invaders would not be dissuaded, though, and who was I to spoil their fun?

I doubt I need to go into the details of the two-hour conga line that followed the popping of corks, or what Marjorie from number thirty-two got up to in the cupboard under the stairs with Albert from number twenty-seven. What I can say is that, by half-past one, when those partiers who were still capable of walking had wandered off, my new house was well and truly warmed.

Sitting on the musty sofa that had come with the place, I looked lovingly at the destruction all around me. All three of my most local parents were nursing headaches. My ex had fallen asleep with his head in the stone-cold fireplace, and Ramesh was still working his way through Abba's back catalogue. It made me glad I'd stuck to hot chocolate.

Not including my rather large mystery library, which would finally be honoured with a permanent home, the grand sum of my earthly possessions amounted to seven large cardboard boxes filled with clothes I didn't like, every school project that I couldn't bring myself to throw away and a small selection of ceramic pigs. I had already picked out a spot in the back lounge to display the books, whereas the clothes were less important, and so I'd probably dump them in one of my – count them! – *two* spare rooms.

That's right! I was the owner of a three-bedroom house!

Incredible!

"Izzy!" My mother suddenly opened her eyes like the supposedly dead monster at the end of a horror film. "In all the chaos of this morning, I forgot to tell you that a letter came." She checked her trouser pockets and, on finding nothing there, reached inside her towering beehive hairdo. "Here we are. It's handwritten, so I thought it might be important."

She just about had the composure to extend her fingers a few inches in my direction to hold out the red envelope, and so I got up from my seat to retrieve it. The address was written in a jaunty, teenage fashion and had a little star over the letter i. It looked rather like an invitation to a children's party, but something about it gave me a queasy feeling.

Izzy Palmer,
31 Hawes Lane
West Wickham

As I tore the gummed flap open, the handwriting brought back memories from over a decade earlier.

Hi Izzy!

I'm writing to let you know that I'm organising a West Wickham High class of 2008 reunion. This year marks the fifteenth anniversary of the end of that formative stage in our lives, and I can't wait to get the old gang back together.

I've secured special permission from our headmistress, Mrs Davies. (Can you believe it? She's still going strong!) And there will be music, dancing, and limited, non-alcoholic refreshments in the school hall that hosted so many happy events during our time there.

I hope you can make it on the 13th of April to party the night away like it's 2008 all over again.

Yours ever so sincerely,
Former school president,
Verity Gresham

The letter dropped from my fingers to the beige carpet beneath my feet. My mother had fallen asleep again, so there was no one conscious to witness the chilling moment – except for Ramesh, but he was busy singing 'Super Trouper' into a hairbrush.

Chapter Two

Perhaps I should explain why I was trying to be more mature. I'd spent my carefree twenties devouring libraries' worth of classic mysteries, drinking hot chocolate by the bucketful and occasionally – though not so much recently – writing the odd poem about life and stuff. But the world was changing around me. But Mum was now a beloved minor celebrity. Ramesh had recently got married, and even former flying doctor Danny had taken a regular job in a Croydon hospital. It was clear that I couldn't cling onto my responsibility-free youth for ever.

And then. in a dramatic turn of events that no one saw coming, I'd become rather successful. The detective agency that I'd opened, with the definite assumption it would soon fail, had surpassed my expectations. In fact, over the past nine months, it had gone from strength to strength and, although sometimes in business success comes from unusual places, I knew exactly why this time. It wasn't the case of the murdered film star that I'd solved on the live television broadcast of Princess Penelope's wedding that propelled me to better things, or the time I unpicked a fiendishly difficult locked room mystery. It wasn't the ancient cold case serial killer I'd tracked down, either, or the billionaire whose murderer I'd brought to justice.

No, it was the story of an old lady in High Barnet who had sent twenty-six letters asking me to find her missing squirrel before I finally gave in and did just that. Although the only direct payment I had received was a rather-too-hard fruit cake, it had turned out to be my most lucrative case to date.

With a little help from my assistant/P.R. manager Ramesh, the press had got wind of the feel-good tale, and the rest is history. I'd been asked in by the Metropolitan Police to work on various tricky cases with hefty fees, swapped pet detection for some juicy jobs working for the elite of British society and finally taken the time to tidy up my office, which, let's be honest, was a disgusting pigsty.

"Wait a second," Ramesh said to interrupt my thoughts (and that unnecessarily long information dump) on the morning after I'd moved. "I have no memory of you ever mentioning someone by the name of Verity Gresham. You spend half your life complaining about the people you went to school with."

"Her name was Flint back then. Verity Flint was–"

"The sister of your first boyfriend Gary!" Sitting at his desk in the corner of our now neat office, his voice became squeaky. "You told everyone in school that he had an embarrassingly tiny–"

"That's the one." I'm not a prude. I just act like one. "And now she's tracked me down."

He sashayed over to the middle of the office to crack the case before we had anything to investigate. "So what you're saying is that you think this girl is out for revenge for the wicked deeds you committed in high school, and that she has devised an elaborate plan to get you back to the site of her brother's greatest indignity?"

"Hey, that's not fair. I'm not the villain. Gary Flint told everyone that I dressed like a cross between a Pizza Hut waitress and a Victorian gentleman."

Ramesh looked unconvinced that this was enough of a reason to cast aspersions on a young man's… manhood.

"He stood me up for the end-of-year disco," I tried again and, though I could tell it wasn't working, I gave it another shot. "He told Martin Thompson that I kissed like a giraffe, which isn't even a very good insult because–" I interrupted myself this time. "Oh my goodness, I'm a monster."

Ramesh came to comfort me. "It was a long time ago, Izzy. We all did things we regret when we were kids. I once forced my father to drive me all the way to Scotland for a Hanson concert. And, worst of all, it wasn't even their MMMBop tour." He paused to let the ramifications of this statement sink in. "It was the one after that."

His words bounced off me, as I was busy accumulating evidence of what a terrible person I was. "I've always thought of myself as a victim, but I printed out a picture of a tiny appendage from the internet and told every girl in school it was Gary's. I could have scarred him for life. His sister is plotting to humiliate me, and I don't deserve any better."

"Is that really what you think of me, Izzy?" A soft voice came poking through the door.

It must have been a strange scene to walk in on. I was pulling out clumps of my hair and Ramesh had got distracted and was doing some sort of line dancing step. He was prone to wearing elaborate outfits, and I hadn't even thought to ask why he was dressed as a cowboy with Day-Glo orange chaps. Having found myself embroiled in such conversations ten times too often, I'd learnt not to start them.

"Verity." I jumped to my feet as though me sitting down was the real issue here.

The busybody school president hadn't changed much in the fifteen years since we'd left West Wickham High. Dressed in what I can only describe as a full-tweed dress, she had high cheekbones and even higher eyebrows that were pointed at diagonals as she attempted to process what she'd just heard. For a moment, I thought she might pull a pistol on me or perhaps chuck a ninja star across the room. From my memory of her, she was just that kind of person.

"I can't say I blame you." Her whole being seemed to relax, and she walked closer with a smile on her face. "I certainly never did anything to win your good opinion when we were at school. I suppose that's why I'm so eager to get everyone together for this reunion."

The best retort I could come up with was "Urrrrrrrrrr?"

"Oh, Isobel…" She bustled forward to take a seat in front of my desk without being asked, then unleashed an unstoppable stream of verbiage in my direction. "It doesn't surprise me that you thought me a rotter when we were at school. I'm sure that I was the last person you would have expected to go through a voyage of self-discovery in a Peruvian rainforest and return to Britain with a clear sense of my personal failings, but that's exactly what happened. I divorced my husband, changed my job and decided to revisit my past."

She had an unusually posh voice for someone who grew up in the centre of Croydon, and I struggled to make sense of anything she'd just told me.

"Allow me to introduce myself." My full-time assistant, Ramesh, sat down rather coquettishly on the desk in front of her. For a moment, I was worried he might cross and uncross his legs, Sharon Stone style, to show off his chaps. "I'm Izzy's secret–"

"No, you're not." I had to butt in before he could say anything ridiculous… well, more ridiculous than normal. "But you were about to make a pot of tea."

He looked sullen for a moment, then pulled his Stetson over his eyes and moseyed off to the kitchenette in reception.

"You'll have to excuse my assistant." I couldn't think of an actual reason why, so I went with, "He was born with a smaller brain than most people."

"How terrible." She clearly hadn't caught the sarcasm in my voice. "That was so good of you to find him a job here."

"I agree entirely. Now, what can I do for you, Verity? Do you suspect one of your neighbours of being a murderer? Or perhaps you've uncovered a criminal drug ring operating out of Bromley." I thought this would sound ridiculous, but quickly remembered a recent trip to that salubrious shopping town where I'd seen a ragged-looking businessman fighting off two stray rottweilers for a cold frankfurter sausage. South East London had really gone downhill recently.

She peered at me over her gold-rimmed glasses, as though trying to decide whether I was sane. I was used to such reactions and didn't take it personally.

"I'm here today because I wanted to make certain that you got your invitation to the reunion. I wasn't sure that you were still living at the same address."

I laughed a little maniacally in response. "With my parents, you mean? Oh, goodness me, no. I'm not some sad-sack who never left home."

"That's right." Ramesh shouted over the sound of the boiling kettle. "She just bought a place three doors down from her folks."

"I got the invitation." I had stopped laughing by now. "You're very kind to check up on me, though. Were you in the area?"

She folded her arms across her chest and narrowed her eyes. "Not at all. I can't stand London. I came from Coventry specially to see you."

"From Coventry? That's a two-hour drive."

"Five on the train... on a bad day." She shrugged off this inconvenience and launched another ton of words at me. "But you see, Isobel, I need a special guest for the reunion. To be perfectly honest, the people from our year at school haven't exactly changed the world. There are plenty of middle-managers, personal assistants and accountants, but I need a star name so that everyone is eager to come.

After that business with the squirrel, you're all anyone talks about."

She sat without blinking for a few moments, as though this was a perfectly normal request to put to someone. I was struggling to understand her motivation, but perhaps that had always been the case. At school, she'd been a rare combination of brainy and popular, cruel but occasionally generous. I took in her manifestation in my office and couldn't work out whether she was Cruella de Vil or a Dalmatian pup.

"Media appearances are my department," Ramesh announced as he bustled in with a tray. "We can talk fees in reception, if you wish. But you should know that Izzy Palmer does not come cheap... Except that one time when we thought a client wanted her to open a new building, and it turned out he was locked out of his house." He poured out two mugs of tea before realising I was glaring at him to be quiet.

"Ramesh, Verity isn't here to book me for a public appearance. She wants me to go to our school reunion." I looked at our guest to check this was true, and she replied with one quick nod. "However, I'm sorry to say that I've got no intention of going back to West Wickham High. When I walked off the grounds for good, it was one of the happiest days in my life. There are medieval prisons I would prefer to spend an evening in, and hearing its name makes my skin crawl."

"I suppose I've had a wasted journey then." She rose to show off her imperious bearing. "But this isn't the end, Izzy Palmer. I will see you at school on the thirteenth of April. I promise you that."

I wasn't some impressionable teenager anymore, and I wouldn't be spoken to in such a manner. "I mean it, Verity. The six years I spent at that school were the worst, and I hope it burns down before I have to see it again."

There was an awkward hush as I awaited Verity's response. She stood fixed to the spot, looking affronted for a moment but said nothing.

In the end, it was Ramesh who would break the silence. "Great. So I'll put it down in the diary as a maybe."

Chapter Three

"I thought we'd decided that *you* were the monster, not your bullies at school."

I could barely hear Ramesh over the sound of deafening music. Nightclubs are categorically not my sort of place. For one thing, they don't have bookshelves. For five more things, they are full of slimy men (and women for that matter). They never serve hot chocolate – I know, as I've asked. They are too warm. They smell terrible, and the music seems to have been programmed by a highly inventive torturer in an attempt to make your ears bleed. So, as I was saying, nightclubs really aren't for me.

"I may not have been perfect – I'm a big enough person to accept that – but, from the moment I hit puberty, my classmates made me feel like a freak."

"Come on, Izzy. School wasn't that bad. I was there too, remember." Shandy, my one remaining schoolfriend, was twerking against Ra as she spoke. We'd fallen out of touch after I left West Wickham High but reconnected at a child's birthday party where an old bully of mine was brutally murdered. I should probably mention that I was not in any way responsible for his death.

"It was terrible. Verity and her gang of stuck-up clones were the ones who popularised my adorable nickname. Being called 'The Freak' somehow followed me through university and into my first job."

Shandy stopped grinding her hips against our friend's leg and considered the point. "Perhaps you're right, but we've all grown up a lot since then. I'm sure it will be different this time."

In order to develop a more assertive personality, I had started going to places that the old Izzy would have found quite terrifying. Nightclubs were close to the top of that list and so, over the last couple of months, I'd assembled a girl squad. There was lovely Shandy, who had been one of the two people at school that didn't treat me like a discarded experiment from The Island of Dr Moreau. Princess Penelope often came out with us (but would inevitably spend the night taking selfies with an endless queue of fans). D.I. Irons was a surprisingly good dancer for someone incapable of expressing human emotion, and then there was Ramesh. We'd invited his wife once, but she was even less at home in The Blue Orchid Bar than I was.

"Come and dance," he yelled before disappearing into the crowd and popping up on a nearby go-go platform.

Don't do it, Izzy! my brain demanded. *In fact, perhaps we should go home and hide under the bed. This place was not built for people like us.*

"Just drink your strawberry-ice-cream martini and stop worrying." The august police inspector waved both her arms to the throbbing beat. "Your problem, young lady, is that you overthink everything. Just try to have fun." I don't know where she got off calling me "young lady". She was only somewhere between five and thirty years older than me – she had one of those faces that was very hard to judge.

"I am *trying* to have fun." Like a nervous toddler with a bottle of milk, I sucked all the harder on my straw.

Just because I was making an effort to be more grown up, that didn't mean I had to like everything about it. In fact, there were some major advantages to being immature. For one thing, I hadn't realised how much work it was to prepare my own meals three times a day. I felt like a slave to the kitchen/nearby café. Every night since I'd moved, I'd been tempted to pop over the road to enjoy my stepdad's wondrous cuisine, and, every night, I'd had to make do with microwave lasagne and cup-a-paella.

"Phwoar, you're alright." A short, hairy guy who looked like the impossible lovechild of Burt Reynolds and Barry Manilow danced towards me with a grin on his face. "I'm Colin!"

He seemed to think that his name was a major selling point and performed a spin on the spot to wow me with his moves. In reply, I hugged the wall a little tighter and wished that my friends would notice my predicament.

"Colin Goode," he clarified. "Goode by name, good in—" I interrupted him then as he was making a thrusting motion which could only lead to worse things.

"Izzy Palmer." Revealing my name was a small price to pay if it meant that I didn't have to hear the end of that sentence. "I'm a detective."

He took a step backwards and looked impressed. "Don't put me in handcuffs, ma'am." He followed this with an inevitable wiggle of his eyebrows. "Unless you really want to."

"I'm not that kind of—" It wasn't worth the effort to explain. "If you don't mind, I was enjoying a conversation with my friends."

"I don't mind at all, love." He not so subtly touched my arm. "Do people ever tell you that you look like a supermodel? An excessively tall supermodel, but less fancy."

"Yes, they do, actually. On a daily basis." I was surprised at how easily I found a retort. Sadly, he didn't get the message.

"How about I buy you a drink and we go somewhere quiet to *talk*?" His whole face was a great big leer that made my major organs want to jump from my mouth and go sprinting from the club (and preferably the country, to be on the safe side).

"Why don't you leave this poor girl alone and check with your parole officer whether you're allowed within twenty yards of any women?" I hadn't started referring to myself in the third person. A tall guy with dark curly hair and West Indian features appeared at just the right moment.

Colin Goode wasn't intimidated. "Eh, mate! I was here first. Hop along."

My knight out of shining armour would do nothing of the sort and placed himself between the two of us. "Get lost, you little worm. It's clear that she doesn't want anything to do with you, so go and annoy someone else."

Goode looked up at his challenger but, in response, could only summon a wheeze and a few vowels. "I... Oh... Eeeee..." He took one last look at me and scrunched up his nose as though to say *she's not worth it anyway,* before dancing off across the club.

I turned to my new favourite person, with perhaps the tiniest fear in my heart that he would be just as bad as the man in the queue before him.

"Sorry about that," he said before I could fail to construct a coherent sentence. "I can't stand slimy idiots like him. That's why I never come to clubs."

I like this guy! Let's marry him!

"I'm used to it," I shouted over the sound of an endless electronic drumbeat. "Blokes like Colin Goode go for the first woman they spy. As I'm the tallest one here, I attract his sort like a lighthouse."

The calm, well-dressed man who, as far as I could see, had no swastika tattoos and possessed a full set of teeth, considered my words. "I take your point, but that's not a very good metaphor. Lighthouses steer boats away from rocks, just as often as they attract them to a safe harbour."

I don't know if it was the deepness of his sparkling brown eyes, or the fact they were at almost exactly the same height as my own, but I was suddenly tongue-tied. "I suppose you're right. But in my defence, I'm not very good at... speaking."

You silver-tongued devil, Izzy. He'll be putty in our hands after a line like that.

I thought he might reply with a cheesy quip. If I was a tacky guy who went up to girls in clubs, I'd have gone with *how about I stop you talking with a kiss?* But he just stood there, looking pensive. There was a seriousness to him that I found rather appealing. He wasn't my usual type – he'd completed a whole minute's conversation without insulting me, for one thing – but, in the gloom of the dank nightclub, I couldn't deny that he was rather yummy.

"My name's Izzy."

"I know." He stopped then, and I was afraid that he would turn out to be a very unambitious stalker, or perhaps my long-lost brother – which obviously made no sense as we looked nothing alike, and my parents had never mentioned a secret child born at approximately the same time as me. Somehow, the truth was even worse. "I'm Gary Flint. We were at school together."

Have you ever had one of those moments when you wished that a bomb would go off to put you out of your misery? Not a really big bomb, just a little baby one with a unipersonal blast radius. Sadly, there were no missile strikes on me that day, and I stood gawping at the first boy I'd ever kissed.

"Gary Flint?" I attempted to say, but instead it came out as, "Gufferlin?"

He apparently didn't think this required a response but did look a little worried about me. It had been fifteen years since I'd last seen him, so it was no wonder I didn't immediately recognise the boy I'd spent much of my high-school career falling in and out of love with.

"What a coincidence."

He shook his head. "It's not a coincidence, Izzy. I came here to talk to you."

It was at this moment that Shandy, our fellow West Wickham High alum, danced past at the front of a conga line – yes, conga lines seem to happen surprisingly often around me for some reason. "Hi, Gary. What a coincidence it is to see you here."

"Not a coincidence," I corrected her. "He came to find me."

"Oh." Usually cheery Shandy attempted to hide her discomfort. "That's really very normal and not in the slightest bit creepy." Luckily for her, the conga line sped up, and she was propelled forward across the dance floor.

"Why are you here, Gary?" I asked once the uncomfortable break in our conversation had lasted too long. "If you're planning on murdering me and rifling through my house for valuables, I hope you know a good antique book dealer who doesn't ask too many questions."

In his typical thoughtful manner, Gary attempted to set my mind at ease. "My sister made me come."

"Oh, great," I replied. "But how did you know where to find me in the first place?"

"Your mate Lady Penelope has been livestreaming the whole evening. She talked about the salt-of-the-earth, practically working-class friends she was seeing tonight, and my sister figured out that was you."

"So you came all this way to see me?" I was a little flattered.

"I live two minutes away."

I was less flattered. "Fine, go back to your explanation. Why did your sister want you to talk to me? And, as a follow-up question, are you planning to murder me and make a suit out of my skin?"

He sighed a weary sigh and un-shrugged his shoulders. "In reverse order, no, I'm not, and she wanted me to come because she's obsessed with you being at the reunion."

Careful, Izzy. This is a honey trap! Verity is dangling her sexy brother in front of you as bait. Run away! Run away while we still can.

I had another question for him. "And why do you think you'll be able to convince me when she couldn't?"

He looked as though he might fall asleep just then. He closed his eyes, dropped his head and released a quiet yawn. "Because she thinks that you'll think that I don't think you should come." It took me a few moments, but I made almost total sense of this sentence. "She reckons you feel guilty about the way you treated me at school."

Ever since I'd realised who I was talking to, I'd been doing my best to stay civil. "The way I treated you? You said I looked like Nelson's column with the figure to match. You stood me up at the end-of-school disco!"

He looked back up at me, and I finally realised that this whole experience was a chore for him. "Yeah, well you told everyone in the school I had a tiny—"

"Hey, Izzy!" Ramesh was dancing along at the back of the conga line, unable to latch on because of the two drinks in his hands in long glasses with even longer straws. "Have you tried the rocky road mojitos? They're something else!"

Gary was not put off by the interruption. "You gave me a complex about my body that years of therapy have done little to address."

Whoopsie!

"I am so sorry." I couldn't think what else to say. Until recently, I'd always considered myself a decent person. "We were just kids. I never meant to…"

Why did my friends only interrupt when I didn't need them to? I would have loved for D.I. Irons to stop by just then to discuss the inadequacies of the club's security protocols. Heck, I'd have been happy if Ramesh had pulled me on stage to pole dance.

You don't need Ramesh, Izzy. Just get up on that platform and unleash your inner stripper! The alcohol in my cocktail had clearly reached my brain.

"I'm genuinely sorry, Gary," I said before I could take the coward's way out and begin a poorly executed dance routine. "I really am. I thought that everything that went on between us was the usual back and forth of young love. I had no idea that I'd hurt you psychologically."

He began to giggle at this point, and I was even more confused than before. "You are too gullible, Izzy. I don't really have a therapist or body issues. I just wanted to see your face." He had a good laugh at my expense, put one hand on my shoulder and said, "I couldn't care less whether you come to the reunion, but it should be fun. Did you hear that Becky and Robert Mitchell got a divorce?" He became more reflexive again. "I always had a crush on her. Of course, she had nothing to do with me after you printed out that photo and passed it around school." His expression hardened once more. "See you around, Iz."

As I struggled to work out exactly what had just happened, he strode off through the crowd.

A voice carried across to me from the nearest platform. "Come and pole dance, Izzy!"

"Seriously, Ramesh? Where were you sixteen seconds ago when I needed your help?" I gave him a grumpy look and marched from the club. I was tired of loud music and sweaty walls. I was tired of grinding crotches and flashing lights that gave me an instant headache.

Clubs are rubbish, and so I went home to bed.

Chapter Four

I didn't sleep well that night.

I don't know whether it was the re-emergence of the twin ghosts from my childhood that had unsettled me, my run-in with the creep in the club or the mind games Gary Flint had played. Whatever the reason, I found myself waking up every hour, aware for the first time of the creepy noises in my new house. Every creaking beam woke me up, and I couldn't find a comfortable position to lie in. By four in the morning, I knew it was no good, and so I got up and went looking for my friends.

This may sound like an ambitious pursuit, but I knew exactly where they'd be. After we go out each night, we end up in 'Fernando's Caff' on Penge High Street. It's not that it's a nice place – in fact, the name alone is enough to put me off – but it was my mum's former hairdresser's lifelong ambition to own a twenty-four-hour café in his hometown, and I wanted to support him. After "Bu-Bu: La Musical" won every award going and sold out its extended run six months in advance, he finally had the money to make his dream a reality.

"I think you should go to the reunion, Iz," he told me as I waited for the others to arrive. It did not surprise me that he already knew the ins and outs of my dilemma. My mother operated a whisper network that would have put the KGB to shame.

"I think I'd like a double bacon bap with a bottle of ketchup on the side, please." I handed him the menu, and he waved it in my direction as though to say, *Good point, Izzy. That's a very good point.*

He wandered off to the kitchen just as Shandy, Danny, Dean… well, a whole bunch of my friends, in fact, thundered into the busy café. I spotted Lady Penelope outside too, but she was busy signing autographs, and D.I. Irons sat at a table on her own for some reason. She was either undercover or she had drunk too many Raspberry Ripple daiquiris.

"I told you Izzy would be here," Dean proclaimed with no small amount of smugness. I thought he might remind us of his impressive IQ then, but Ramesh was on hand to do it for him.

"You truly are a genius. Which is all the more reason we should work together to launch my sure-fire money-making invention; The Half Scarf." We waited to hear of this earth-shattering new idea. "A half scarf is half the length of most scarves, so it's the perfect accessory for when a regular scarf is too long. Best of all, though, you can buy two half scarves and combine them, for when one simply isn't long enough."

He raised his eyebrows and waited to hear what our richest ever friend thought of the proposal.

Dean Shipman from Bromley turned to me instead. "So, Izzy. I hear you deserted your friends in a huff this evening."

I admit that, out of context, this sounded bad. "Yes but, in my defence, at least I didn't jump out of a window." He did not look as though this was much of an argument and so I continued to fight my corner. "When I was a teenager, I was forever making dramatic exits by jumping from balconies and low windows. I thought everyone would be amazed but... well, they weren't. Tonight I merely walked out of a club, got on a tram, then a bus and then walked home from there. It's a far more grown-up method of escape, and I'm not the slightest bit embarrassed by my behaviour."

Shandy hadn't said anything until now and was happily hiccupping away to herself. "Hey, I remember that! You jumped from the first floor of the North Block at school when Mr Peters told you off for daydreaming."

"Yes, but... in my defence..." I began but couldn't think of anything to say.

My dearly beloved ex looked a little worried about me. "Izzy, isn't it possible that the kids at school didn't call you *Freak* because you were tall, but because you were really very odd?"

I buried my head in one arm on the tabletop and wished that I had a normal brain.

Oi! Who are you calling abnormal?

"Don't worry, Iz." Dean put one hand on my shoulder in sympathy. "I never had any friends when I was young and look at me now!"

Ramesh gave him a high-five, which I had expressly forbidden in my presence, but no one ever listens to me.

"Dean's right," he insisted. "Don't worry about silly things that happened in your childhood. You're bound to have suppressed all that shame and embarrassment by now. It's working away in your subconscious, and there's nothing you can do about it." Funnily enough, this did not make me feel any better. "I remember when I was at school and there were four girls who wanted to go out with me at the same time, plus a boy who offered to carry my bag every day."

I had to look at him then. "Sorry, why are you telling me this?"

He peered up absentmindedly at the white-tiled ceiling. "Ummm... I can't remember. Weren't we reminiscing about happier times?"

Fernando came to take their orders just as something occurred to me, and I fired a suspicious comment at Danny and Dean. "What are you boys doing here anyway? You weren't out with us tonight."

They looked to Ramesh as their spokesperson. "I was texting them in the club, and Danny came up with a solution to your problem."

The dreamy doctor hesitated before putting forward his grand plan. "We thought... or maybe it was just me... So, I thought that perhaps one of us could... pretend to be your husband."

"Nope!"

"Hear him out, Izzy." Dean was surprisingly keen on the idea.

"No, I will not. I'm perfectly happy on my own, and I don't need a man to complete me."

"You tell 'em, Iz!" Shandy was half asleep on her paper placemat but managed to mumble this much.

"It fixes everything," Ramesh put in. "If you turn up alone to your school reunion, you'll be too nervous and spend the next two weeks worrying about what everyone thinks of you. But if you go there as Izzy Palmer, the famous detective, with any one of us hunks on your arm, you'll go down in West Wickham High history!"

The three hunks...

Ha!

... stared at me hopefully.

"I've already told you; I'm not going. I don't care how many members of the Flint family ask me. They can send their grandparents as far as I care. I have no interest in suffering any further humiliation at that cursed institution."

They looked at one another, as though deciding who should commence the next wave of persuasion. It turned out that it was Dean's turn. "Yeah, but you always say that. You spend your life saying no to things that you eventually do."

"I do not."

"Yes, you do!" they said as one, and Shandy drunkenly echoed the comment.

"Fine, I do. But this time will be different."

No, it won't.

Oh, shut up, brain. I'm trying to win this argument and you're not helping.

"We've got your interests at heart, you know." Ramesh hit me with the full force of his puppy-dog eyes. "We know that brain of yours will be tied in knots wondering what Gary's real intentions were in coming to see you tonight. And we know that, by this time tomorrow, you'll have decided that you have to go to the reunion. You can't just leave a mystery unsolved, and so the best solution for everyone is that you take a sidekick for backup."

I scoffed at this. For one thing, my brain was busy singing the theme tune to 'Knight Rider', and I hadn't been paying attention, but I also objected to the idea that any one of them could be considered a real detective's assistant. "You're not my sidekicks. You're a small selection of the irritating people I have collected over the years."

Dean took this as a sign I was wavering. "Great! So which of us will it be? May I remind you that I have experience pretending to be your fiancé from the time you took me to your family party? Passing myself off as your husband shouldn't be too much of a stretch."

Danny took exception to this. "Hey, I dated you for real. Surely you'd prefer to pretend to be married to someone you've actually kissed? I'd do a better job than *Dean*." He shot our tetchy techy friend a contemptuous look.

"Say what you like, mate." Dean crossed his expensively tailored sleeves over one another and looked through the café window to the street beyond. "I think we all know who she'll choose."

"Me!" Ramesh wouldn't be outdone and threw his hat into the ring (or onto the table, at least). It was the Stetson he often wore to work. "She'll choose me. After all, there's a key characteristic that you're all forgetting. I'm the only one of us who's ever been married. It won't be difficult for me to play a husband, as I am one!"

"Who said I'm even ready for a pretend husband?" I thought

this was a salient point, until the words were out of my mouth, and I realised that I was talking just as much nonsense as any of them. "Perhaps I'm not looking to pretend settle down just yet. Perhaps I'm pretend playing the field!"

"Tell 'em, sistah!" Shandy's eyes were fully closed by now, but she managed to make this sororal exclamation of support sound quite heartfelt.

"Hey. I'm open-minded." Danny relaxed back into his seat to suggest just how chillaxed he was. "As the only one of your serious ex-boyfriends who is not currently incarcerated, I'm happy to pretend to be whatever takes your fancy. I'll be your pretend friend with benefits if that's what you want." He pouted seductively, and I realised that it was time to call a halt to this spiralling conversation of the absurd.

"No, no, and also no. When I go to the reunion, I'll be going alone." I thought about this for a moment, before realising that I would have at least one friend there. "Well, me and Shandy are going alone, and it'll be great."

I was hoping for a chat-show style whoop of approval from my old schoolfriend, but she had passed out entirely and was snoring away. And that is how my friends distracted me from the real issue so much that I ended up agreeing to go to the dreaded event without meaning to.

Chapter Five

They were right, of course. I was always going to change my mind and go to the reunion. My curiosity was too great for anything else. In fact, I'm pretty sure that's why reunions were invented in the first place. Who can resist the temptation to see all the bullies and bright stars of high school with beer bellies and triple chins?

Even more than that, I had to find out what damage I'd done to Gary Flint. I'd spent my life feeling hard done by for the series of horrors I'd endured at high school and not knowing the truth would have haunted me for the rest of my days.

I suppose that life itself is one big mystery. Each person is a puzzle, made up of a million moments that shape our character and behaviour for evermore. And if there's one time, more than any other, that moulds who we become in life, it's our adolescence. I'd long since realised that my time at West Wickham High was hugely formative. Kids there ragged me for being tall, knowing how to read, and possessing a brain. Their taunts and cruelty turned me into an outsider, but all of that also drove me to fulfil my greatest ambition when the opportunity arose.

I'm not going to thank a lot of monstrous teenagers for abusing me through my formative years, but perhaps I would never have made anything of myself if they'd ignored me. So, whether I'd treated Gary Flint unfairly or not, I know that I wasn't the only one to blame. I didn't just go to high school; I survived it. And, as there were no West Wickham Alumni support groups for me to attend, a reunion might be the next best thing.

I can also admit that it was gratifying to know that Verity had pursued me quite so eagerly. Was I really the most successful ex-pupil from our year? Becky Mitchell had been a yummy mummy Instagram sensation the last time I'd met her, and her husband was one of those people who did something with money.

They're called bankers, Izzy.

Right, yes, he was a high-level banker before their Instagram careers took off. Had I outshone the pair who had been voted West Wickham's cutest couple three years in a row?

At the back of my mind, there was a little voice telling me that it was all a trap and that the Flints really had organised the massive party in order to serve me an ever-so-cold dish of revenge. Even this possibility wouldn't dissuade me, though. I'd made up my mind and was determined to find out the truth.

Wouldn't you prefer to stay home and watch telly? Legally Blonde is on ITV3 tonight!

Legally Blonde is on ITV3 approximately twice a week. We're going to the reunion.

Of course, that was easier said than done. In many ways, that night was the culmination of who I was. My whole life had been building up to this point, and I had to get every detail right. I'm not normally the kind of person who worries about what clothes I wear, and most of my makeup is so old that I need a screwdriver to get it open, but I was determined to do all that I could to show my old demons from school that I wasn't such a freak after all.

Sadly, this meant resorting to something that I'd been avoiding for years.

"Makeover!" Ramesh screamed as I opened the door to him a few hours before the reunion. He was dressed in a baby blue tuxedo with a frilly shirt, which should have made me suspicious. It was no stranger than his normal outfits, though, so I thought nothing of it. "I've been waiting for this day for so long, Izzy. The closest I've come was when I bought your dress for my wedding. To be perfectly honest, a large part of my decision to get married was the chance to choose your outfit."

"I know, Ra. I know." I opened the door wider to let him in.

He held his hand to his chest and attempted to smile. It was clear that the emotion of the day was getting to him. "We've only got three hours, so we'd better be quick." It was at this moment I spotted the full-sized rolling suitcase, which, like a loyal hound, followed along behind him into the house.

I helped him carry it up to the spare bedroom where I'd dumped my boxes of possessions. "These are all my clothes. I didn't bother unpacking them yet as I've mainly been wearing pyjamas since I moved in. I wore them to work one day and, as you didn't realise, I figured I could get away with it." I pointed to my snowflake onesie, and he reeled in horror.

"Are you trying to poison me, Izzy Palmer? Is that what our friendship means to you? I never thought I would die surrounded by brushed cotton." He apprehensively approached the first box and poked it with the end of a well-manicured finger, as though checking to make sure it was dead.

"Aside from pyjamas, my clothes largely fall into two categories. There's workwear from our time at Porter & Porter and spangly stuff that my mother bought me, and I try never to look at." Emptying another of the boxes, I proved my point. I also found where I'd packed my copy of Agatha Christie's 'The Pale Horse', which I'd been reading before the move.

"It's like going through the possessions of a dead pensioner in an overly sexualised retirement home." He shook his head in dismay. "I've got my work cut out, but I think I can perform a magical transformation, just like in every teen movie from the nineties!"

Teen movies from the nineties are to Ramesh what whodunits are to me. I didn't begrudge him his moment but, as he unzipped the extra-large Lewis Vorrton suitcase, a wave of fear passed over me.

Izzy, if he goes anywhere near your hair with a pair of scissors, run to the hills!

We're in South London, brain. Not the Alps.

He delved headfirst into the case and, after thirty seconds of rumbling, raised one hand with a lipstick clutched triumphantly between his fingers. "Tell me, Isobel, how do you feel about the colour puschia?"

"I feel that it doesn't exist."

"They said that about varlet, and now look at us."

I had no idea what he was talking about, so I sat down on a chair in front of the wardrobe mirror and closed my eyes until it was all over. I'm not one for new-age concepts, but I must admit there was something freeing about the experience. All I could do was sit there and relinquish control. Perhaps I achieved Zen or mindfulness or something of the sort but, instead of worrying what was about to happen, my mind seemed to dance off through space.

Ramesh prattled away about shades of mascara and why his wife no longer allowed him to do her makeup, but I was on a higher plane. I didn't even think about the thugs and drama queens I was about to reconnect with at my school. I accepted what the universe had to offer and, when Ramesh had finished, I opened my eyes and said, "Bleedin' heck. Who's that?"

The girl in front of me was a real stunner. She had finely accentuated misty grey eyes and long lashes. Her skin was smooth and unblemished, her cheekbones pronounced but unaggressive and her smile was, dare I say it, really very pretty, thank you very much. I'd never looked so good.

"Ramesh Khatri, you're a miracle worker."

"Isobel Palmer, I know!" he emitted a cackling laugh and went to the bed where he'd picked out an outfit for me.

"No, not again. Please, not that!" Suddenly, I didn't feel so confident.

Sometime later, he gave me his arm, and we walked downstairs to wait for Shandy to pick me up. Though I really couldn't fault the "hair and makeup reimagining" that Ramesh had conducted, I felt less than a million dollars in sheer black tights, sparkly red shorts and a gold lamé top. I looked like a children's TV presenter who'd fallen into a vat of glitter. I don't think that people over six foot should be allowed to wear hot pants, and I cursed my luck for not leaving them behind in my old house. I have no doubt that my mother would have looked sensational in them, but sadly I'd inherited a genetic tendency towards gigantism from my father's side of the family and was resigned to the fact that all clothes made me look like a heron that a child had adopted as a pet.

"You look…" Ramesh began as we waited on the doorstep. "You look just… well, there really aren't words."

"Yes, there are. Tarty is one. Ridiculous is another. The deformed lovechild of Elizabeth Taylor and Arnold Schwarzenegger are a few more."

"Well, I think you look great."

I caught my reflection in the mirror by the door and couldn't help but disagree. "I've seen disco balls with less sparkle than me. I was trying to impress my old schoolmates, not offend their sensibilities."

Or blind them.

Damn, that would have been a better joke than mine.

"You're worrying about nothing. You look fierce, my dear friend.

No two-bit Tommy or dull-as-dishwater Dave is going to mess with you tonight."

"Yeah, but only because looking at me directly would cause blinding."

Ha! You're right. That was a good one.

Ramesh didn't reply but shook his head in wonder at his brilliant work.

"Actually, you know what?" I asked the mooning fool. "I'm not the slightest bit comfortable and feel like an idiot. I'm going back upstairs to get changed."

I dashed to the clothes mountain before he could complain. Rather than actually think about what I wanted to wear, I stuck my hand into the pile and came away with a black sequin-infested gown. It was almost as shiny as the hot pants, but at least it went down to my ankles. Paired with some sturdy leather boots, it made me felt quite confident.

"You look…" Apparently Ramesh hadn't recovered his breath by the time I got downstairs. "You look… much more like yourself. It's a good choice, Izzy."

He nodded contentedly, and it was at this moment that a stretch limousine pulled onto my road. A rather curvaceous woman with long curly hair was sticking up through the sunroof and waving ecstatically.

"Here we come!" Shandy bellowed. I should have examined her choice of subject pronoun, but I was too surprised to see my part-time chauffeur/full-time dad parking his limo in front of my house. "Climb aboard, Iz!"

"Hello, darling," Dad said on jumping from the vehicle. "I'll be your driver this evening. If you need to do any passionate necking with a young gentleman, feel free to put up the rear privacy screen."

My sweet, loveable daddy only knew the most antiquated terms for the rigours of modern existence. I should have been nice to the dear old teddy bear, but instead I acted like a teenager. "Urghhh! You're so embarrassing! I'm not going to kiss anyone tonight. I'm going all on my own because *sistahs* are doing it for themselves."

"That's right, Izzy!" Shandy ducked into the vehicle and returned with an open bottle of champagne to tip down her throat. "*Sistahs* are doing it for themselves!" She let out a whoop as I climbed into the limo.

"What are you doing here?" I said to Dean, Danny and, just entering through the far door, Ramesh.

"I'm Shandy's date!" Danny sounded quite proud.

"I can't believe it."

It was my supposed 'sistah' who inspired the most disappointment.

She looked guilty for approximately three seconds. "Sorry, Izzy, but my ex-husband will be there tonight. There's no way I'm going to turn up alone to our school reunion like a sad sack."

"But what about sisterhood and all the stuff you said the other week at Fernando's Caff?"

She at least had the decency to shrug and look unapologetic. "I don't know if you noticed, but I wasn't exactly sober that night. And besides, have you seen your ex-boyfriend? He's like a walking Ken doll! Tim is going to be so jealous."

In case I hadn't realised that he was handsome, Danny now pointed at himself and grinned. My only relief was that he didn't prove how muscly he was by striking a bodybuilder pose.

"What about you two?" I directed my ire at Tweedle Dumb and Tweedle Dean.

Dean could at least make eye contact. "Shandy has set me up with your old classmate, Lorna."

"Lorna Inglis? She was so quiet that she made it through the whole of Year Ten without speaking. Don't expect much in the way of conversation."

"Ah, don't be mean, Izzy." Shandy reprimanded me whilst also laughing. "Lorna might have been quiet at school… and on our course at university, for that matter, but she's really nice when you get to know her."

Dean clearly didn't have a problem with a quiet date. "To be honest, I'm not looking for love this evening. In fact, it was my girlfriend's idea that I should accompany one of your single friends. I think I've been getting under her feet recently."

Ramesh still wouldn't look at me but was humming a medley of Tina Turner anthems. I cleared my throat to get his attention, and he finally capitulated. "Fine, I'm coming because I didn't want to be left out."

"You didn't even go to school in London. You grew up in Watford."

"That's right." He grabbed a flute, and Shandy filled it with champagne. He looked far too cool, even in an ugly tuxedo. "I'm crashing your high school reunion!"

"Off we go, driver," Shandy yelled. "Time and tide and bad discos wait for no man."

Chapter Six

The good thing about spending my life surrounded by idiots is that there's rarely time to focus on my real issues. I was about to enter the lion's den – to jump headfirst into a frying pan of my own making. Yet, instead of worrying about the night ahead, I passed the short journey bickering with Dean about the correct pronunciation of *library*!

How difficult is to pronounce in the first place? It's only got three syllables.

Thank you! It's nice to know that one non-verbal entity agrees with me.

"I thought you were supposed to be a genius?" I barked.

"Oh, so now you're saying that only well-spoken people can be clever?" He sounded genuinely offended.

"No, I'm saying that…" It was at this point that I realised we were alone in the back of the limo.

"Would you like me to put up the privacy screen?" Dad asked with a tip of his chauffeur's hat.

"No, Dad," my fourteen-year-old self huffed again. "We're just leaving."

I scrambled from the car on all fours. It turns out that there is no graceful way for a six-foot-three woman in a prom gown to exit a limousine. To be honest, the car was so long we could have got in through the back door, left through the front and made it halfway there, but then I wasn't the one who had booked the most expensive method of transport available.

Stepping onto the pavement in front of my old school sent shivers through me. Though I'd never left my hometown, I'd intentionally avoided Croft Avenue since our last day of school. I can't say the building had changed very much. It was still a squat, bulky box of beige bricks that had been plonked on the residential road like a spaceship crushing whatever was in its landing zone. I'd always felt that the playground and football field looked like the aftereffects of a meteor crashing to Earth, and this impression had only strengthened over time.

A big banner on the front of the school read, "Welcome Back,

Class of 2008," and fairy lights had been strung along the path up to the entrance, but this did little to make it more welcoming. As I trundled behind my friends, I could only think of the time that Martin Thompson had told everyone that I was a man in drag, and half the kids in our year had believed him. I remembered hiding in the South Block toilets with my best friend Simon until half an hour after the bell had rung each day to make sure that no one was waiting to steal our bags or punch poor Simon in any number of painful places. So, it wasn't exactly a happy return to my alma mater, but I took a deep breath and adopted a fake smile.

Ramesh held back to thread his arm through mine. "You poor thing. This must be very trying for you."

"It is, but that doesn't mean I'm going to let you pretend to be my husband. My record as an internationally renowned detective should be enough to impress everyone. I don't need you making up fantastical stories about me."

"Are you absolutely sure?" He wrinkled his brow and considered this conundrum. "What about if I tell people that you're tipped to be knighted in the King's Christmas honours list?"

"Too big."

"That you're a good tipper in restaurants?"

"Too small."

He clicked his fingers as another idea popped into his truly unusual brain. "Then how about I drop a few hints that you were voted your local Chick 'o' Mansion's favourite customer two years in a row?"

"I'm not sure that's something I'd ever want to boast about. And besides, it's far too close to the truth." I knew I'd have to let him down gently (again). "I appreciate the effort, Ramesh. But this is something I have to do alone."

"Way to make me feel like a spare wheel, Izzy. Thanks very much." He looked a bit grumpy, but I knew he'd soon be distracted by something shiny and forget all his woes. It was one of his greatest talents.

In front of the school was a large grey arch of the type you walk through at airports to check for weapons and ham sandwiches (I forget what you're allowed to take on planes these days!) There was something of a queue as security guards checked bags and solemnly waved revellers through.

"What's all this for?" I asked Shandy, who was already dancing to the muffled sound of a Black-Eyed Peas song that was floating out of the school.

"These days, anywhere you get teenagers, you get a whole load of security that we never had back in our time. The school where I work is the same. Kids are always stealing stuff or getting into trouble with the police. I have to enter a one-time password to get into the staff car park and another to leave. It's like working in the Royal Mint."

"That's so sad," I said, as nothing gets a party started like worrying about the safety of young people in modern society.

"Please, Izzy, can we not?" Shandy put her hand out to stop me. "This is my one night off from my kids for the next two weeks and I want to have a nice, easy-going time. So can we focus on the positive and not worry about knife crime or what a load of psychos our classmates were when we were kids?"

I gave her a sad smile – which hardly helped. "Of course we can. Let's just have fun."

She squeezed my arm affectionately and ran off to drape herself over her rent-a-stud-muffin for the evening.

Stud muffin? Are you ninety years old?

My first thought would be, *no, that's impossible…* However, it would certainly explain my taste in comfy footwear.

As we got closer to the school, I noticed more security devices that had not been there fifteen years before. There were bars and metal shutters all over the windows, and we walked through a thick, reinforced door to get into the front hallway. I wondered if they were planning ahead to the day all South London residents would walk around with Uzis, or perhaps they were hoping for a visit from the Pope. I already felt nervous as I stepped over the threshold; I didn't need any bonus dark thoughts, but I certainly had them.

More tiny twinkling fairy lights were laid out beside a red paper path, which led us to a table outside the school hall. Our headmistress Mrs Davies used to have assemblies in there three times a week and, from the look of things, it hadn't changed a bit. There were still ugly brown curtains covering the long rows of windows, just to make sure no daylight could penetrate the gloomy sanctuary, and the exterior walls were that uninspiring grey colour they reserve for schools.

"Izzy, you came!" Verity Gresham stood up from her table. She already had my name badge in hand and bristled with excitement as she nudged the woman next to her. "You really are the cherry on the top of this whole celebration."

I think I blushed. "No one's ever said that about me before. A guy I dated once said that I looked like a pork chop dressed as bacon, but I wasn't sure if that was a compliment or an insult."

"Oh, Izzy!" Verity let out a chortle. "You are so funny. Make sure you keep some of that winning humour for the speech."

I don't know how I'd managed to keep it together until now, but it was at this point that my stomach decided to check out what the floor was up to. I might have uttered a pained, "*Speech?*" but my voice had largely stopped functioning.

"Now let's see who else we have here." Verity scanned the faces of my companions and looked for matching name badges. "Who could forget Shandy Duchamps?" As so many people did on meeting my beautiful, well-proportioned friend, Verity drew an outline of Shandy with her eyes. "And what about these three handsome gentlemen?" To be fair to her, she was just as flirty with the boys.

"This is my boyfriend, Danny." I think the champagne must have gone to Shandy's head as she proceeded to paw her fake beau like she was a sexy cat. "He's a… *doctor!*"

"And I'm here with Lorna Inglis. Have you—" Before Dean could finish his question, the human equivalent of a piece of plain white paper emerged from the hall and ran squeaking towards him.

Lorna Inglis was the most unremarkable person I'd ever met. I know that she and Shandy had won the environmental technology prize for their recycling invention in Year Ten, and that she was once knocked unconscious by a volleyball that our psychopathic P.E. teacher Mr Bath threw at her head, but beyond that I could recall very little about her.

"Eeeeee!" was the only sound she would make as she felt the quality of Dean's Armani suit. I could tell that he instantly wished he'd made less of an effort. For her part, she was dressed in a black and white pinafore dress, like she'd stepped out of a Victorian photo album or a haunted house.

"And this is your—" Verity began, but Ramesh had turned away and was waving to an imaginary friend.

"Bill? Is that you, Bill?" He wandered off along the corridor and embarked on a lengthy conversation, though there was clearly no one there.

I realised at that moment that Verity knew exactly who he was as she'd met him at my office.

"Yes, that's my assistant, Ramesh. I tried to convince him not to come, but he hates being alone in his house when his wife is away on business. She does leave the windows cracked open, but he still gets scared of the dark. I would also like it noted that he is not my husband."

Verity and her helper looked confused but nodded politely. "Very good. Yes, that's excellent. You're all very welcome here."

Shandy leaned over the table and scanned the remaining nametags. "Just out of curiosity, has Tim Cornish turned up yet?"

Tim was Shandy's childhood sweetheart, who had made her the happiest woman in the world by marrying her at twenty-three, giving her two beautiful children and then deserting her for a younger woman a few years later. He was a scumbag, and I hoped for all our sakes he wouldn't be coming.

"Yes, he's inside with any number of the stars of our year. I'm sure we'll have a special night." There was a glint in Verity's eye as she said this, and I found myself questioning her intentions again. A large queue had built up behind us, so there was no time to probe the possibility that the whole event had been staged as an elaborate trap.

The tide of bodies carried me into the hall, which was decorated just like in so many American movies. Whoever had planned the evening (and booked us a limo) seemed to be under the impression that this was a prom rather than an unnecessary meeting of no longer connected people in their thirties. There were balloons *everywhere*. There were balloon arches, a balloon pagoda and even a mobile balloon water feature.

Any inch of space not occupied by inflated plastic was hung with shiny paper. A large sign on the stage welcomed us to "The Enchantment Under the Sea Dance", though there did not appear to be much of a nautical theme anywhere else. If anything, I'd have described the theme as *children's party full of soon to be drunk people.*

I caught sight of a few old faces. They were fleshier in some cases, thinner in others, but I still recognised them as the kids they'd once been. Some grinned at Shandy, others gawped at me, and I couldn't help feeling like I'd made the biggest mistake of my life going back there. It wasn't just the humiliation I was surely about to endure; it was the psychological damage that I'd spent a decade and a half resolving. My time in high school was hellish and, for some stupid reason, I'd decided to relive it.

"Izzy Palmer!" a voice beckoned me towards the stage. It was not one of my teenage enemies desperate to make amends for the way they'd treated me. It was our headmistress.

"Mrs Davies, it's so nice to see you." I didn't really know whether this was true. The only time I'd spoken to her as a pupil was when she'd found out about the incident with Gary Flint.

Instead of chastising me in front of everyone for a foolish mistake from my adolescence, she gripped both my hands in hers and shook them. "We are all so proud of you here at West Wickham High. Izzy Palmer, our most famous alum… Well, we did once have a pupil who appeared on an advert for shaving wax, but you've definitely pipped him."

"You're so kind." I think I sounded slightly surprised that this was the case. I might have said more, but I noticed that Gary was leaning against the wall in the far corner of the room. He had a look on his face that was somewhere between desperate for revenge and completely unconcerned.

We'd better watch out for that one. He's impossible to read!

He wasn't the only figure from my childhood I'd located by this point. Former school heartthrob Robert Mitchell was glaring across the room at his ex-wife Becky, and their respective friends were gathered around them like bodyguards. It felt like a scene from an insensitively cast remake of West Side Story. I'd expected everyone's attention to be trained on the former dream couple all night, but Verity had mounted the stage, and the screech of the microphone pulled focus.

"Good evening, everyone. It's such a joy to be back with you. I won't talk too long as the reason I organised this whole thing was to give everyone a chance to chat and catch up on what the world has done to us." I thought her phrasing a little odd, but she barrelled on, before I could think much about it. "It is a great honour that so many of you have turned up this evening, but there's one person in particular whose presence means a lot to me, and I'm hoping she'll come and say a few words."

Next to me, Mrs Davies adjusted her red and white spotted neckerchief. I'd never seen anyone else wear such an item of clothing, and it typified her old-fashioned style. She smiled, cleared her throat, and I felt a little sorry for her. I was fairly certain that she wasn't the guest of honour to whom Verity was referring.

"Ladies and gentlemen, here with us this evening we are lucky to have an old friend: the much-admired private detective, Izzy Palmer!" Our host pointed to me and, as I'm too polite to walk away when I find something deeply terrifying, I tottered up the steps towards the lectern.

She welcomed me with air kisses and mouthed a few words as she handed me the microphone. I thought she might at least stand next to me for support, but no. She stalked off in that proud, horsey manner of hers and watched from the floor as a hundred people looked up at me, and my whole body froze.

Chapter Seven

I'd addressed bigger crowds before. I'd had to unmask a killer at a village fete for one thing, and I believe I've already mentioned my appearance on international television at the last royal(ish) wedding. But this was different. I knew these people and, to a man (or woman), every last one of them intimidated me.

Everywhere I looked, grim ghosts from my past stared back at me. Near the door was Pete Boon – one of a pack of bullies who had followed me home from school one day and painted the word *Freak* on our garden wall. By the drinks table was Shandy's ex Tim Cornish – who once paid a girl from our class to steal my clothes during P.E. and replace them with a fancy dress costume. And perhaps the most malicious figure of all, standing beside the exit to the playground was my P.E. Teacher, Mr Bath – the man who, instead of letting me wear my games kit to the rest of my lessons, made me put on said costume so that I had to walk around school for the rest of the day dressed as a carrot.

Well, scumbags, I would have the last laugh. Not only had I grown up to be a ginormous success, deserving of my own speech at our high school reunion, I'd told everyone I met on that fateful day that I was dressed up for charity. That ugly orange costume raised over twenty-seven pounds for the Red Cross.

Of course, none of this helped me know what to say into the microphone.

Tell them about the time the boy you fancied mistook you for a man!
That is one of your worst ideas ever.
Maybe, but it would still be funny.
Afraid that I might say something equally embarrassing, I scanned the crowd again to look for a friendly face. Thank goodness for Shandy, Lorna and my three favourite boys. For the first (and possibly last) time that night, I was really glad they'd come. Ramesh scrunched together his eager little face and raised one fist in the air in solidarity.

I knew in that moment what to say. I had to tell the truth.

"High school is torture." Okay, the words came out in a strangled squeak, and I doubt anyone understood them, but just saying this short sentence gave me the confidence to continue. "It took me years to get over what went on here, but then I kind of think that's the point. This was an ordeal we all had to get through. I'm sure I'm not the only one who feels that way and, though it might not have seemed like it at the time, it made us stronger."

I tried not to be put off by the blank looks that floated up to me. I should never have been on that stage, and I was sure that everyone knew it. If Becky and Robert Mitchell hadn't imploded, they would have been there in my place, telling everyone how wonderful their lives were compared to ours. Perhaps it was an unwarranted fissure in our dimensional timeline, but life hadn't played out how everyone had expected, and so it was my job to keep talking.

"I've spent the last fifteen years feeling sorry for myself. I went from school to university with the idea that I would forever be the victim of bullies and preening 'it' girls. But the adult world is less predatory than West Wickham High, and it isn't nearly as bad as I was expecting. It took me a while, but I found my people. People who don't quite fit in, but who love me and support me through every minor disaster. I found my own path through life too, which is something that not everyone can say. A couple of years ago, I opened a detective agency and have solved over..." I had to think for a moment... "Seventeen murders. I've met royals and Hollywood actors. I've unpicked the schemes of several brilliant criminals, and I did it my way."

Izzy, sing a song!

Nope.

The fear in the pit of my stomach had dissolved like an antacid tablet, and I was starting to enjoy myself. "So what I want to tell you all tonight — the reason I agreed to come up here in the first place — is that it doesn't matter who we were back then. It doesn't matter if you were a big macho guy in high school and went on to open a poodle parlour. Nobody cares anymore if you were supposed to be famous by now but you're still working at a supermarket in Addington. All that matters is the world you've built for yourself." The room was silent as I took one last dry gulp of breath and uttered my closing line. "And so, let me tell you something about myself. I play a mean accordion, bowl a 210 average and speak Spanish to a C1 level. My name is Izzy Palmer, and I'm a private detective."

My words left a vacuum and my skin prickled as I awaited the boos. I hadn't known what I would say when I stepped onto that stage. I hadn't realised that what I'd been fantasising about my whole life was about to come true. But no matter how my old schoolmates reacted, I felt incredible.

I looked about those highly strung, narrow-eyed faces and took their silence as my cue to make a swift exit. I turned to go, and the strangest thing happened. The room erupted.

"Izzy, thank you so much." Verity was so desperate to shake my hand, she practically pulled me down from the stage, and she wasn't the only one.

"Wow, Iz." Top bully Pete Boon was close to tears. "I never thought someone could put into words exactly how I feel about this place, but you did it."

The crowd was still applauding as someone pressed a cup of non-alcoholic punch into my hand, and Queen Becky Mitchell pushed through the crowd to get to me. "I always knew you'd be amazing, Izzy," she attempted to say, but there were too many people in front of her, and she was squeezed back out again.

If this were a teen movie, it would have ended right there. The football team would have raised me up on their shoulders, and I would have enjoyed the applause and adulation as they paraded me around the school in front of all the jocks and teachers, nerds and geeks. I would have my fifteen seconds in the spotlight and then the credits would roll.

Sadly for everyone, this isn't a teen movie. Not that we knew it then, but like all of my best stories, this is a murder mystery. As the noise in the hall swelled, and I saw my old P.E. teacher rumple his grey moustache in quiet respect, the lights went out and everyone screamed.

Chapter Eight

"There's no need to worry." Mrs Davies's confident voice cut through the panic. "We've been having some problems with the electricity supply recently. But there are back-up generators that should kick in at any—"

Before she could finish her announcement, the lights turned back on, and the noise died down. "There we go. Nothing to worry about in the slightest."

A murmur of relief spread about the hall, but it would be short lived.

"The shutters," an unidentified voice declared, and we all turned to look at the heavy metal slats that were closing over the windows that gave on to the playground. "They're sealing us in."

Mrs Davies looked a little more nervous this time and tugged on her neckerchief. "I'm sure it's just a safety feature. We have a high-tech ant-burglar system designed to protect us from thieves, hurricanes and minor nuclear disasters. The power cut must have triggered the shutters. It's nothing to worry about." She cast about for a familiar face. "Lorna, go to the office and check that a fuse hasn't blown. I'll go to the security room and reset the system."

Dean's date for the night emitted a squeak which sounded a little like, "Yes, Miss!" and scuttled off to do as she'd been told.

The briefly panicky atmosphere died away, and most in the crowd forgot about my inspirational words and returned to their friends. To keep the party going, Verity put some music back on the school speaker system and songs from the early noughties blared across the hall. I hadn't thought too highly of Eminem and Westlife the first time around, and they were doing very little for me now – though I had a sneaking suspicion that, if I had another cup of sugary punch, I would soon find myself dancing like a loon.

"Bit weird all this," Dean was still studying the shutters as though their war-grey glossy paint might help him decipher the electrical issue. "I don't see why a power cut would trigger a full system reset."

Dean owned X-Tec Spyware, a company which produced technological... Well, I'm not entirely sure what they did, though he'd told me in great detail on several occasions. All I know is that, while I didn't understand a word he was saying, he seemed quite concerned.

The drama appeared to have concluded, and I was readying myself for a procession of repetitive conversations with old classmates who would surely never have remembered me if I hadn't just given the most barnstorming speech since 'The Dead Poet's Society' wrapped up filming.

"Sorry, who are you?" See what I mean!

A rather well-spoken chap in an incongruous three-piece suit had popped by to look unimpressed. He had an arrogant air, as though the fact he couldn't remember me offended him.

"Hello, Michael. I'm Izzy Palmer." I waited for this name to sink in. "We sat together in physics class with Doctor Phillips."

No reaction. Michael Andersen, the richest boy in school, had always been a snob, and I had to wonder if he was putting on an act to annoy me.

"I was friends with your sister in primary school?"

"Oh, you're Sally!" he incorrectly concluded.

"Nope, I just told you, I'm Izzy. Isobel Palmer. You walked in on me getting changed in your pool house one summer when I was thirteen?"

"Doesn't ring a bell." He looked truly clueless, and I thought I'd give it one last try.

"I sang Robbie Williams's 'Angels' at your sixteenth birthday party to make Becky Mitchell feel better after she caught Robert kissing the exchange student?"

He shook his head. "I do remember the Belgian girl. Celine Delacroix, I believe her name was. But I'm afraid that, otherwise, I'm drawing a blank."

"Celine?" I might have lost my temper at this. "You remember Celine Delacroix, who only came to our school for two weeks, but you don't remember me? We were in class together for thirteen years. Our mothers used to play squash every Thursday!"

He smiled and released a *what-am-I-like?* sort of laugh. "Well, anyway. I only wanted to say that you had a jolly good stab at a speech up there, and I'm glad you're enjoying the evening." He shook my hand like a politician pressing the flesh and then moved away to schmooze someone else.

You should have told him about the time you solved a murder on international television. People are occasionally impressed by that.

Oh, shut up.

He'd certainly knocked the wind from my sails, as did seeing Danny sitting on Shandy's lap at the side of the hall. The fact that two of my favourite people had their lips locked together should have made me happy. Although I'd loved Danny for half of my life, we'd both come to see that we were totally wrong for one another, and Shandy deserved a good partner more than anyone I knew. So why did watching them smush faces make me feel so odd?

"It's because you secretly hope that all of your exes harbour undying love for you." Ramesh delivered this verdict in a knowing tone as he walked past with three drinks in his hand.

"Urmmm... no I don't. I never think about that Danny or Nigel or that guy who ended up in prison and wonder if they think of me when they're kissing other people."

Ramesh turned his head in a sign of undying pity. "You keep telling yourself that, Izzy." He glanced about at the crowd that had dispersed around the hall. "I have to get these drinks to my new friends Lilly and Paul. You should mingle, Izzy! Mingling is the name of the game."

Before I could tell him that I hadn't the first clue what game we were playing, Shandy's hard-man ex rushed over to offer an observation on the new lovers' display.

"It's disgusting." He managed to say this through gritted teeth without even moving his lips. "People shouldn't do that kind of thing in public, especially when..."

"Especially when you left that beautiful woman and your gorgeous children in order to sleep with a twenty-one-year-old?" I should perhaps have shown some solidarity as we were now united by the fact our exes were making out with one another, but it was hard to feel much sympathy for the grimacing thug.

He could summon no reply and continued grinding his teeth so loudly that I thought the enamel would wear off.

"Where is little Martika tonight, anyway?"

He finally tore his gaze away from the show of affection that continued beside the dance floor. "We... broke up."

I'd be lying if I said I tried to suppress a grin just then. "No way! She left you, didn't she?"

He bowed his head, clearly unable to think of an excuse. "Well, yes, if you want to put it like that; she left me. But only because she found someone better to go out with." He wasn't doing himself any favours. "She said I was too old for her!"

Ahhh, poor chap.

Urggghhh, what is wrong with me? I should have laughed out loud and told him he deserved it. Instead, I found myself patting him on the shoulder and making a frowny face. "I'm sorry, Tim. I hope the next woman you date is more suitable."

Hey, at least you managed to sound judgemental whilst comforting him. Great job!

"Thanks, Izzy." He sniffed loudly and put his hand on top of mine. "Hey, are you here with anyone tonight or…?" His sorrow quickly forgotten, he raised his eyebrows and winked.

"Yuck! What is wrong with you? I was trying to be nice, not chat you up."

He immediately acted as though I'd led him on. "Don't be like that. I thought we could make them jealous with a bit of the old tongue tennis."

I looked at my friends again and realised that they still hadn't come up for air. "Urmmm… no. I don't think that would work even if we tried. Run along now."

He balled up his fists and, with a low growl, walked back to his posse. It was as though no time had passed for the popular boys in my year. Pete Boon, Robert Mitchell and Tim Cornish might have lost a little hair and piled on the pounds, but they still had the sophistication of a pack of randy weasels.

Weasels don't hunt in packs. They're largely solitary animals.

Why don't you know anything useful?

I do! The European Least Weasel is the world's smallest carnivore!

I was about to continue this argument when Dean appeared. I actually felt quite popular for once and could have stood by that stage all evening for people to come and talk to me as though I were the guest of honour… which I suppose I was.

"Are you having fun at my high school reunion?" I had to ask him.

"Yeah, I've always wondered what these things were like. I got expelled from my school for hacking the headmaster's computer. They wouldn't have me back, even if I wanted to go."

"I bet they would now that you're a millionaire."

He considered this and gave a quick shrug. "I suppose so. Money erases all evils, don't they say?"

"Something like that, yeah. How's your date going?"

He had a quick look around. "Well, Lorna is certainly keen on me. She made that quite clear from the start. I've tried mentioning my girlfriend to show I'm not available, but she didn't get the hint. I don't think I've ever spoken so much about Fiona since we started going out. I sometimes wish she was the jealous type, so that I could avoid situations like this."

"Oh, come on. Pretending to be my boyfriend that time wasn't too painful, was it?"

"No, I enjoyed that." His smile illuminated his normally deadpan face. "But I don't know what I was thinking, trying my luck a second time."

When I first met Dean, I'd found his nerdy awkwardness (and outright rudeness) seriously off-putting. To my infinite surprise, he's grown up over time and can actually be quite a charmer.

Dean's date reappeared at that moment and whispered a few words which sounded a lot like, "The fuses are fine. Has Mrs Davies returned?"

"I haven't seen her." Perhaps it's all the time I spend falling over dead bodies, but I made this sound far more dramatic than it should have.

"Perhaps we should check on her," that suave chap Dean suggested.

Lorna muttered something, and we followed her out of the hall. I hadn't considered the ramifications of the technical malfunction that had occurred, but the anti-theft shutters now separated us from the outside world and there was no escape from the building. Clearly Mrs Davies had been unable to address this problem, and I thought it lucky that I'd brought my very own tech genius to the festivities after all.

We carried straight on past the school office along a narrow corridor that led to the West Block. It was a real trip down memory lane to walk through the upper-school locker room and around my GCSE religious studies class – where Mr Coleman had occasionally taken his glass eye out of its socket to scare us. This was one of my happier memories from school, and I had to smile as I recalled Becky Mitchell (nee Taylor)'s disgusted expression as the little ball rolled around in the palm of our teacher's hand.

The security room was next to the computer lab where I'd first learnt how to waste endless hours on the internet. We tried the door and, though it would open a fraction, it wouldn't budge all the way.

I think that, despite his claims to the contrary, Dean was enjoying the attention our mousy friend offered. He rolled the sleeves of his dinner jacket up to the elbows, so that he looked like a detective on Miami Vice, and prepared to barge the door. Lorna let out a pre-emptive romantic sigh.

"Ready?" he asked, as though we might need to prepare ourselves for such a sight. "One, two... three..."

He charged. He hurt his shoulder. The door stayed right where it was.

"Perhaps the three of us should try at the same time?" I suggested, and the fake couple nodded their agreement.

"One... two... three..."

My plan was far more successful, and we managed to push the door open just enough for me to slide through. I really should have been prepared for what I found there. As my friends always tell me and I attempt to deny, I attract dead bodies the way that honey brings the bears.

At first, I couldn't make sense of what I was seeing. There on the floor, crushed beneath the weight of a large fallen cabinet, were two people I barely remembered as being with me in my Year-Nine maths class. That's right; Tommy Hathaway and Clara Higson were no more.

Chapter Nine

"Who are they?" Mrs Davies asked when she returned to the room, having gone off in search of the caretaker.

"Just two kids from my year. I think I remember hearing that they got married. Perhaps one of their friends can tell us why they left the party."

"It's a bit odd, don't you think?" This was Dean's catchphrase for the night. "Why would they have come in here? And why would that server have fallen over?"

There was one thing we were all ignoring. "Well, Tommy has his pants around his ankles. That might explain it."

Mrs Davies pulled her neck in as though she'd never heard of sex before and wasn't sure she approved of the whole darn concept. "You mean that they came in here for a bit of…"

"Nooky!" Lorna squeaked so that our headmistress didn't have to.

"Thrill seekers," Dean explained. "It happens everywhere. I once had to go to my factory in the middle of the night after a couple of kids set off the silent alarms. I found them on the roof of the building, stark naked except for two full-face horse masks."

"Wait, what were the masks for?" I asked, before deciding I didn't want to know. "Actually, don't answer that."

Mrs Davies got us back on track. "So you think they leant against the server cabinet, and it fell and crushed them?"

I thought I'd let Dean field this question as I hadn't a clue how to answer it.

"You'd expect the engineers to have screwed it to the wall, but if you employed a bunch of cowboys to do the job, I wouldn't be surprised that it wasn't up to scratch. People don't think carefully enough about housing and installation in server rooms these days. Everyone thinks you can just throw a few switches and servers together and hope for the best, but let me tell you—"

He would have continued like this for some time – there's nothing Dean likes more than discussing networking requirements… or cowboy workmen, for that matter – but I noticed something on the other side of the room and stepped around the bodies to take a look.

There was a long desk with a number of monitors that showed different parts of the school on low-resolution monochrome feeds. I looked around the small space and realised that there were no cameras visible.

"Dean, can you show us what happened in the corridor outside this room in the last half hour?"

He cracked his knuckles as he came to join me. "It shouldn't take too— There you go." With a few mouse clicks and a press of the enter key, he had called up a video that he set to fast forward until we saw a pair of grinning former students grace the screen. Tommy had a particularly wicked expression on his face and had undone his trousers before he'd even entered the room. Poor Clara tiptoed after him, looking guilty.

"So..." Mrs Davies crossed her arms in her usual efficient manner. "Mystery solved. The only problem now is the shutters. I spoke to the caretaker, and he says that his override key isn't working, and he hasn't the first idea about, in his words, 'this new-fangled technology.' Do you think you might be able to open them, Mr..."

"Shipman," my friend responded, and I knew he was living out a long-standing James Bond fantasy. "Dean Shipman from X-Tec Spyware. I'll see what I can do." As though he'd spent years in that room, and knew everything about it, he reached under the desk and pulled out a black tool bag with pockets all over it. "I don't have a code to disable the system, but there should be another room somewhere in the school that provides the power to the electric shutters. If you can show me the way, I should have us out of here in no time."

"Wonderful." Mrs Davies hadn't looked so cheerful all night. "Lorna, call the police and wait here with the bodies. I'll be back as soon as I can."

The headmistress turned to leave, and Lorna gave a terrified squeal as I followed Dean from the room. Back in the hall, Outkast's 'Hey Ya!' was blaring from the speakers. By this stage in the evening, Ramesh had inevitably made friends with everyone there, taken control of the party and arranged a dance-off. Two boys from my drama class were strutting their stuff against the Simpson brothers, and the rest of the crowd were egging them on.

"Go, Malcolm! Go, Malcolm! Go, go, go, Malcolm!" Ramesh

hollered as I tried to get his attention.

"Pssst." I stuck out my head over his throne-like chair, which I could only assume he'd commandeered from the staff room. "I need to talk to you."

Gary Flint was standing next to him, and Ramesh signalled for my first boyfriend and possible current-stalker to take his place. "What is it, Iz? I'm a bit busy at the moment being incredible."

"Tommy Hathaway and Clara Higson are dead."

"Who are Tommy Hathaway and Clara Higson?"

"It doesn't matter. I just need you to keep the party going so that no one freaks out."

He looked confused. "So you interrupted me to tell me to do exactly what I'm already doing?"

"Pretty much."

Malcolm Simpson had just performed a sweet backflip, and Ramesh was about to return to his task when a thought occurred to him. "So you'll be busy investigating another murder, I suppose?"

"No, they weren't murdered. They're just common-or-garden dead people that you might find at any high school reunion."

He was still dancing as we conducted the conversation. "So how did they die?"

"A computer server stack fell on top of them while they were…"

Whatever you do, don't say 'playing mummies and daddies!'

"Making whoopee in the security room."

He wrinkled his nose up. "Okay, Izzy. Sure. They *weren't* murdered." His voice was less than serious. "An innocent server just innocently fell on two innocent people whilst you innocently stalked the halls looking for dead bodies. Admit it; they were murdered!"

I adopted a neutral tone. "Honestly, they were just unlucky. They chose the wrong server to bump up against."

"Come off it, private detective Izzy Palmer! They were slain to death. Wherever you go, killers are never far behind."

"I'm not going to argue with you, Ramesh. I just need you to keep the dance-off going for another half an hour until the police arrive or Dean can get the shutters open."

"Only half an hour?" he sounded a little disappointed. "Fine, but don't blame me if my people beg for more." He turned away and instantly re-engaged with *his people*. "Go, Benjamin! Go, Benjamin! Go, go, go, Benjamin!"

Gary Flint took a sideways look at me as I retreated and, for a moment, I considered what Ramesh had said. I really wasn't in the mood to investigate a double murder, but it might not be the maddest idea. Perhaps my still furious first boyfriend had killed them to test my abilities as a detective… or incriminate me! Perhaps he was planning to bump off people from my past in order to make it look as though I'd gone on a killing spree.

Or perhaps he really is totally over you and those poor lovers were simply crushed by falling computer equipment. It happens all the time.

Does it?

I don't know! My point is that not every man who has kissed the great Izzy Palmer is still hung up on you years later. Look at the love of your life over there. You and Danny had a will-they/won't-they romance to rival Caesar and Cleopatra, and yet he seems perfectly content pashing with Shandy.

Perhaps you're right…

Or perhaps I should still have a chat with the dead couple's friends just to make sure.

Chapter Ten

"Tommy and Clara are great, aren't they?" I asked, ever so naturally.

"Yeah, they are! I'd say Tommy is my absolute best friend in the world, and I would be lost without him. My girlfriend Samantha is the same with Clara. They do everything together. They even work together."

I was talking to one of the only two people I could remember having anything to do with the recently crushed couple. Barry Travers was part of the four-member photography club that used to hang out in the dark room in the South Block.

"I don't suppose you know much about what they get up to in their spare time?"

"You mean bird watching?" Barry was wearing an orange suit for some reason. He was the kind of quirky, wacky guy who wanted everyone to know just how quirky and wacky he was. It was almost as ugly as the carrot costume I'd been forced to wear.

"No, not bird watching. I was thinking of something a bit more *adult*."

He looked around us then, but we were in a corner, far away from the still raucous dancing, and there was no chance of being overheard. "Oh, you mean their casual shoplifting? Yeah, I can't say I approve of it myself, and I've told them on a number of occasions. But my buddy Tommy says it's just a bit of fun, and I'd trust him with my life. He's the best."

"Sex!" I have no idea why I can't say such words discreetly. For all my attempts at subtlety, I practically screamed the word at him. "I was wondering about what they got up to *in the bedroom*. Or rather, *out of it,* if you know what I mean."

He didn't look as though he did, but luckily the fourth founding member of the West Wickham High Photography Club returned at that moment to explain. "She's talking about their *outdoor* habits, Barry." He still looked uncertain, but Samantha kept talking as though she was used to her boyfriend not understanding much. "They're always at it. They're off right now in one of the staff rooms." A strange look crossed her face. "Why are you asking? Are you interested in joining them?"

"Urghhh, no. That's the last thing I—" I managed to hide how disgusting I found the idea. Well, I didn't vomit at least.

"Oh, their *outdoor* habits!" Barry had finally cottoned on. "You should give it a go. There's a group of us who meet on Thursday nights in the car park of The George pub."

Ahhh! Izzy! Get us out of here, I think they're—

Before I could think it, Barry made it absolutely clear. "We always have a *swinging* good time!" He winked at me, and I felt dirty just talking to him.

"Leave it out, Barry." Samantha elbowed him in the ribs. "You always do that. You should probably indulge in a bit of light conversation before going in for the hard sell." She turned to me with a sympathetic expression. At least she was a polite swinger. "I'm sorry about him, Izzy. But I'll give you my card just in case you're interested."

She rummaged in her bag and pulled out a cardholder before extracting a bone-white rectangle with her information on it. After the conversation we'd just had, I half expected it to say:

Samantha Goulding

Husband Swapper

Instead, it said:

Samantha Goulding

Senior School Inspector

So that was a surprise.

"You didn't go into photography then?" I considered asking, but instead I ran away as fast as I could.

Look on the bright side. At least it seems as though Tommy and Clara weren't murdered.

Yeah, that is good news. But it doesn't change the fact I just had the ickiest conversation in my life. I know I said that I wanted to be more grown up, but there's a limit. And now I feel like taking a very long shower.

As I sped across the hall, I kept catching people's eyes. In fact, everywhere I went, people smiled at me and called my name. I even got a few comments of "Great speech, Izzy." Why couldn't my time studying there have been like that? It was all well and good being nice to me now, but why couldn't they have evened it out a bit back then too? I saw Becky Mitchell cutting a line through the crowd, but before she could catch me, Lorna Inglis returned to the hall.

"Sorry, Izzy," her tiny, high-pitched voice was barely audible over the sound of Ramesh singing 'Another One Bites the Dust'. I have no idea how he'd ended up with a microphone, but he was clearly making the most of it. "I don't mean to bother you, but…" She searched for her words, and so I tried to reassure her.

"It's no trouble, Lorna. What's the matter?"

"It's just that… Well, Mrs Davies relieved me of my watch with the d… dead…"

"Dead bodies?"

"Yes, that's it. The d… dead…"

Not again!

"The poor unfortunate people who were crushed by the falling equipment?"

She let out a sigh of relief. "That's right. She took over in the security room, but she told me that Dean can't get the shutters open because they've been sabotaged."

"Sabotaged?" This seemed like a rather dramatic point, and so I felt I had to repeat it. "Is that really the word she used?"

She nodded just a tiny bit, much as a mouse might shake its whiskers.

"So we're stuck in here?"

"I'm afraid so. Perhaps you should—"

"Noooooo!" Verity Graham had been standing nearby, watching the dance-off, but had evidently overheard our conversation as her face now fell. "Please don't say that. This evening has to go right. It simply has to! We can't be stuck in here."

"We're stuck in here alright!" Dean had returned and was wiping grease off his hands with a rag. It was a surprisingly macho gesture for him. "I've done all I can, but the physical override for the anti-theft shutters has been damaged. I got the main power back on, but until someone comes with a battering ram or an industrial strength blowtorch to cut us out, we're locked in the school."

"Nooooo!" Verity was wailing by now and went running from the hall to examine the front shutters. "This can't be happening. I wanted everything to be perfect, and it's all going wrong."

The woman flailed about desperately, and I had to wonder why she cared so much. It was only a high school reunion, not… urmmm… something more important than a high school reunion.

A baptism?

Exactly! It wasn't a baptism. If she'd planned a baptism and ended up baptising the wrong baby, you could kind of understand why she was so upset. But we had non-alcoholic punch, a sound system, and the world's best children's entertainer to keep the crowd happy. No one was going anywhere in a hurry and there was nothing to worry about.

"That girl is weird," Lorna (of all people) pronounced as Verity fell to her knees like Charlie Sheen on the poster for Platoon.

Actually, that's not Charlie Sheen on the poster. It's Willem Dafoe.

And I ask you once again, why don't you know anything useful?

Oooooh, I'm sorry!

I turned to an expert for help. "Dean, explain to me what's happened in the most basic terms you know."

He thought about it for a moment. "Right… Well… You see, what's happened is that, for some reason I have yet to ascertain, this school has the kind of security system you get in high-end, private banks." He waved his hands around as he spoke, as though he were talking to an idiot. I greatly appreciated it. "When you try to mess with the computerised security system, it shuts everything down. There's a password-protected override lever in the basement that should reset everything, but someone has broken in there and short-circuited it."

"So we're stuck."

He looked bemused by my conclusion. "Yes, Izzy, we're stuck, as I told you two minutes ago, and I assume that Lorna had told you two minutes before that. The bigger question is, why are we stuck?"

"Why are we stuck?"

"That's right."

"No, I'm asking; why *are* we stuck?"

He scratched his head. You'd think that would be more of an expression these days, rather than an actual thing that people do. But Dean is one of the most literal people I've ever met, and he often scratches his head when thinking. Perhaps that's the secret to his success.

"Well, the anti-theft security in this school was designed to keep people out, but I can only imagine that someone wanted to keep us inside."

"Brilliant detective work, Dean. How do you do it?" For the first time that evening… no, wait. For the first time in the last fifteen minutes, there was a bad feeling rising up within me.

"Oh, and I bet your I.T. work is top notch, though, isn't it, Izzy?" He might have had a point. "Come on, Lorna. Let's dance. Actually, I have a very weak bladder and I need the toilet after all that punch, but then we can go for a dance."

The shy character released a gentle yelp and hurried after her new partner. I knew for a fact that Dean hated dancing, so this was one sick burn on his part. I was about to comfort Verity – and find out why she was making such a fuss – when her brother strolled over to make me feel worse about the world.

"Looks like you're in a spot of bother again, Izzy. Like that time Mrs Davies called you to her office. Remind me, why did she have to talk to you that day?" He pretended to think. "You were always such a good girl. Surely you hadn't done something incredibly cruel."

I slumped my shoulders and turned to face him. "Seriously, Gary, can you make your mind up whether you're annoyed with me or not? This whole thing is becoming boring. Yes, I did something very unkind, but I fancied you for the best part of two years, and you never once admitted that you were going out with me in front of your friends."

I couldn't stop there. It was my turn to get something off my chest. "You also stood me up for the end-of-school disco, which I'd made the stupid mistake of looking forward to for months. I allowed my mum to choose my clothes for once, dressed up in a very flouncy dress, and her hairdresser Fernando came to do my makeup. And then, when I was ready, I sat in my lounge for two hours with my father holding a camera for the moment when you arrived. It was nine thirty by the time I gave up and accepted you weren't coming. So which of us is the real monster here?"

My brain had become a little emotional. *You told him, Izzy! That was amazing.*

It was enough to make Gary crumble too. "Oh, heck, I'm so sorry.

I'd forgotten all about that. I just thought it would be a laugh to tease you. I know you didn't mean to be nasty. We were kids, and we were both horrible to each other. The only reason I didn't tell anyone about us was because I fancied the pants off you and didn't know how to say it."

"Is that why you said I kissed like a giraffe? And why you told Martin Thompson I was flatter than— Wait. No, stop. I'm not going to go through this again. I'm not a teenager anymore and I don't care why you did all that stuff or whether my revenge was way out of proportion."

If I'm being honest, he looked pretty distraught. I think he was about to apologise again when a shriek ripped between us on its way to the moon.

"It's all gone wrong." Still on her knees, Verity looked up to the sky – or rather the nicotine-stained ceiling of the entrance hall, which hadn't been decorated since the seventies (when, I can only assume, smoking was mandatory in British schools).

Gary directed a slightly embarrassed look in his sister's direction. "She really takes this sort of thing seriously. I was hoping that she'd chill out a bit after she had a reawakening in the Peruvian rainforest, but she's more uptight than ever."

"Yeah, someone should probably do something to calm her down."

He nodded and looked a bit sad. "Totally."

"Well, go on then!" I kicked him in the back of the leg. It felt pretty good. "She's *your* sister!"

"Oh, right. I see." He hurried off to do just that, and I decided that I'd spent enough time with the Flint family for one evening/lifetime. Instead of going back to the party, I wandered along the corridor towards my old classroom. The walls were lined with cases of trophies and old photos from years gone by. I noticed that most of the sports prizes still bore the name of our school heartthrob, Robert Mitchell. He'd won everything from the county badminton championship to the county basketball championship. He'd represented Great Britain at archery and been tipped to compete in the Commonwealth Games until he broke his hand jumping off the roof of Michael Andersen's greenhouse into the swimming pool.

I had an awful feeling that there might still be a photograph of our school year there, and I was about to come face to face with my eighteen-year-old self. Thankfully, wall space only permitted leavers' photos going back to 2012, and I was spared such an ordeal. Still, it wasn't hard to spot a girl in each of the pictures who looked just like I had. There was always one of them, lurking at the side of the shot, or looking back over her shoulder as some dumb kid put bunny ears over her head. They were the girls with uniforms that didn't sit right on their tall, skinny frames – the girls who wouldn't make eye contact with the camera, let alone the other kids – and I felt sorry for each and every last one of them.

I wanted to send them a group text telling them not to worry. I would have told them that, even if they didn't realise it, there were people like us all over the world and we should never give up.

That was what I was doing as another scream rang out. I didn't think anything of it at the time, as I assumed that Gary had made a truly ham-fisted attempt at comforting his sister. The two of them hadn't been close when we were kids, and so it was something of a surprise to see him at the end of the corridor with his arm around her. Verity even looked as though she was feeling a bit more positive about things.

Of course, that raised the question of who had produced the scream. If I'd managed to hear it over Ramesh's *dance-frontation* (his word), that would suggest it had come from somewhere close by. I was standing ten metres away from the entrance to the headmistress's office. The door was ajar too and there was faint light coming from inside. I tiptoed closer, realising in that moment that I still held a child's reverence for such forbidden territory. I was just as nervous peeking in as I had been when summoned there for the stern telling-off that I'd received in my last week of school.

"Mrs Davies?" I decided to let my voice enter the room ahead of me, in the hope that I wouldn't have to, but there was no reply. "Mrs Davies, are you in there?"

I touched the door, and it seemed to jump open like in every horror film ever.

Hey, the caretaker may not have time to paint the ceilings or learn anything about computers, but he clearly keeps the door hinges well oiled.

I ignored the nerves that were jumping in my stomach, heart and head and stepped inside the room. There was a man in a green tracksuit leant over the desk with a tiny sword-shaped letter opener in his… No, wait a second. That was another case. But this guy also looked like he was having a nap, and I might have left him there if it weren't for the fact he had a phone in his hand. He was gripping it ever so tightly and I knew then that he wasn't asleep.

"Mr Bath, are you…?"

I didn't finish that sentence, as it was pretty damned obvious that he was dead.

Chapter Eleven

It's hard to know what to do when I find a body. It seemed a bit mean to leave him there on his own, but I had to go off and tell someone. Ringing the police would have been the obvious thing to do, but they'd already been called for a previous (increasingly suspicious) death and didn't need me bothering them again. They couldn't get into the building, anyway, and so... Well, I wasn't sure what the protocol was in such a situation.

I had a look around the room to see whether the killer had foolishly left any clues behind. Wait, was I looking for a killer? Isn't it possible that this was another tragic accident? Let's be honest, Mr Bath hadn't been in the best of shape when he was in his forties. Well into his fifties and still running around the field every day or chasing after footballs with a beer belly in front of him must have been a physically demanding existence. It seemed more than possible that he'd felt a bit peaky and gone looking for somewhere to sit down before having a heart attack and reaching for the phone. Perhaps he was trying to call an ambulance as he expired.

The only problem with this exceptional piece of detective work was the slightly burnt smell rising from him, and the thick black cable which curled around the telephone cable and, I could only assume, led to a wall socket behind Mrs Davies's computer. Yep, he'd been murdered. He'd picked up the phone, touched a live wire, and received more than he'd bargained for. The only question was why he'd come to that office and why he'd even needed the phone when he had his mobile right in front of him. Oh, and who had killed him, and why—

In fact, there were clearly a lot of questions still to answer.

Sadly, the screen on Mr Bath's mobile was off and my guess at his password – S@disticTe@cher123 – was never going to do the job. There was something else that I found a little unusual too. On the desk beneath the monitor was a tube of neon-pink lipstick that I couldn't imagine our headmistress (or our P.E. teacher, for that matter) ever using. I was instinctively reaching towards it when I heard someone arrive behind me.

Mrs Davies sucked in a sharp breath as she spotted her colleague's slumped body in her chair. "Ernie?"

Huh! I never knew that Mr Bath's name was Ernie. I would have imagined something more sinister.

Like?

Atilla maybe? Or how about Adolf?

Adolf Bath? It seems a little unlikely.

"I'm sorry, Miss." Was it weird that I still called her "Miss" after so long? "I'm afraid he's dead."

To my surprise, the woman I'd always thought of as restrained and sparing in her emotions burst into tears. "The poor chap. He was going to retire at the end of the year."

I took a step back to comfort her. "I know. It's terrible."

"To think of all his grandchildren who will grow up without their pi-paw."

It was hard to imagine they'd miss such a brute, but I wasn't about to tell her that. "I know. It's terrible."

"And the charity work he's done over the years! He's raised millions for the homeless. Millions! He once told me that it was his greatest accomplishment in life."

"Wait, are you sure you're thinking of the right person?" I didn't go into the details of the psychopathic behaviour he'd exhibited in our games classes, as I figured she must have known all about it.

"Well, his greatest accomplishment after the work he did with you children, of course." She dried her eyes then. "You know, Isobel. When you first came to this school, Ernie told me that he'd seen something special in you and would do all he could to bring it out. He was so proud of the progress you made in your time here."

I was speechless. Truly speechless.

"And now he's gone!" She started crying again, and I was knocked from my stupor.

"I know. It's terrible." Apparently, this is the only type of comfort I am qualified to give, so I gave up trying. "In the absence of the police, I'm afraid I'll have to ask you some questions." I was about to do just this when my phone started ringing. "Sorry, I'll be right back."

I didn't recognise the number on my screen and went into the hall to answer. "Hello, the Private I Detective Agency. Izzy Palmer speaking. How may I be of help?" Ramesh had been unfairly critical of my phone technique recently, and so I was trying to sound more accommodating to clients.

"Izzy?" I recognised the gruff voice as my dear (sort of) friend, D.I. Irons of the Metropolitan Police. "It didn't sound like you."

"Yes, it's me!" I replied with just a hint of irritation.

"Ah, that's better."

I tried to be more polite again. "How can I be of assistance?"

"I was just wondering if you happen to be in West Wickham High School this evening."

"That's right. How did you know?"

"Well, I'm outside with a team of fifteen officers attempting to access the dead bodies that have been found in the school. The problem is that it's sealed tighter than a pair of my handcuffs around some snot-nosed kid's wrists."

"And?"

"Well, it all sounded like the kind of ridiculous situation you would find yourself in, so I had to wonder whether you were here."

"I might be."

There was a short pause before Irons replied. "You just told me that you were."

"Fine, I'm inside the school. What of it?"

Her flat voice perked up a fraction. "When the call came in, I thought it had all the hallmarks of one of your cases, and so I tagged along with my colleagues. I was just wondering whether you reckon that the dead bodies that were found could have been murdered."

I think I scoffed then. "I would say that is highly unlikely. They were merely crushed to death by some falling computer hardware."

"Right you are then. Well, if you—"

"However, I have since discovered another body that I am fairly sure was, in fact... murdered."

"Another body?" She sounded a little bemused. I often have that effect on people. "So it's just a big coincidence that three people have died on the school premises this evening?"

It was hard to be reasonable and grown up about everything when, wherever I went, people insisted on being murdered in a ridiculous fashion. "Fine! There's a small possibility that the deaths are connected and, now that I come to think of it, there's a chance that the real target each time was my old headmistress Mrs Davies."

"Gotcha. And where is she now?"

I had to raise the phone just then to bang it against my forehead. "She's in with the last victim who was killed by what looks like a booby-trapped phone."

"Gotcha. But you told her not to touch anything, I assume?"

I was already running back to her. "Of course, I did." Who says grown-ups can't lie from time to time to make themselves look less like idiots? "I wouldn't just leave her in there to die."

"That's a relief." Irons whistled down the phone.

"Hello, Mrs Davies," I said very loudly so that the detective inspector could hear. "I'm just on the phone to the police. They should be able to gain access to the school in a jiffy." I might have covered the mouthpiece at this point. "Please make sure you don't touch anything in the office. It could interfere with the investigation and also potentially kill you."

She looked uncertain why I'd run into the room, speaking ever so quickly, but she nodded and took a step back from the desk all the same. I returned to the corridor as the booming bass-line of Robbie Williams's 'Rock DJ' pounded out of the hall.

"You *are* going to get us out of here in a jiffy, right?" I whispered to D.I. Irons.

She whistled once more, but not in relief this time. It was the kind of whistle a plumber might make when you ask how long it will take to repair the boiler. "Ooh, a jiffy might be pushing it. But we're certainly doing our best."

The line fell silent for a few seconds and so I asked for clarification. "What does that involve, exactly?"

"Well, I've got several officers here who have had a very close look at the situation, and they've all come to the conclusion that we do not have the tools required to get you out of the school."

"That's brilliant." I had to put the phone in my mouth and bite it just then to stop myself from swearing.

"Don't worry, though. PC Atkinson's best mate's uncle is a locksmith, so we've got him on the phone to see what he thinks."

"And?"

I'd love to have seen her face then. It wouldn't have displayed any emotion – Irons never does – but it would have been a pleasure to know that, deep down, she was squirming. "Mr Smith from The Happy Locksmith Company has confirmed that he also lacks the tools required to force open an anti-theft system of this calibre."

What the heck were they thinking when they installed those shutters? Are there rare gems stored on the property that they didn't want anyone taking?

"And so your next step would be?" I gave her one last chance.

There was some muffled chatter as she conferred with her colleagues. "Our next step would be to brainstorm other ideas for how to get you out and, short of that, call in the fire brigade."

"Thank you, D.I. Irons. You've been a great help."

Chapter Twelve

Irons and I promised to keep one another abreast of any developments, or, as she put it, I should "ring back if anyone else gets topped." With the call concluded, I returned once more to the scene of the (definitely a) crime.

"I don't understand what's happened here, Izzy." Mrs Davies was still distraught. "I've been looking at the body, and I don't think that Ernie died of natural causes. It's pretty clear that he was…"

"Murdered? Yes, I came to the same conclusion. The phone on your desk was hooked up to an electric current and, when Mr Bath tried to make a call, he got a million volts straight through his body."

Her sorrow faded a little, and she looked frustrated in the way that most teachers do when one of their students says something ignorant. "A million volts isn't very realistic, Izzy. British mains power is around two hundred and thirty volts and, from what I can see, the cable that killed Ernie was hooked up to the battery from an electric car that would offer anything up to 400 volts and could more or less guarantee death in a man of his size and physique." She peered under the table to confirm this fact. "Yes, it's a battery from a Nissan Leaf."

I didn't feel too bad about not knowing such information and responded with a catty, "Well, you certainly didn't teach me anything so practical when I was here. Have you thought of eliminating physical education and offering something more useful such as detective studies, perhaps?"

She wasn't keen on the idea. "Izzy, the more pressing question is why anyone would have murdered him."

I sidestepped along the gap between the desk and the window to look at the body from a different angle. "Perhaps he wasn't the intended victim. Perhaps the killer set this up for you. I've been wondering about Tommy and Clara in the security room too. What if they stumbled into a trap?"

She put her hand to her mouth. "I don't see what you… Wait, the power cut!"

"That's right. What if the killer triggered the power cut in order to close up the school, knowing that you would go to the security room to try to fix it?"

My dear old headmistress was crying again but for a different reason this time. "This is awful. I can't..." She moved as though to sit down at her desk but then had second thoughts.

"I'm sorry, Miss. But everything suggests that you were the real target. Unless you can think of a reason why Mr Bath came into your office."

She peered at her hands as though she blamed herself. "No... I... I can't think what he was doing in here. I suppose he just came to call his family away from the noise and decided to use the landline. Perhaps there was a problem with his mobile."

I was more focused now and decided to go slowly with her. "I understand, and I'm sorry to have to point this out, but that does suggest that you were the person the killer expected to sit in this chair. So can you think of any reason why someone would want to hurt you?"

In one jarring movement, her eyes clicked onto mine. For a second, I thought she was about to reveal some dramatic secret that could explain why the school had invested in their insane security system. I mean, Dean's completely paranoid and even he doesn't have tungsten-reinforced plates over his windows.

Instead, her eyes widened, and she shook her head. "No, I really haven't a clue. I have the odd run-in with my students, but I think everyone knows that I'm a fair teacher. I'm never excessively strict."

This fitted with everything I remembered about her. The truth was that she was a thoroughly good egg. Though I'd been at the point of imploding whilst waiting to go into her office back when I was eighteen, the hardest part of that day was the fear I had before entering the room. Once inside, she listened to what I had to say, told me I'd acted like a moron, and let me off with a warning. She even gave me a lollipop, but that was mainly because I was crying. I think I might have gone into too much detail about the problems in my relationship with Gary Flint.

"What about back when we were your students?" I thought I'd shift the focus of my question. "There were some nasty kids here then. Was there anyone in particular who stood out?"

She leaned against the wall as though she couldn't support her weight for one moment longer. "To be perfectly honest, Izzy, fifteen years have passed since I even thought of most of you. I had to go back through the files to put a few faces to your names. I hadn't a clue who Verity was when she came to ask whether she could organise the reunion."

"So you don't remember any of us?" I definitely showed more disappointment at this than I'd intended. "I mean, you can't recall anyone who had a grudge against you?"

She breathed in softly and considered the possibility. "Well... I think that there are pupils in every year who take against their teachers. Back in your time here, there was a group of boys who caused a lot of trouble. Robert Mitchell's friends were forever ending up in my office, but I doubt any of them hated me so much that they would do something like this."

I let out a disbelieving huff, as it was that very gang who had made my life so unbearable.

Mrs Davies clearly sensed my mood on the matter. "Maybe you thought that we teachers didn't know what went on when our backs were turned, but we did. Any good head will know who the kind-hearted children are and who deserves a good kick up the behind."

I loved her old-fashioned manner. She'd already looked ancient when I'd arrived at secondary school, and she'd grown into a rather loveable grandmother figure.

"I suppose you're right."

Her face clouded over all the same. "Mind you, there was one boy who was particularly cruel. It's not often that I come across a pupil to whom I take an instant dislike, but he was that rare example."

In my mind then, I scanned the faces of every last thug and ruffian who'd called me Freak or tried to pull down my skirt in the playground.

She beat me to it. "His name was Martin Thompson." Her voice had become cold and hard. "It was certainly a happy day when he left this place for good. Ever since I saw his face again on my computer, I've been dreading the thought of seeing him. As far as I can tell, though, he hasn't appeared."

I was happy to deliver a nugget of good news. "You don't have to worry about Martin Thompson. Someone stuck a cake knife through his heart at a children's birthday party. I solved the case myself."

She really smiled at this. "Oh, wonderful. Well, that is nice to hear." She pulled her quilted jacket down so that it was tighter around her hips, nodded and marched from the room.

Weird.

Yep. Weird.

I took a moment to take stock of the facts. To start with, we were trapped inside a building with a killer who possessed a surprisingly extensive knowledge of wiring and security systems. If I'd been trying to electrocute someone, I'd have gone to a shop and bought a standard car battery, but our killer clearly knew (or, at the very least, searched online to discover) that a normal one wouldn't do the job.

I don't think this was my biggest worry at that moment, however. What was really upsetting was the idea that there were over one hundred people in the hall, all dancing to the beat of Ramesh's drum 'n' bass anthem. Any one of them could have sneaked out to set a couple of deadly traps. How was I supposed to identify the culprit?

The first thing I needed to do was to get my gang of helpers together. Danny and Shandy were… Well, the last time I'd seen them they'd been pressed up against the climbing bars at the back of the hall. If I talked to Ramesh, he'd only chastise me for telling him what he already knew – i.e. me + any kind of public function = guaranteed killing spree. So that only left Dean and Lorna.

I have to say that I felt a little sorry for her. When I arrived in the hall, she was dancing a few inches from Dean as though Britney Spears' 'Toxic' was a romantic ballad. Back when we were at school, she'd made me look like Little Miss Charisma. I'd always wanted to be nice to her, but that was easier said than done when she hardly spoke and spent most break times hiding in the physics room. And now here she was, falling in love with Dean. I couldn't help feeling responsible. If I hadn't gone to the reunion, my idiot friends wouldn't have joined me, and poor Lorna would never have fallen for the wrong guy.

This flashed through my head in the two seconds before Dean realised I was standing staring at them. He rushed over, happy for an excuse not to have to dance.

"Any news from the police?"

"Yes, but none of it is good."

Lorna made some sympathetic sounds that were entirely

incomprehensible over the noise of the music or, I can only assume, a light breeze.

"That's not the worst of it, though." My mother always says that a problem shared is a problem halved, but even a tenth of a reduction would have made me feel better. "I just found Mr Bath dead in the headmistress's office."

Dean made a *what are the chances?* sort of face before realising it wasn't a coincidence. "You mean he was murdered?"

"Yep, he was electrocuted with a booby-trapped phone." I remember a time in my life when this would have been an unusual sort of declaration to make. I remember a time when I'd never seen a dead body, and my greatest concern was who'd stolen my steak from the freezer. Oh, for those happy days once more!

"What next?" I am fairly confident that this is what Lorna asked.

"I haven't a clue. All I know is that it's not a good idea to get everyone else worked up. We should keep it quiet until the police can unlock the shutters."

Dean uncrumpled his very crumply face. "Surely there's something we can do?"

"Like what, oh wise and brilliant one?"

"You know, investigating and that kind of thing."

I had to take a deep breath to stop myself slapping him. "Don't you think I've considered that? Don't you think I'm aware that all my old schoolmates will expect me to catch the killer after they heard how brilliant I'm supposed to be? There are far more suspects than on a normal case, and I have no idea how to whittle them down."

Instead of making fun of me, or casting aspersions on my allegedly incredible skills of deduction, Dean licked the end of one finger and smoothed both eyebrows. This was his rather disgusting way of concentrating, and he soon came up with a response.

"Let's start by thinking things through. Obviously, the fact that the killer struck tonight is proof that the motive harks back to fifteen years ago when you were all at school. So what links your victims? What big event occurred back then that could explain why three people are dead?"

I was about to snap at him again, but reluctantly came to realise that this was a sensible approach. "You're right, but I've tried that.

I can't even say that our victims were the real targets. It seems to me that Mrs Davies should have been in both of the locations where people were killed. Or maybe that's what the killer wants us to think. Maybe the victims were lured there in order to suggest that this is all linked to our old headmistress."

Lorna whispered something else that whistled past me unheard.

"Good point!" Dean put his hand out for a high-five, and she looked overjoyed to reciprocate. Neither of them was used to high-fiving and so it turned into a clumsy wave. Whatever her suggestion had been, Dean led us outside to enact it.

The two of them sped off, chitty chattering away like Muppets, and I tagged along behind. We didn't stop at Mrs Davies' office but kept right on to the security room.

"Yes, that is a good idea to re-examine the first crime scene in light of the second," I stated in a (hopefully) casual voice as my brain finally deciphered Lorna's previous comment. "Now that we know that there is a killer on the premises, we should see whether Tommy and Clara really were just unlucky to come in here."

The door still only opened a fraction as the fallen cabinet blocked the way, but we managed to sidle in one at a time, and I walked further into the room to have a proper look around.

I don't often say this, but Ramesh was right. By this point, you really should expect any dead body you find to be a murder victim.

I ignored my own *told-you-so* thoughts and inspected the now dark monitors. "Lorna, did Mrs Davies turn these off?"

She shrugged, and Dean came to see what was going on. "They're not just turned off. Someone has smashed up the computer that was controlling everything."

He ducked under the table and returned with a demolished drive… thingy. Fine! I don't know much about electric wiring, and I can't tell you the first thing about computers. But ask me who starred in any of the Poirot movies, and I'll reel you off a cast list that makes me look like a savant.

I thought of a perfectly valid question. "Are the cameras still filming around the school?"

"No. They could be if we had another computer to control them, but I'd have to install new software and configure it. It would take me a while and there's no guarantee I'll have access to everything I need. If only I had my geek squad here. They could lock this place down and catch our killer in minutes." Dean had a pack of tech-nerds in his office for just such emergencies, but they wouldn't be much use beyond the iron curtain.

I let out a downhearted purr to which Lorna was surely quite receptive as she shot me a sympathetic look. "Couldn't we…" she began, but she was just as stumped as I was.

Despite the well of indecision I was wallowing in, I spotted something on the floor beneath the smithereens of computer hardware. "Wait, that's odd." I walked over for a closer look at the brightly coloured, towelling band that was half concealed by shards of plastic. "I swear this is the sweatband that Robert Mitchell wore on our sports day in 2006."

They looked at me as though I was weird for remembering what the most handsome boy in school had been wearing as a sports accessory during a particularly sweaty eight-hundred-metre run seventeen years earlier. "Hey! Don't judge me. That was the day he broke the county record. It's not like I fancied Robert Mitchell or anything. I knew he'd never go out with a girl like me; I was too clever."

Aww, you still like telling yourself that. It's so sweet.

"Izzy, you're imagining things." Dean sighed a little. He often did that when talking to me. "We're looking at you in the same completely normal way we always do. If anything, I think facial expressions are overrated."

Lorna nodded in agreement.

"Fine, but the headband could be significant, especially as I found a tube of Robert's ex's exact shade of lipstick at the scene of Mr Bath's murder."

I thought this was an interesting twist, and the perfect thing to spur us – Famous Five style – on to the next part of the investigation.

Dean's eyes flicked over to his fake date before he addressed me once more. "Alright," he conceded. "I wasn't judging you the first time, but I am now. It is a little odd that you know so much about two people you've had nothing to do with since you left school. I barely remember my nephew's name, and we live on the same road."

"Well, thanks for looking down on me." I parsed his comment for information. My brain is more of a nineteenth century typewriter than a supercomputer, and it would take a minute. "Hang on a second. Does that mean you have siblings? We've been friends for three years and you've never mentioned any." I clapped my hands together and yelped in glee. "Ha! Now who's the weird one, Dean? Now who's the weird one!?"

From the look on Lorna's face (as I danced the Macarena in celebration) this was an easy question to answer.

Chapter Thirteen

Our really quite inconsequential discovery in the security room had given me a boost of energy. I ran back to the hall like a team leader on a corporate trust-building weekend. I was determined to get to the bottom of the strange run of events before (too many) more people were murdered.

The mood in the party had changed. The dancing had become wilder and there were occasional shouts of disagreement between old rivals.

"I don't know what's got into them, Izzy." Ramesh yelled from across the room as soon as he saw me there. "They were putty in my hands, but things have started to go wrong."

As he came closer, I noticed a couple of Robert Mitchell's laddish friends pushing one another, and I thought I knew what was causing the problem.

"The punch!" I clicked my fingers and felt like Robin to Ramesh's cheesy 1960s batman, so I made a mental note not to do that again. We rushed over to the drinks table and, sure enough, there was a slight aftertaste to the fruity drink. "It's been spiked."

Ramesh looked confused. "Is there something I missed while we were playing a game of spin the human disco bottle?" He held one hand out to stop me before I could answer. "No, let me guess. I was right all along and there really is a murderer here? One of your former teachers has also been killed, and you've found a minor piece of evidence to link the two crimes together?"

I was a little in awe of this. "How did you do that?"

"It's not so difficult, Izzy. I've watched enough high school reunion comedies and a billion whodunits with you over the last couple of years. If you know your tropes, it becomes rather formulaic."

I had to blink a few times to check that I wasn't imagining things. "So does that mean you know who the killer is?"

He raised one finger as though supremely confident on the matter. "Nope... I haven't the foggiest. But don't get ahead of yourself. First, you might want to consider who spiked the punch and go from there."

I cast my gaze towards the party and noticed once more that

Pete Boon was bumping his chest up against Michael Andersen's. They were clearly a good few cups drunker than the dancers around them and, if my calculations were correct, this made them the likely culprits... of this one minor offence at least.

"Who do you think would consume more?" I asked. "The people who know that a non-alcoholic drink has been spiked or the people who don't?"

"Pete Boon!" Ramesh replied, as he'd apparently got to know every last person in the room whilst I was dealing with those of the post-life persuasion. "He's been running around like a madman. I thought it was just excitement to be here, but he must have read the invitation and done what he could to correct the lack of alcohol."

As he said this, Pete ripped his shirt open and roared like the Incredible Hulk – which is the second and last superhero reference I will be making today (and possibly for the rest of my life).

My top-three former bully wasn't the only one who was acting out of character, though. Verity Gresham had apparently forgotten her woes and was riding Robert Mitchell around the room. She'd found an old school tie from somewhere and was whirling it about her head like a lasso. Even more surprisingly, she occasionally gave his neck a tiny bite and let out loud woofs. I considered telling her that someone had got the party drunk, but she seemed to be having a good time, and I didn't want to make her sad again.

"It's actually very good," Ramesh said as he helped himself to another cup. "You can barely taste the vodka but, once you know it's there, there's no mistaking it." He knocked it down his throat and let out a crisp breath.

"Ra, do what you can to get the party under control. There's someone I need to talk to." I should probably have told him not to drink too much, but I had bigger things to worry about. I'd also lost my temporary sidekicks at some point, though I couldn't blame them for ditching me. I'd been acting funny all night, and no number of Enid Blyton and comic book comparisons could make it seem normal. They'd either deserted me, or Dean's weak bladder had sent him off to the toilets again.

Someone who already looked sad was Becky Mitchell, the onetime princess of West Wickham High. If I haven't made it clear yet, Becky was everything I dreamed of being when I was sixteen. She had tons of friends, great hair, and the boyfriend everyone wanted. She was like South London Suburban Barbie, and who wouldn't want to be South London Suburban Barbie?

I marched over to see the woman who was sitting alone, looking glum. In truth, if I hadn't been bouncing about the place in full detective mode, I would have probably done the same thing. I'd yet to suffer some terrible embarrassment that night, but that didn't make the reunion any more bearable. I thought I would get a buzz from seeing how my classmates' lives had turned out, but it was a little depressing to discover what had become of everyone. I just had to hope that we wouldn't all meet again when we were older and more miserable.

That's the spirit!

"Hi Becky." I tried to sound jolly for her sake. "Is there anyone sitting here?" It wasn't the most sensitive question to put to her.

"No, go ahead, Izzy. Do whatever you like." She masked a sob by clutching a balled-up tissue to her mouth. "You normally do anyway!"

It wasn't exactly an invitation to chat, but then I'm supremely talented at ignoring *the hint* and began to blather away. "I'm sorry we haven't had a chance to talk until now. I've wanted to catch up ever since I got here, but I've been a bit busy."

Her head was pointing in my direction, but her eyes were fixed to the floor. Even when crying, she looked excruciatingly pretty. I'd always been jealous of her as a kid, but I just felt bad for her now. My mind flashed back to a similar moment when we were both sixteen and, instead of talking to her to check that she was okay, I'd started singing a pop song.

I would not be making that mistake today. "I'm sorry, Becky. I really am."

"What for?" Each word was a sniff.

"For everything. For me being up on the stage instead of you. For turning your son's birthday into a murder investigation when Martin Thompson was stabbed, and for giving your six-year-old a bottle of vodka as a present." I was trying to think what else I might get off my chest but drew a blank.

She sat up straighter in order to look down her perfectly symmetrical nose at me. "Oh. So you're not sorry for tearing my life apart?"

I was more than a little surprised at this response. Before coming to the reunion, I'd been scared that everyone would laugh and make fun of me. Being blamed for Becky Mitchell's divorce was nowhere to be found on the bingo card in my head.

She had more to complain about, of course. "Until I bumped into you in the supermarket and invited you to Jasper's birthday, my life was perfect." She had a jug of punch in front of her and, instead of pouring out a measure for herself in one of the brightly coloured spotty paper cups, she chugged it straight down. "I had my angelic children."

Angelic? They make Hannibal Lecter look like a really rather reasonable chap!

"I had a wonderful, successful, well-toned husband, and an Instagram that I could be proud of." She looked into the nostalgic fog of the middle distance. "I truly was 'The Yummiest Mummy'! But then it all went wrong."

This didn't make much sense to me as, from what I'd heard from Mum, who heard it from her friend Sarah, who was told by Becky's dad, the Mitchells' fame had exploded after the party I'd attended. "But I thought you transitioned to true crime and made a killing?"

She didn't blink once throughout the conversation but trained her eyes on me like laser beams. "That's right. Our company, 'Mumspiration and Murder,' mined an on-trend seam of internet-based content. We hit six million followers, and the money just flowed in." She allowed herself a brief, evil laugh – as is the right of anyone who becomes filthy rich. "We counted David Cameron and the drummer from Coldplay among our subscribers. We had synergetic influencing arrangements with Softust!"

"Isn't that a toilet paper?"

She put one hand out in melodramatic shock. "No, Izzy. It's not just 'a toilet paper'. It is *the* toilet paper – the very best available – and we were their true-crime-and-parenting-focused Instagram influencing partner. The day that we signed with them was the happiest I can remember; I thought that all of our dreams had come true."

I'd lost my patience by now and decided to stick up for myself. "So how can you blame me for whatever went wrong?"

Crossing one leg over the other, she leaned in closer and dropped her voice a few decibels. "Because if it hadn't been for you, we'd never have achieved all that. My darling Robert and I flew too close to the sun; we lost sight of the things that mattered. And yes, I made it into the top five sexiest Insta-babes in Real Detective magazine. And, okay, we were tipped as one of the best non-fiction podcasts of 2021 by Ozzy Osbourne's book club. But all the fame and the countless celebrity endorsements sent us on different paths. They split my family apart."

She was even more self-centred than I had remembered.

"And that's my fault?"

"Yes, it is! My daughter Angelica was signed by an under-elevens modelling agency. Little Jasper got a lucrative e-gaming sponsorship, and Robert…" Her voice broke at this moment, and she struggled to complete the sentence. "Robert made a fortune advising up-and-coming mummy-bloggers on how to be successful entrepreneurs. If we'd never changed to true crime, we'd never have become so famous, and my husband wouldn't have left me for a cakestagramer called Sprinklez3000!"

She was weeping by this point, and I figured I should at least try to comfort her. "That must have been terrible for you. I honestly can't imagine what you've been through."

"Of course you can't!" She looked at me in that appreciative way that vain people do whenever you say something complimentary. "They have their own podcast called 'Cakez 'n' Crimez'. It doesn't even make any sense. What has baking got to do with murder?"

I would have asked her what "mumspiration" had to do with murder, but she was in a dark place, and I didn't want to make things worse.

"You should see the woman's black velvet dribble! It's a thing of beauty, Izzy. I can't compete with that." It took me a moment to realise that she was talking about a cake. "People have always been jealous of my brand. If anything, I would say it is my defining feature. Remember in archery class in year eleven when Verity accidentally shot my target? I swear that arrow was meant for me. But I doubt that anyone would try to shoot me now!"

She was clearly disappointed that she was no longer a likely murder victim. It was hard to empathise with this position, especially considering all that had gone on that evening.

"Maybe they wouldn't kill you," I began, having remembered that I was supposed to be investigating a murder or three, "but can you think of any reason that someone might want to frame you for a crime?"

She bit her pretty pink lip and considered the question – or possibly thought about how wonderful she was for a few seconds. With Becky, it was hard to say what was going on behind that glossy façade. "A few months ago, I could have listed any number of people who would have wanted to knock me from my lofty perch. After all, I did make it into the top five sexiest Insta-babes in Real—"

"Yes, you told me." I had that particular issue filed in my office somewhere, not that I'm obsessed with Becky Mitchell or anything. It had an interesting article on surveillance techniques that I hope to get around to reading one day.

"Wait, you didn't let me finish. They've just published this year's list and…" The sorrow stormed her body once more, and I doubted she'd be able to complete this sentence. "…I was only at number nine."

The poor girl really was a mess. It didn't matter that I thought her priorities were twisted beyond all reason or that I found her to be the most superficial – yet beautiful and occasionally charming – person I'd ever met. She really was suffering, and she deserved my sympathy.

Sing to her, Izzy! It will make her feel better.

No! I'm not going to sing. You got me into that mess the last time.

♩♫♩

Brain! Stop whistling Robbie Williams's 'Angels'. I'm not going to sing that bloody song!

"Tell me, Becky…" I began without knowing what I would say. "Do you have anything against our old headmistress?" It wasn't the subtlest question, but then I didn't think she could cry any more than she already had. I was wrong.

"You mean Mummy?" Her eyes widened and tears as big as pear drops fell from them.

I'd forgotten that suck-ups like Becky had called Mrs Davies that. It was so schmaltzy it turned my stomach. "Yes, I mean *Mummy*."

"Please tell me that something hasn't happened to her."

"No, don't worry. It's just that she's…" Talking without thinking is a stupid thing to do, but I came up with a half decent lie. "Well, she's been receiving some nasty letters and such. She believes they could be from someone in our year."

She shook her head as the thought of something happening to our teacher ran through her brain. "I loved dear old Mrs Davies. I still do. I would never wish her any harm."

"What about the rest of your friends? Is there anyone who took against her?"

She glanced back to the raging throng of dancers, and her sweet tone was suddenly gone. "That lot? Where do I begin? Every last one of them had some grievance with her. Pete Boon used to claim he was going to knife the wheels of her Volvo whenever he got into trouble. Verity got a talking to when Mrs Davies found her in the boys' toilets with her cousin Steve." Becky's voice fell to a conspiratorial whisper. "She never confessed what they were up to in there, but we all saw the love bites."

Urgggh! Her cousin?

"Oh, and I mustn't forget Mandy Johnson."

"Your best friend Mandy Johnson?"

"No, Izzy, another Mandy Johnson." She rolled her eyes, then continued in an even more impatient tone. "She can't stand the woman. Not only did Mrs Davies give Mandy a B minus on her geography essay when we were in year ten, a few years after we left school, she had an affair with Mandy's dad."

Yeah… I think I would have started with that.

"Lovely old Mrs Davies was Mr Johnson's mistress? I might be remembering him wrong, but didn't he look like a werewolf?" It was all coming back to me now. "I can picture him; he had hair on his eyelids."

"Apparently Mrs Davies didn't notice. The two were madly in love. Mr Johnson left his wife and children to be with her." I thought this would be the end of the sordid tale, but there was more to come. "And on the day he left home to start a new life, he was mowed down in the street by a hit and run driver. Mrs Davies found him in the street, but they never found out who did it."

My synapses fired as I took in her story. This had to be the killer's motivation. I'd barely seen Mandy that night – and, no I haven't mentioned her before because I didn't realise that she would be of any significance whatsoever – but she'd just shot to the top of my suspect list.

"Tell me honestly, Becky." I paused and held her gaze to show just how serious I was. "Do you think that your friend could be trying to get her own back on Mrs Davies?"

She bit her lip and thought about herself some more... or considered my question. I still couldn't say for sure. "She did say she wasn't looking forward to crossing paths with 'the old witch' again."

"But do you think she would have gone further and sought revenge?"

It was a rare moment when Becky Mitchell wasn't entirely sure of herself. "I... I can't say for certain. She does talk a lot about her father. And I know her mother has never got over what happened back then. I suppose it's possible."

This was all I needed to hear. I was up on my feet before she'd finished speaking.

"Izzy, wait!" Becky shouted after me. "I haven't spent enough time making you feel guilty. We were supposed to be talking about me!"

Chapter Fourteen

The disco lights sent a flashing red beam across my path as I darted through the crowd, determined to track down the culprit. It surely all fitted together. Mandy had found a way to cut the power in order to get her nemesis Mrs Davies into the security room. When Tommy and Clara fell into her trap instead, she rigged up her plan B and waited for her intended victim to come to the office and make a phone call. The only problem was that saintly Mr Bath happened to wander by and took the full four hundred volts through his body before I found him. Who could say what else Mandy had cooked up? All I knew was that I would not let her get away with such wicked deeds.

"Mandy Johnson!" I yelled, seizing her by the shoulder in the middle of the melee. She turned around with an unusual look on her face… and a different haircut from the one she'd had earlier. "Oh, sorry, wrong person."

On I went, weaving through the throng in search of the killer. I was worried that she was busy somewhere arranging her next attack. I was about to leave the dance floor when I heard a voice from behind me and spun around to find her standing right in front of me.

"Izzy, it is you!" Somewhat puzzlingly, she sounded pleased to see me. "Do you still go to the same supermarket?" It was just the kind of question that a killer would pose to throw a bloodhound detective off the scent. "Do you remember the last time we met, and we realised that we both go to the same supermarket? I mean, what are the chances? Just think how many times we must have been there at the same time and not even realised. It was back at Becky's son's sixth birthday party. Do you remember? That was the party when Becky wore a white mini dress and Martin Thompson was stabbed to death."

She waited a good ten seconds without me saying anything before continuing as if I had. "Do you remember? I said that I liked the selection at Sainsbury's, and you said they have really good cakes. I laughed at that because I don't eat gluten, or sugar, or dairy, or food beginning with C. Except for carrots, celery and cabbage, of course." I was still a little hopeful that this incessant droning was a ploy to hide her guilt, but I had also come to remember that she was the most boring person I'd ever met. "Oh, you made me laugh, Izzy. You really did. I don't think I've had such a giggle since."

My heart sank lower in my chest, as though it had turned to lead. "So what are you up to these days?" I asked, despite myself.

Indulging in a spot of murder, perhaps?

She laughed inappropriately loudly. "Well, it's all change at chez Johnson-Marenghi. That's right, I kept my maiden name when I married Gav. He didn't mind, and I thought that Mandy Johnson sounded better than Mandy Marenghi. That's right, I married Gavin Marenghi. Do you remember Gav? He was a real joker when we were at school. That was how I knew he fancied me. He tried to play so many tricks on me in chemistry that, one day, I said to him, I said, are you going to ask me out or are you going to keep playing the idiot? Anyway, as I was saying, it's all change at Chez Johnson-Marenghi. We had the spare bedroom re-wallpapered recently, and I can't tell you the difference it's made. I really can't. It's like a new room up there, it really is. You must come round sometime and see it. I mean, I know you don't know what it was like before, but I can't tell you what an improvement it is, and I've got plenty of photos of the old décor. I'm sure you'll appreciate it."

Have you ever had a conversation where you know in your heart you'd be better off bludgeoning yourself to death with the nearest blunt object as the very fact of listening to the barrage of senseless verbosity is somehow more painful? No, neither had I until that moment. She had somehow become more inane in the two years since I'd last seen her. It was quite uncanny.

Every fibre in my body was pulling me in the opposite direction, but I managed to get another question out. "And what do you do for a job?"

"Me? A job?" She laughed again. I have no idea why. "I don't think anyone's ever asked me that before. I work for my brother's company. He sells sand to double glazing companies. Only he doesn't really sell the sand, so much as the chance to buy the sand. It's very interesting, actually. Though, as it happens, I don't have anything to do with the sand, or the selling. I'm more what you might call a connections specialist. You see, it's my job to…"

I think it was at this point that I passed out with my eyes open. The woman's capacity to bore was an all-potent superpower. I could only imagine that Gavin Marenghi had married her because he'd lost the will to live in a middle of a conversation and fallen into a coma. When I finally came around, I would have given her a kidney or let her move into my house as long as she stopped talking.

"Nothing to do with computing or electrical engineering, then?" I got my final question out and was champing at the bit to run away as soon as she'd delivered her answer.

"Well, now that you mention it, I do have a computer and, as far as I know, it is connected to an electrical supply, but I'm no Brain of Britain. I only really use it for checking my socials during my coffee break. To be perfectly honest, I don't—"

"Thanks, Mandy." I was hopping from foot to foot in desperation. "It was great catching up, but I have to… go… now."

"We've only just—"

"Yeah, sorry. I think I'm going to wet myself." The embarrassment that this statement could provoke seemed insignificant when compared to my need to escape, and I sprinted through the crowd towards the front of the school.

"Don't forget about the spare bedroom!" she called after me. "You can pop by at any time. We're at number twenty-four, Collingtree Road, Sydenham. We'll have a really—"

I'm sorry/glad to say I didn't hear anything more. I'd put my fingers in my ears and was rushing through the double doors and into the corridor. I pushed my back up against the wall like I was escaping from a hand grenade. When the force of Mandy's boredom didn't come blowing through the exit in an explosion of brick, wood and dull comments, I knew I was safe.

To my surprise, the world had kept turning while I was being tortured. Dean and Lorna were sitting in the comfy seats in the foyer having a civilised conversation.

"It's interesting you should say that," my friend declared in response to some typically hushed utterances. "I tend to use Japanese-made conductors in my prototypes for new products."

I stalked towards them to find out what techy nonsense Dean was babbling, when my phone started vibrating in my purse. "Hello, the Private I detective Agency. Izzy sp—"

"It's me again," a voice at the other end interrupted my spiel.

"Oh, hello, D.I. Irons, I mean Victoria." I'd never got used to calling her by her first name, which certainly made hanging out at nightclubs with her a strange experience.

"Hi, Iz. We're making big progress out here. The lads and ladies from the local fire station are about to arrive, and we'll have the school breached in no time. In fact, that's why I'm ringing. I just wanted to check that no one is in the foyer right now and, if they are, perhaps you could clear them out in approximately the next seven seconds before our armoured vehicle ploughs through the front shutters."

"Dean! Lorna!" I screamed their names when an imperative sentence would have been the more direct way to save them. "Move, now!"

I think that my tone communicated the necessary urgency, whereas the expression on my face put across the danger they were both in as they shot up to standing, ran in my direction and leapt through the air as we heard the mini-tank hitting the concrete steps outside the school.

The three of us fell to the floor with our heads in our hands just as the impact was felt. The impressive sound echoed around the foyer and when it was over, I remained there motionless for a few seconds.

Confident that I was still alive, I put my phone to my ear.

"Nah, that didn't work." I could hear Irons scratching her cheek as she assessed the damage. "We've dinged up the truck pretty badly, but there's not much of a dent on the shutters." She shouted across to one of her colleagues, "Oi, John! I told you it wouldn't work!"

"You could have given us more warning." I had just about returned to my normal state of mild panic, but my voice came out in a shriek. "What were you thinking?"

She became a little defensive. Even hints of emotion were out of character for her, so I certainly paid attention. "I didn't know the idiot was going to drive like that. I thought we were going to call a welder or something, but Brabazon had a better idea. Ever since he bought a Kia Sportage, he thinks he's Michael Schumacher."

Dean was busy making sure that his companion for the evening was okay when Irons found she had another question for me. "By the way, has anyone else been killed?"

"Not yet. And I'd appreciate it if you could do whatever it takes to prevent that from happening."

She gave a long sniff before responding. It sounded a little hard done by, but then I'm always psychoanalysing Irons and doubt many of my conclusions are close to the truth. "We're doing our best. If the welder can't cut through the shutters, we've got a team searching the perimeter for another way in. We'll have you out of there in a—" I hung up before she could finish that thought.

I was perfectly happy on the floor, but a boy from my GCSE history group walked out of the hall at that moment on the way to the toilet and stopped in his tracks to cast me a funny look. I figured this was a sign that I should get up.

"Are you guys okay?" I asked as I got to my feet.

"I've got a hurty knee," Dean revealed, but Lorna squeaked some assurances that she was fine.

On the one hand, I was happy that they hadn't been squashed by a marauding armoured vehicle. On the other, I was disappointed we were still stuck in the killer's playground.

It's all swings and roundabouts, Izzy. Try to look on the bright side.

"This isn't like one of my normal cases," I told them once we were no longer so afraid of imminent death. "For one thing, I'm rarely the potential victim."

"Why would anyone want to kill you?" Dean sounded quite bemused by the idea.

"Oh, thanks very much." I suddenly understood how Becky had felt at not even passing muster as the target of a killer's rage. "So I'm not the kind of person that a savage murderer would bother killing. Is that what you're saying?"

He shook his head despairingly. "Not quite, Isobel. I was asking whether you had reason to believe the culprit had something against you."

"Oh. I see." I thought this was a pretty solid response under the circumstances. "In that case, no. I have no reason to believe they're after me, but three people connected to my year at school are already dead. There's nothing to make me think that the killer has finished for the night, so I'm just as likely to be next as anyone else."

He crouched down on his haunches and supported his chin with his fist. It was another of his classic thinking poses. "Tell us what you've discovered."

I thought back through my interviews with Mandy, Becky and Mrs Davies. "I discovered that my headmistress isn't the goody-goody we all thought she was. And I know that one of my classmates has recently wallpapered her spare bedroom but, beyond that, not much."

"Good." He didn't need to squat there for long and popped back up to standing. "You're obviously getting nowhere, so there's only one thing for it."

I can always trust Dean to get me through a crisis of confidence. He marched off along the corridor, trying each door he came to until he found one that was unlocked.

"This is so much fun!" Lorna bobbed with excitement as she followed him into the onetime nurse's office turned general first-aid-room. I heard they'd given dear old Nurse Crouch the sack because of cutbacks a few years earlier. To be honest, there can't be many school nurses left in the world and she was lucky to have lasted as long as she did. This did raise the question of how they'd paid for the ridiculous security system, though.

I thought about getting Ramesh, but he was busy in the hall, and anyway, his idea of brainstorming was to accuse all the suspects of being secret lovers and think that was enough to solve the case. I might have looked for Danny and Shandy to round off the numbers too, but it turned out they were already there.

"Urghhhhh! What are you doing?" I did not mince my words. "That's disgusting."

The pair of them were laid out on the examination bed, their legs knotted together like a love spoon. I had to console myself with the fact that they were fully clothed.

"Hi, everyone!" Danny beamed at us as though it was perfectly normal to find him stuck to a woman he'd met a mere fifteen to twenty times before.

"Hi, Izzy." Shandy at least had the decency to titter like a naughty child.

"I thought you were just pretending to be into one another to make Shandy's ex jealous!" This was an incredibly optimistic conclusion to form.

"That is exactly what we were doing..." Danny smiled at Shandy, and they both looked a bit shy. "...to begin with."

"Yeah, to begin with, that's all it was." Shandy was full on blushing and couldn't take her eyes off my ex. "Danny was being nice to me and held my hand. Then we started dancing together, and he just smelled so good that... Well, one thing led to another and... Have you seen what he looks like in a V-neck t-shirt?"

This might not sound like much of an argument, but Danny disagreed and pointed to himself cheerfully.

"None of that is relevant," Dean interrupted and slammed down a home medical guide onto the nurse's desk – which I now noticed was all muddled and messy.

I'll give you one guess why!
Noooooope!
Danny and Shandy, lying on the desk, K-I-S-S-I-N—
Shhhh!!!

"All of you, shut up and pay attention." Whilst I'd been feeling grossed out for no sensible reason, Dean had produced some tiny pieces of technological equipment and connected them together using Bluetooth or magic or something. "Izzy needs our help to solve this murder, so that's what we're going to give her."

Danny and Shandy made no reaction to this sensational news.

"Why are neither of you at all surprised that someone's been killed?" I had to ask.

Shandy shrugged. "It's just the kind of thing that happens around you, isn't it? Some people win lots of raffles and lottery prizes, you discover dead bodies. We all have our thing."

Lorna did not appear to be listening but was overjoyed as a light beam popped out of Dean's small black box to cast an image onto the wall. After a few seconds, a picture came into focus. There was a blue pleated curtain and several office chairs arranged in a semi-circle in front of it. It reminded me of a tiny conference room, but something about it looked oddly familiar.

"Hello, darling!" Mum stuck her head into view as two of her husbands mumbled in the background.

"Mother, have you turned my bedroom into a media centre?"

She looked apologetic for approximately three seconds. "I'm not going to lie to you, my sweet. That's exactly what we've done.

However, in my defence, it will be very useful for conducting interviews from home."

I was appalled. "That's not a defence so much as a reason. What happened to my James Blunt posters?"

I heard my dad whispering loudly. "Ohhh, she'll be in for it now! Those posters went in the recycling bin the same day that Izzy left home."

I considered falling to my knees and crying out in pain at the thought of the callous bulldozing of my shrine to my childhood self. Luckily, Dean was still there to keep us on track.

"I've been liaising with your mother throughout the evening, and she's assembled a team to help us." To this day, I have no idea why my friends text my mother so often. I often go weeks without replying to her messages.

"That's right, Izzy! I've reassembled The Hawes Lane Amateur Detective Society." She was clearly very excited and waved her hands towards the camera as a roll call of figures from her entourage appeared to take their places. "The whole gang's here! My personal stylist, Fernando. Mrs Dominski from the newsagents. Will Gibbons from Porter & Porter. Your ex-ex boyfriend's Auntie Val. Mrs Curtis, who taught you when you were eleven. And Brian from the supermarket."

They waved as they took their seats like guests on a chat show.

"So hit us with the evidence, Izzy." Mother sounded like an army general as two loveable old fellows came into view. "Your fathers are standing at the ready with flip pads and pens. We'll solve this case if it's the last thing we do."

I looked at all those expectant faces back in my bedroom and all those expectant faces in the nurse's office, and I mumbled an answer. "I don't know what to tell you. I know I'm supposed to be more confident these days, but there's something about this case which feels all wrong."

"Ahh, there's a pity," dear old Auntie Val declared in her melodic South-Walian tone. "Take a deep breath, Izzy, my love, and tell us all about it."

"You can do it, Iz!" the guy who collects trolleys in our local supermarket declared, and I felt oddly empowered by his belief in me.

"Okay, I'm ready."

"That's the spirit." There were cheers of approval, and Mum said her recently under-used catchphrase. "Let's crack this case wide open!"

Chapter Fifteen

"It's not that there isn't any evidence. In fact, we've got an abundance of clues. It's making sense of how they might fit together that's flummoxing me."

"Flummox!" Fernando chipped in. "That's a good word!"

"Thanks." I was pacing up and down in front of the webcam that Dean had hooked up to his phone and then to... you know what? I have no idea how he'd done it, but we could see them, and they could see us. What's even more impressive is that he'd concealed all the equipment about his person without ruining the line of his nicely tailored suit. He really was a man of—

Izzy, focus!

"I think the second killing is key. With the first, we still can't say for sure that Tommy and Clara were the intended victims. They were such peripheral figures at school that it seems very unlikely that they would be targeted. I keep coming back to the idea that Mrs Davies should have died in the security room and again in her office. But if that was the case, it would mean the killer had worked out a truly elaborate back-up plan and arranged to bring a car battery into the school in order to achieve the desired result."

"Unless..." our nice Polish newsagent began. "Unless it isn't so much a back-up plan as an either/or situation. Perhaps this psychopath wanted to make totally sure that your headmistress got what was coming to her and set two different traps."

I had to consider her point – it was a lot more sensible than the rubbish my friends normally spouted. "It's possible, but that's still a very high level of planning. At the scene of each crime, I discovered artefacts that could connect the killings to specific former classmates. First Robert Mitchell and then his ex-wife Becky. Becky and Robert were the golden couple of our year, and I can't understand why their sweatband and lipstick would have been planted there."

"That seems fairly obvious," Danny surprised me by suggesting. I was frankly impressed that he'd managed to keep his mouth off my friend for long enough to speak. "Surely the killer is trying to incriminate them."

"Hmmm," Dean replied, and I must say that I agreed with him.

"Yes, on the surface that might make sense. Leaving a key item from each person definitely connects them with the crime. But Robert used that sweatband fifteen years ago. He doesn't walk around in sportswear these days and wouldn't have brought such an item to a school reunion."

"So what are you saying?" I think that Dad mainly asked this question to know whether to add the sweatband and lipstick to the list of evidence on his paper flip pad.

"I'm saying that it doesn't fit together with the elaborate plan that the killer has constructed. We're clearly looking for a person with knowledge of I.T. systems and some basic understanding of voltage and electrical wiring."

"The internet!" Lorna whispered rather dramatically.

Shandy clearly caught her meaning and seemed rather impressed. "That's a very good point, Lorna. You can find anything on the internet these days. I could probably knock up a half decent Taramasalata with the help of YouTube, but that doesn't make me a Greek chef."

There was some murmuring of agreement at this, but I continued with my point. "Fine, they don't necessarily have to be experts, but the fact that they went to the trouble of formulating an extremely technical plan means that they're smart enough to know that leaving a piece of evidence to link a particular person to a crime scene would not make them the killer."

This produced a burst of animated discussion, which buoyed me as I continued. "It also distracts us from the real target. Imagine that Mrs Davies had died in the first attack. What's the connection between her and the Mitchells?"

"More to the point," my stepfather Greg said in his wonderfully calm voice, "why would anyone want to kill the headmistress of West Wickham High?"

"That's what I've been focussing on since Mr Bath was killed. I thought I'd discovered a key point when Becky Mitchell told me that her painfully boring best friend's father had an affair with Mrs Davies. What I'd forgotten was that Mandy has the intelligence of an earwig and the charisma to match."

"There's nothing to say that boring people can't be killers, Izzy."

Dean was at his pernickety best. "I think you're being close-minded."

"Trust me, if you spend two minutes talking to Mandy, you'll know she isn't the monster that we're looking for. I'm not denying that she's evil incarnate, but in a whole different way. Now that I think about it, I should have known that she couldn't have come up with such an intricate plan. In general studies when we were seventeen, we had to do a presentation on women who had changed the world and she chose Sporty Spice."

Pfff, that's ridiculous. Everyone knows that Scary Spice was the real innovator.

"Lots of people hold grudges against their teachers," Auntie Val on the wall pointed out. "Perhaps there is one person in particular who sees that their life started going wrong when you were at school. Who's the biggest failure in the year? Who really went off the boil? That's the suspect I'd start with."

"Pete Boon!" Shandy, Lorna and strangely even Dean uttered at the same moment.

"That petty bully with the shaved head?" Mother clearly remembered the little worm.

"That's the one, and he had a real grudge against the school after he failed his A-levels." I could remember plenty of the stories Shandy had told me about him. "His family put in a formal complaint about the teaching, but that's not all. He spent the next decade working for his friend Martin's family garage. But after Martin was killed in a presumably unrelated incident, Pete lost his job. He's been sleeping in his parents' spare room in a flat in South Croydon for the last couple of years."

"He's not the only mess-up though, is he?" Shandy's normally smiley face was terribly serious.

"I've spent a few years in the wilderness. But I wouldn't describe myself as a mess-up!" I replied instinctively as, until a few months before, I'd been used to people telling me I'd done nothing with my life.

"Not you, Iz," she put her arms out in apology and, even though it was unnecessary, I did go over for a nice comforting hug. I have to admit, I could see why Danny was attracted to her. She was the ultimate yummy mummy without all the pretences of the Becky

Mitchells of the world. "I was talking about my ex. Tim Cornish's life isn't so different from Pete's, except that he also has two kids who he hardly ever sees. Whenever he's with them, he makes excuses for what a damp squib his life has become. If anyone has a chip on his shoulder, it's Tim."

My stepfather diligently wrote up each new name, and our suspect list was growing.

"Maybe you and Danny can talk to Tim?" I suggested to Shandy and, for some reason, Danny took this as a sign that he should make it a group hug. I enjoyed it at first, but it went on far too long, and I soon felt weird sandwiched between them.

"Who else could be involved?" Greg asked with his pen poised. "Is there anyone we're missing?"

"Gary Flint!" I sounded a touch too eager.

"Your boyfriend when you were at school?" Dad asked.

"That's right." Good old Dean was happy to add some gloss to this detail. "The one who Izzy claimed had a miniature…" Rather than say the word, he held up his little finger at a grotesque angle.

"Isobel Louise Palmer!" My mother was horrified. "How could you be so cruel? Especially after the way people make fun of your height. Body shaming is not acceptable."

I extricated myself from the platonic embrace of my friends in order to elbow Dean. "Thanks a lot for getting me in trouble. Snitch!"

He didn't seem bothered and displayed a smug smile. I don't have a brother, but with Dean, Danny and Ramesh around, I doubt I'm missing out on much.

"That's not the point," I continued in the hope Mum would forget about my greatest crime. "The point is…" I really didn't know what the point was. Luckily, there were a lot of people involved in the case by now, and one of the extras helped me out.

"The point is that Gary might still be angry at what happened," Brian from the supermarket explained on the video feed. "But then, if he was out for revenge against you, Izzy, why would he kill an ex-teacher and get rid of a couple of feisty swingers who you barely knew?"

I looked at Dean as he was the only person I'd told about Tommy and Clara's extra-curricular activities. It turned out that he really had kept my mother abreast of every last development.

"Which brings us back to my very first thought." I paused to give them the chance to catch up. "None of it makes any sense. The evidence planted at the scene of the crime, Mrs Davies' role in everything, and the choice of victims. It's all muddled up."

"Becky and Robert!" Dad cried out with glee. He even did a little dance on the spot whilst waving his coloured markers in the air. "They're our killers. They left evidence pointing to themselves in order to make us think that someone was trying to frame them."

Shandy tried to make sense of this. "But Becky and Robert hate each other since Robert cheated on her with a craftstagrammer."

"Cakestagrammer," I corrected. "But just because they're making a public display of hostility, that doesn't mean it's real." My brain was full of possibilities. I hadn't interviewed Becky as a suspect, but perhaps I should have. "Robert runs a true-crime podcast too. I wouldn't put it past them that this whole thing is a way to create new content for their followers."

The two-dimensional, illuminated rendering of Will Gibbons was having none of it. "So they became murderers to have something to talk about online? That's ridiculous. If they were going to plot a murder just like they plot their Instagram stories, they'd surely come up with an elaborate narrative to link everything together." My ex-colleague was like a snappy dog when he got worked up about something. He was practically snarling by the end of this comment.

His scepticism served to stop my father's dancing and left an uneasy atmosphere in its wake.

"So... we're no closer to the truth than we were before," I said in the hope that someone would contradict me.

"That may be true, dear." Mother wore a pouty frown. "But we're working together now. It won't be long before we identify the killer."

I felt bad that we'd left Ramesh out of our meeting. This would have been the perfect moment for him to say something completely inane. He'd probably have put forward the idea that Gary's sister was in love with the headmistress and had sown a path of destruction because of her unrequited feelings.

"That's almost a good point, actually."

Urmmm, Izzy... I thought you would have realised by now that only you can hear what's going on inside your head.

Whoops!

I let out a cackling laugh, as surely that made me look more sane. "I mean to say, one person we haven't considered is Verity Gresham. She was the one who got us all here in the first place, and she's been acting madder than Tom Cruise on Oprah all evening."

"Exactly! What was all that fuss about in the foyer when she found out that we were locked in the school?" Lorna produced two audible sentences in a row for the first time that night. "You'd think she'd staked her house on this evening going off without a hitch."

"Yep, as I said, she's as mad as a Hollywood star. And ever since then, she's been dancing and singing and having more fun than Ramesh. There's something not quite right with that one, and I don't think it's got anything to do with her sticking up for her brother."

Back in my childhood room at 34 Hawes Lane, Greg had been scribbling away on the evidence sheet. He'd written down…

- **Sweatband**
- **Lipstick**
- **Car battery**
- **Gary Flint's questioned manhood**
- **Mandy Johnson's dad**
- **Cakestagrammer (what's that?)**
- **Tom Cruise**

With his job done, my stepfather recapped his pen and turned to the camera. He pointed at the third and final easel where a flip pad had only one word at the top of a clean page. It said 'Hypotheses' and the more that he tapped his pen against it, the worse I felt about our progress.

"Is there anything you'd like me to write here, Izzy?"

"Yes, that's a good idea. You can write, *anyone could have done it for any reason*, and we'll leave it at that."

"Very good." Being an obliging chap, he selected a different coloured marker and was about to do as he'd been instructed when Shandy interrupted.

"Stop," she said this in her teacher's voice, and so we all did as she suggested. "There's no need to be so negative, Izzy. You've barely started investigating for one thing; it takes time to get to the truth."

She and marched confidently across the room. "Before you know it, you'll find the key piece of evidence that will pull everything together. You wait and see."

"I don't think that it's really so—" I started, but my tone was not to her liking.

"Enough of that." She held her finger to her lips, and I found it strangely hypnotic and was no longer able to speak. "Each of us is going to leave this room and follow up on one point that we've discussed. Danny and I will keep an eye on Verity. Lorna can look for Mrs Davies who, if I'm not mistaken, hasn't been seen for quite some time, and Dean can strike up a conversation with Tim and Pete."

"Actually, can I go to the bathroom first?" Dean asked, with his legs crossed. "I've really got to stop drinking so much punch."

I felt a little left out. "What about me?"

"You're the detective. I can't tell you what to do." Her curly hair bobbing as she turned back to me. She was all charm and confidence, and I wished that she'd been my teacher when I was at school. "You're Izzy Palmer, you play the accordion, you're good at cricket—"

"Ten-pin bowling."

"You're good at bowling. You speak Spanish far better than anyone else I know, and you're going to solve this case."

"You're right!" A rush of positive energy travelled through me. "I have a driving licence and a mortgage and two spare bedrooms." I looked around at my friends, who couldn't decide whether to be inspired or worried about me. "I'm Izzy Palmer, I'm a grown-up and I'm going to solve this case."

Chapter Sixteen

I doubt I was the only one who left that room feeling invincible. The only problem was that we were all so up for the challenge that we deserted our centre of operations without ending the video call.

"Ummm, are you forgetting something?" Mum called after us.

"Sorry, Rosemary," Dean returned to say goodbye.

"Yes, what should we do?" I heard Auntie Val enquire, so then we all had to go back. It certainly broke the momentum, but I couldn't be angry at the dear Welshy.

We left it to Shandy to address the live stream. "Well, we're trapped in here. The police can't break through the shutters, and it doesn't look like we've got much hope of escaping for quite some time. So it's your job to stay hydrated, keep your phones close at hand in case Izzy needs you, and have a good old think about who the killer might be."

She'd worked her magic again, and I could see the whole lot of them perk up. They were positively beaming. Forget teaching primary kids, Shandy should have been a motivational speaker. She should have had her own Instagram!

So, after that false start, we gave it a second shot. We left the room full of hope and self-assurance. I knew I was going to find the killer because Miss Duchamps had told me that I would, and that was good enough for me. With one last knowing wink for my team, we dispersed in search of our quarry. Well, the others did at least, but I still hadn't decided what I should be doing.

From the beginning, I'd assumed that the killer was motivated by some great injustice that had occurred way back when, but perhaps I was wrong. Perhaps the real cause was something more recent, and the culprit knew a nostalgic event staged to help us relive our youth would be the perfect cover to settle a grievance. I had to consider the possibility that the killer wasn't even part of the reunion but was skulking about the school setting traps.

I stood in the doorway to the hall as the party raged. Someone had changed the music so that Nu Metal screamed out of the speakers in place of the pop bangers that Ramesh had overseen. A big group of men were pogoing about and pushing one another as the guitars on the record clanked and jangled. But they weren't the only ones. Mandy Johnson and her ilk were just as up for it. A big group of them were jumping in time with the music, their arms wrapped around one another in a circle.

Over in the far corner, Barry and Samantha – the dead couple's friends – had found a dark spot and were… let's say, making the most of their time. However, there was no sign of Becky, Robert or the majority of their old companions. Pete and Tim had disappeared, and I hadn't seen Michael Andersen since he'd denied knowing me.

I tried to imagine one of that posse of former bosom pals being responsible for the deaths of three people. I can't say I was the most impartial judge. I'd both admired and despised every last one of them. I wanted to be their friend but hated them through and through. When we were at school, I barely existed to kids like Robert Mitchell. And no matter how hard I stared and willed him to look at me when I went to watch his tennis matches or saw him collecting prizes in assembly, it made no difference whatsoever. We might as well have been different species.

That's it in a nutshell: different species. There were two types of people at West Wickham High. The Mitchells were of a higher order that we mere Palmers and Inglises could not aspire to. There were few people who spanned both groups, and even those willing to slum it, like Shandy and my would-be first beau, were soon kicked back into their rightful world.

The music pumped in my ears like an angry metronome, and the present and the past melded together in my mind. It was like I was back there. Back in 2006, with my classmates all around me. We were sitting in a circle in the hall listening to Mr Bath give a top-up class on sex education. If it hadn't been embarrassing enough discussing such things in front of a teacher when I was eleven, it was even worse at fifteen.

But it was Mr Bath himself who seemed most nervous. He was holding a banana and presumably questioning how he had arrived at such a stage in his life. "Right, the thing is…" He had to clear his throat every two or three seconds. "The thing is, and this is very important… you see, what you have to know is that… Well, first of all, you have to know that I wouldn't have to be doing this if Nurse

Crouch wasn't off sick today. But the other thing is…"

Becky Mitchell was sitting a few seats away from me and kept laughing behind her hand as she and Mandy whispered to one another. I don't think they were paying any attention to the class as she never took her eyes off her new boyfriend Robert and kept flicking her tongue across her lips as though she were terribly thirsty.

"Enough of that laughing." Mr Bath stopped what he wasn't saying to point across the room at me. "You girl, come to my office after class."

"But it wasn't even me, sir!" My teenage indignation immediately shot to the heavens, and I crossed my arms across my chest. "I didn't do anything, it was—"

"No answering back." He narrowed his eyes and focused his pent-up anger on me. "Just because you're bigger than all your friends, that doesn't mean that you can blame everyone else."

"Ha, Izzy Palmer, you massive freak!" This was Martin Thompson's observational comedy at its finest. He put his hand out for a high five from Pete Boon, and I took solace from the fact that puffed-up Daddy's boy would end up murdered at a children's birthday party, fifteen years later. I also now realised why I hated high fives so much.

"To get back to what I was saying, can anyone tell me…" Mr Bath studied his notes. He clearly had no idea what he was doing and appeared to be repeating a recent biology lesson we'd had. "…the different stages an unborn baby goes through?" He scanned a class of nervous faces before inevitably choosing the most helpless student there. Nope, not me! "You girl." He didn't know her name but pointed at Lorna.

The very fact that she'd been selected elicited peals of laughter from Pete Boon and his posse of savage clones.

"Fertilisation, blastocyst implantation, embryo development and the foetal stage," is what the poor girl tried to say, but it was drowned out by howls and insults.

"Lorrrrrrrrrrrrrrrna!" Pete said in a spooky voice. "You died in a mysterious accident in a Victorian orphanage and have returned to reap revenge!"

It was true that, with her pale skin and ruler-straight haircut, Lorna looked a lot like a nineteenth century ghost, but that didn't mean it was okay to say it.

"Alright, lads," Mr Bath made a token effort to control his favourite students. "We all like a joke, but let's concentrate on the lesson."

My only friend Simon sunk lower in the chair next to mine, clearly hoping that he would not catch the bullies' attention. Sitting opposite me was a boy with beautiful brown skin and curly black hair. He looked just as unhappy to be there as Simon, Lorna and me, but he was sitting right in the pack of the most popular kids in our class. That was the moment when I noticed Gary Flint looking at me for the first time. He stared in my direction and, even when I caught his eye, he didn't shift his gaze away. I thought for a second that he would make a nasty face or lob an uttered *Freak!* in my direction, but he smiled, and I felt as though I'd been popped into a microwave at a medium heat for thirty seconds.

I must have been daydreaming – yes, within this daydream, I was having a daydream; it's all very 'Inception', try to keep up! Time passed without me knowing what happened and, suddenly, Pete Boon and Michael Andersen were sword fighting with inflated condoms. Rather than telling them off or actually trying to teach us, Mr Bath was in fits of laughter. His bristly face had turned bright red, and he was clutching his stomach in agony. I could tell that he would have loved to be messing about with the boys, just like when he was at school.

Seeing Mr Bath in his element – ignoring the nice kids, treating the idiots like the stars of the school – made Mrs Davies's comments about him even harder to believe. How could he have taken such an interest in me when he never remembered my name? And it's true that, when I'd started at that school, I'd been unable to kick a football or run more than a few metres without wheezing. And yes, by the time I left I could just about remember that you weren't allowed to pick up footballs and managed to complete a whole cross-country run without fainting, but was that really the highlight of his career? I went from pathetic to slightly less pathetic. Nothing I knew about Mr Bath added up.

Don't do yourself, down Izzy. You won the four-hundred metre sprint on sports day in Year Thirteen.

Yes, but that was only because I was really desperate for a wee. I didn't even stick around for my medal; I kept going all the way to the

West Block toilets.

"Sir, shouldn't we be talking about sex and not babies?" Mandy Johnson asked, and I swear she didn't realise that the two things were related. "This is sex education, isn't it?"

"Sir?" Robert Mitchell was giggling to himself before he even thought up the question. "What does dry humping mean? And does it make girls pregnant?"

"Oh, Robert, that's so funny." Verity made dreamy eyes at Becky's future husband, and I remembered just how much she'd been in love with him back then.

Mr Bath had stopped laughing and was about to change the subject when our drama teacher Mr Cody came into the hall.

"Excuse me, but my class is coming in here now." Dishy Mr Cody, with his tight-fitting black sweaters, did not look happy with his colleague.

"Alright, mate. Calm down." Bath immediately shot to standing and inflated his barrel-chest like an exotic bird during a mating ritual. "There's plenty of space for your kids to flounce about. We don't take up much room."

I could see that the teacher I had fancied since the day I turned twelve did not think much of our makeshift sex-educator. "We're not here to flounce about. We're rehearsing a scene from Macbeth."

Ai ai ai! Mr Cody was so sexy when he was angry.

Uggggggggg! I know. I still dream about him sometimes.

We both do!

Mr Cody's Year Nine students cowered in the doorway as he marched up to the burly northern P.E. Teacher. "If you'd bothered consulting the book in the office, you'd have seen that the hall was reserved until eleven o'clock."

"I don't give a damn. We were here first, and you lot can push off back to your cave in the South Block."

The two of them stood glaring at one another for a few seconds and a piece of my heart snapped off as Mr Cody let out a slow huff through his nostrils and accepted defeat. That was probably the moment that my schoolgirl crush became a fully fledged infatuation. Poor Mr Cody was just like me. He was bullied and beaten by the big boys even as an adult, and I was sure I would never love another man in quite the same way.

Anyway, the upshot of me standing alone as the disco rumbled on and thinking back on the past was that I realised one very important fact; I'd been ignoring a key group of suspects. Rather than a bunch of no-longer kids they hadn't seen for fifteen years, it was the people that still worked there who were most likely to stage an attempt on Mrs Davies' life or murder Mr Bath in cold blood.

I finally knew what I needed to do. There were loads of teachers there that night, and I was going to chat to every last one of them.

Chapter Seventeen

"It's so nice to see you again, Miss," I told my German teacher, Frau Schmidt.

"I'm going to let you in on a secret, Izzy." She peered at the people next to us at the drinks table to check that no one was listening. "My name isn't really Schmidt, it's Smith. I haven't got a drop of German blood in my body. I was born in Yeovil!"

My mind was less than blown by this revelation, but she was in a chatty mood, and I was determined to find out whatever she might know that could help me solve the case. "You don't say! And what other secrets of the school can you share? Was Samuel the cleaner really in love with Miss Salmon? Did Mr Moore run off with the money from the school fundraising drive when he left like everyone says?"

She leaned in a little closer. "Yes, and yes, as it happens. But far worse went on back then that we'd never get away with today. Did you know that—" Before she could spill the beans, we were interrupted by my geography teacher Mr Roberts.

"Hello, Palmer." He always called us by our surnames, but he got points for remembering who I was. "Caught your speech earlier. Hope I wasn't to blame for any of the nastiness around here." He spoke like he was about to lead his troops into battle but, despite his rather old-fashioned manner, he was a thoroughly good bloke.

That's the perfect cover for murder!

"No, don't worry, sir. We all loved your classes after you took us on a school trip to Wales and made us stand in a cold pond for three days taking water samples."

He tipped his head back to examine me. "I imagine you're joking, but I'll take the compliment all the same. You weren't a bad bunch, all in all. Isn't that right, Maureen?" He turned to his colleague and winked.

"That's right, Mel." She giggled a little, and it didn't take much detective work to realise what they were up to. "I was just telling Izzy here about all the scandal and secrets that went on among us teachers."

"Oh ho ho!" He laughed like he was a person doing an impression of someone laughing. "Yes, you thought that you students were up to no good! Tell her about Old Edmund Bishop. He was a real character."

There was some nudging and giggling, and I was beginning to wonder whether I should have warned everyone that there was vodka in the punch. Of course, there was a good chance that some of them had realised and were making the most of it.

"Mr Bishop was the deputy head when you first started here, Izzy. Do you remember?"

A picture of a fuzzy-faced old man who I hadn't thought of in decades popped into my head. "He wore a long black robe and looked like the grim reaper! I remember him now."

"That's the chap." Mr Roberts grabbed hold of the story once more. "Well, the head told everyone that he was retiring, when in actual fact, he'd run off with one of our school leavers. She was eighteen, an absolute stunner and the head of the volleyball squad. No one imagined old Edmund had it in him. The last I heard, they were happily married with five kids and a caravan in Hastings. Of course, such behaviour would probably land him in jail these days."

"And rightly so." Frau Schmidt/Mrs Smith nodded sagely before adopting a suspicious tone. "You noticed she was a stunner then, did you?"

"Objectively speaking, of course." Mr Roberts pulled at his tie and squirmed until his colleague let him off the hook.

"Oh, come here, you." She grabbed hold of her boyfriend and gave him a great big kiss on the cheek. "If you'll excuse us, Izzy, we're off to do some serious necking behind the North Block. Now that I come to think of it, isn't that where I caught Gary Flint with his hand down your top? Whatever happened between the two of you? I thought you made a rather nice couple."

I let out an exhausted sigh. "It's a long story."

"Oh well, Izzy," Mr Roberts said before pinching his partner on the behind. "It's never too late to find love."

His own late love put her arm around him, and they bustled off to a quieter part of the school to act like teenagers.

"It's rather heartwarming, don't you think?" a deep voice asked me, but I was still watching the flirty couple retreat across the room and didn't turn to see who it was.

"Totally. It couldn't happen to a nicer pair."

"Oh, I don't know. I always thought you were rather a good sort, Miss Palmer."

I spun round, my eyes inflated to the size of blimps, and there he was. Older and a total silver fox, but still recognisably the sexy drama teacher I'd never stopped dreaming about. "Mr Cody, what are you doing here?" Have I ever mentioned how terrible I am at talking to men I fancy?

"Well, Izzy, I've worked here for twenty years, and Mrs Davies begged us all to put in an appearance as the girl organising was terrified that no one would come." His voice was as smooth as Galaxy chocolate and fell quieter as he confided in me. "I was also rather hoping that I might bump into you."

Kiss him, Izzy. Kiss him right now!

He's old enough to be my father!

I know. Swoooooon!

Luckily, I still had some self-control and managed to resist this slightly odd urge. "Little old me?" I said instead.

"I was always disappointed you didn't continue your studies in my class. You were one of the best actresses in the school."

This sounded like a total line, and I had a sneaking suspicion that he'd said it to five other girls that night, but I did not mind in the slightest.

I replied in a sort of trance. "You were one of the best drama teachers in the school, too."

"Did you really think so?" I'd forgotten that he actually sounded a bit smug, but who could blame him. His eyes looked like they'd been retouched for a magazine cover and the fact he'd ended up teaching in a scruffy secondary school in South East London – and not acting the pants off an American co-star in a bad Hollywood movie – was a mystery that would forever perplex me.

Lick his face, Izzy. Lick him!

Shut up, you moron. I'm not going to lick anyone. I have a job to do.

"To tell you the truth, sir. I'm not just here to enjoy myself. I've been hired by Mrs Davies to investigate some threatening letters she's been receiving." This lie had worked once already. I figured I'd give it another shot. "Is there anyone on the staff who doesn't get on with her?"

He pulled back and suddenly looked less seductive. Well, marginally less seductive. "That's terrible." He had a wonderfully pensive look that was perfectly suited to his profession. "But I honestly can't think of anyone with anything against her. She's been the head here ever since I arrived, and you don't stay in a job for that long if people don't like you. There was the odd teacher who left under a cloud, but that was always their own doing, and I don't think anyone blamed Frances."

It took me a moment to realise that Frances and Mrs Davies were the same person. It was always a bit weird learning a teacher's name. It was hard to imagine them existing outside of the strict environment in which we first knew them. I was happy not knowing what Mr Cody's friends called him. If I'd discovered his name was Bob or Jimmy, he might have lost his allure.

"What about Mr Bath? He was such a nutter when we were at school. He must have rubbed someone up the wrong way."

He looked surprised. "Ernie Bath? A nutter? He might have some traditional ideas about teaching, but I've rarely met someone who cares so much about his job. He once told me that his educational philosophy was to treat the pupils who struggled educationally with kid gloves and to push the rest of you on with an iron rod. He can be hardheaded at times, but I've grown to respect him over the years, and I'd even describe him as a friend."

"But when I was fifteen, you almost had a punch up when you wanted to rehearse Macbeth here with your Year Nine class."

His head wobbled as though he was suddenly drunk, and he had a brief laugh. "Oh, you remember that, do you? Yes, he was a bit full on that day, but he apologised after. He absolutely hated having to teach sex education, and I couldn't blame him. Besides, halfway through the argument, I remembered I hadn't actually put my name down in the book to reserve the hall. I didn't have a leg to stand on. We both laughed about it later."

I was even more shocked by the confirmation that Mr Bath was a good teacher and a beloved member of staff than I was by the fact Mr Cuddly… I mean Cody, was so into me.

He became a little shy and, with his eyes cast to the floor, made a confession. "Izzy, I must admit, I've been following your career in the press, and I think it's wonderful what you've made of yourself. You really are something special."

Those eyes – those incredible pale green eyes – were brighter than the disco ball that spun above our heads. I wanted to dive into them and swim around his body like a tiny Olympian. I wanted to take a picture of each of them, blow them up to ten foot by eight, and paste them on the walls of my bedroom. I wanted to—

"Help!" a voice screamed in the distance. "Someone, please help!" It was Shandy. She was standing in the entrance to the hall screaming the place down, so I sprinted over to her as fast as I could. Admittedly, another little part of my heart snapped off as I pulled away from my long-desired encounter with Mr Cuddly. I mean Cody! But this was more important.

"What is it, Shandy? What happened?"

"Danny!" she said with her voice low in her throat. "The killer knocked out Danny."

Chapter Eighteen

I was amazed to see that most people went back to their dancing as though a woman hadn't just run into the room screaming but, once I understood the problem, there was someone I had to tell. Nurse Crouch was at the party, and I was fairly confident that her first-aid skills would be better than mine.

"Of course, this sort of thing wouldn't happen if they'd kept a school nurse on the payroll," she exclaimed. Although I somehow doubted this was the case, she was willing to come along with us, so I wasn't about to argue. "They invest all their money these days in computers and security systems, but there's no dedicated member of staff to put a plaster on little Billy's knee or take Suzie's temperature. There's no one to make sure kids are getting their daily carton of milk or to talk to each class about the food pyramid. This world isn't what it used to be."

She was a big woman with shoulders that were broader than an ox's back and a round, fleshy face that was stuck in a constant state of disapproval.

"That's very interesting, Nurse Crouch," I told her, before turning the discussion back to more useful topics. "Perhaps we should listen to what Shandy has to say before we get to Danny."

"Good idea," she grumbled, as she stopped at the door to her old room. "I'll just need one thing." She popped inside, then reappeared a moment later looking very confused. "There's a very polite man being projected onto the wall in there. He's pouring out cups of tea for a group of chatty, middle-aged people and he could see me as I walked in."

"Yes, that'll be my dad. I'd explain what they're all doing but…" I didn't know how to finish that sentence, so I turned to my friend, who was apparently still disturbed by whatever she'd seen. "Shandy, can you tell us exactly what happened?"

She kept her eyes dead ahead as she navigated the corridor back to the West Block. "Well… Danny and I followed Verity. She was looking very pleased with herself, and we knew she was up to something. But just before we got to the toilets, we lost sight of her around a bend. We couldn't follow her too closely, as she'd have spotted us otherwise."

She'd fallen into that gloomy sort of hush that witnesses often adopt, and so I prompted her for more. "What happened next? Did you go into the toilet or find her somewhere else?"

She looked at me as though she'd forgotten I was there. It was rare to see Shandy being anything but cheery and bright. "There was no sign of Verity in that corridor, and I felt sure she must have gone into the toilets; it was the only obvious place. Danny waited outside because he said he wasn't the sort to go into a ladies' toilet without permission. I thought that was rather sweet, and so I gave him a big kiss and—."

I didn't want her getting stuck on to the topic of how adorable her new love was, so I interrupted. "What did you find in there?"

We'd reached the arched walkway that led between the blocks. Normally it opened onto the playground, but the shutters were down even here, and so it was more like a tunnel in an underground bunker.

Shandy took a deep breath before finding the courage to relive that moment. "The lights were off in the toilet, and I couldn't see much, so I took my phone out and used the screen as a light. I walked inside ever so quietly and carefully. I walked past the sinks and towards the cubicles, looking to see whether any of them were locked. But when I got there, one of the first doors burst open and someone shot out."

"Did you see who it was?"

"No, I fell backwards and whoever it was escaped. I eventually started after him, but I was a little dazed from my fall."

"What about Danny?" I asked in the softest manner I could muster, whilst still urging her on.

"I heard a thud and a scream and, when I got back to the corridor, he was laid on his front. There was no sight of the assailant."

As she finished her tale, we reached the area in question. I was expecting my dear friend to be lying unconscious in a pool of blood but, fortunately, it was less dreadful than that.

"Hi, Iz!" Danny called in his usual cheerful tone. He was sitting on the floor with his back to the wall, clutching a wad of wet paper towels to his head.

"Gosh, are you alright?"

Shandy accelerated over and the affection she had for him was quite endearing.

"I'm fine! There's nothing to worry about. All that happened was that the killer came out of the toilet, and I was looking in the wrong direction, so he whacked me over the back of the head. I fell to the floor and woke up a minute later when Shandy came to look after me. It's really not a problem." As he said this, a drop of blood trickled down his forehead and his bravado abandoned him. "Or, on second thoughts, help!"

With her nurse's bag at the ready, Nurse Crouch went to inspect the damage. "Calm down, you baby. It's only a drop of blood."

She was just as maternal as I remembered. When I was eleven years old, I'd gone to her office feeling sick. She'd given me an aspirin and told me to stop making a fuss over nothing, and that was the last time I ever asked to see the nurse.

Danny's face had turned white, though I could only think this was out of fear rather than any medical issue. "Sorry. I'm a bit squeamish."

"But you're a doctor," I reminded him. "How can you be scared of blood?"

"It's not any old blood that bothers me, only mine."

"You poor man," Shandy was blinded by love to the absurdity of the idea of a squeamish doctor. I certainly was not and had a good laugh at him.

"I'd say that was a pretty reasonable fear, thank you very much, Izzy."

Nurse Crouch was concentrating hard as she wrapped a bandage around his crown and under his chin.

"I can't feel my face anymore," he succeeded in mumble, despite the fact his jaw had been tied shut.

"You're welcome," the big woman displayed an enormous grin. "That's how you know it's working."

Although I had a lot of sympathy for poor Danny, something that distracted me at that moment. I got up from where I'd been crouching to look at the position he was in. There was a hefty trophy lying on the floor that must have been used as a weapon, and I could see the display where the killer had taken it from. What surprised me most was where Danny was lying, just a little way from the toilets. He'd evidently moved back along the corridor in the direction he'd come from before the killer knocked him out.

"Danny, what were you doing when you got hit?"

He looked up at me and tried to think. "I heard something... I was. You know, I can't remember. I think I went to look in the room next door, but I can't say for certain."

He was only a few feet away from the door in question. I remembered it being an art studio and, looking inside, I could see that the objects on Mr Archer (or whoever had replaced him)'s desk had been knocked onto the floor.

We all know what that means!

Please don't.

Someone and someone sitting on the desk, K-I-S-S-I-N—

Nope!

"Is it possible that Verity hid in here?" I called over my shoulder as I inspected the room.

Shandy came to see what I was looking at. "I suppose so. She definitely disappeared very quickly. I assumed that she was the person in the toilet, but maybe she came in here instead."

"There's another door," I said as I hurried over to the far exit.

I turned the handle and looked out onto the walkway at the edge of the block. Whoever was in there could have avoided detection without much trouble and gone running as soon as they heard the commotion. It begged the question why anyone would be so secretive, but then there were any number of explanations, and I preferred not to conclude that everyone there was a murderer.

For once.

We left the art class to return to the others. Danny looked like he'd started to dress up as a mummy for Halloween, then run out of bandages. Nurse Crouch, meanwhile, was celebrating a job well done with a nice, relaxing cigarette.

"There's something that doesn't make sense," I said to myself more than anyone and floated towards the door to the girls' toilet. I had a pair of latex gloves in my bag – because who doesn't take forensic supplies to a school reunion? – and I slipped them on just in case. "If Verity was in the art room and it was the killer you met in here, why did they run?"

"How do you mean?" Shandy replied from behind me.

"I mean, you wouldn't have thought it strange to meet someone in the toilet. They could have just slipped past you without making a scene. Instead, whoever it was pushed you over and knocked out Danny. They must have had something to hide."

I stepped inside the dark toilet. Why the light was off was anyone's guess, but it took me a minute to find the switch and nudge it on with a knuckle.

The room before me was much like any toilet I'd visited – though admittedly with lower hand basins for kids. I looked about the floor for any evidence that might have been dropped by the fleeing killer, a scrap of paper with their home address on, or perhaps a signed confession. I was out of luck; there was nothing but an abandoned crisp packet and the plastic wrapper of a chocolate bar.

By the time I'd made it to the cubicles, my heart was providing a rather jazzy soundtrack to the proceedings. It was almost a relief when I kicked the first door I came to and there was no one on the other side. Far more horrifying, though, was the fact that the neighbouring door swung open at the same time. I had to take another step to see whether there was a ghost, a devil or merely a dead body waiting to greet me there.

And the winner is... option number three!

That's right. Once I'd plucked up the courage to see what the fleeing Danny-batterer had been doing there, I discovered the body of one of my least favourite people. Pete Boon was lying on the floor in a crumpled heap. There was a knife poking out of his chest, a perfectly circular bloodstain surrounding it, and he was dead... Wait! You already knew that...

Pete was dead, and he was also wearing a tie covered in little yellow suns.

Ha! You didn't see that coming!

Chapter Nineteen

The fact he was dead seemed less significant at that moment than the fact his mobile phone was poking out of his pocket and emitting a faint light in the gloom of the toilet. I was about to fish it out when I heard someone approaching and Shandy appeared at my side.

"It's horrible, Izzy. Just horrible." She put her hand to her mouth, her anguish plain to see. "I know Pete could be a pain, but look at the poor guy…"

Before she could finish this thought, she turned away to dry retch. So, instead of poking around for evidence, I had to look after my friend, as if we were two drunk girls in a club.

"Izzy, why are you holding my hair?" she asked after a few seconds of me rubbing her back and saying, "There, there, everything's alright."

"Oh, sorry, I was trying to be supportive."

She shook her head and remembered the body she'd just glimpsed. "I don't know how you do this job. I could barely see the blood, but it was still too much to bear. Don't you find the whole thing terrifying?"

I thought about telling her how my youthful embrace of genteel murder mysteries with very little gore had desensitised me to the reality of real-life killings. However, I was really eager to look at Pete's phone before it locked itself or the battery went dead so, instead, I just said, "Nope, not really. Now perhaps Nurse Crouch should have a look at you while I finish in here."

She nodded, still a little sensitive after the experience she'd just been through.

Izzy, the first time you found a body, you went in for a closer look. I don't know why people make such a fuss.

Yes, brain, but most people are less… what's the word…

Weird than us?

That's exactly it!

My brain whistled "Zip a Dee Doo Dah!" whilst I went to rifle through the pockets of yet another one of my murdered bullies. I'm not going to lie; I was actually quite excited. I thought about ringing D.I. Irons and making sure that I was allowed to investigate while she was unable to attend, but I was scared she might say no, so I dived straight in.

It was a standard touchscreen phone with no identifying features, so he'd probably spent a fortune on it. Pete was just the kind of person who would set his password to 1234, but it was even simpler than that; the phone was already unlocked.

I looked through his messaging apps first, but the last thing he'd received was a note from his mum reminding him to feed the cat. Somehow, this made me much sadder that he'd died. When I'd thought he was just an overgrown bully living in his parents' flat, I hadn't even worried about the human impact of his death, but the feline impact really got to me. A determination rose up within me, and I made a silent promise to find poor, dead Pete's killer… for Mog's sake!

I moved onto his social media – mainly posts about beer and football with very few likes – before striking gold with his text messages. Pete was a big texter. It was like he'd never moved beyond his first phone and only approved of technology up to the year 2009. He had an ongoing flirtation with a girl, though the early messages gave nothing away about who she was or how they'd met. There were no names anywhere and whoever was writing to him was saved in the phone as "G.G." The most important messages came last of all, but I scanned through the whole conversation which had started several months earlier.

Fine. Meet me in the girl's toilets in the West Block, right now.

There'd been a bit of a negotiation between them as G.G. had suggested Mrs Long's history classroom and Pete had said the toilets were, and I quote, "sexier" before G.G. signed off with that last line. It was hardly a startling insight into what was happening there that night. Was Verity G.G.? Shandy and Danny had seen her heading over that way. Was it for a tryst with Pete Boon? She'd been in love with his friend Robert Mitchell when they were at school, so perhaps she'd gone for the next best thing. Her married surname was Gresham. G.G. could be Gresham Girl. Or perhaps Gary's Girl, because Pete knew her brother better?

I skipped on through the phone, travelling to the calendar (no entries since 2017 when he'd met his gran for lunch) his voice notes (mainly him singing Guns 'n' Roses covers – badly) and I ended up in his photo app. That was when I discovered why he'd left his phone on in his pocket. It was still recording when I went in, and all I had to do was press stop and skip back to the beginning to watch a dark, blurry image of the murder. I couldn't make out any image as it had been filmed through his pocket, but I could just about hear it.

"That's it, baby," Pete said as, I can only imagine from the rustling and murmuring, he rubbed his body up against his killer. "That's how Daddy likes it."

Vom! Please tell me they weren't his last words!

Nope, it gets worse.

"Oh yeah, right there... Sweet like chocolate." He moaned a bit more and then let out a squeal of surprise. "Wait, what are you..."

His assailant said nothing as Pete collapsed to the floor. I heard doors opening and closing, but not another word was spoken. It was a sad testament to the end of a sad man's sad life. I looked at the body once more and realised that, though there was a wooden handle sticking out of him, it wasn't a knife that had pierced his chest. It was some sort of tool from the technology lab – a chisel, if I wasn't mistaken. I wondered whether this was the killer commenting in some way on the standard of education we'd received. The handle was certainly rather shabby and dented. Was this a cutting rebuke at the state of the school's equipment? It seemed plausible, but surely a strongly worded letter of complaint to the local council would have done the job. Murder seemed a little over the top.

Just beside his feet, placed rather deliberately with the cover facing upwards, was a worn paperback book with a plastic cover like you get in libraries. It was spotted with blood, but still easy to read. In fact, I didn't need to look too carefully at the title as I'd have recognised the cover anyway. It had a picture of a dead girl wearing an old-fashioned bathing costume on a sandy beach. The name 'Evil Under the Sun' was visible in heavy type at the top.

I had to assume this was another murder memento. Becky had her lipstick, Robert his sweatband, and the killer had chosen an Agatha Christie novel to stand in for me. At this point, I felt confident in calling her *she*... unless there were two people working together. It had been a while since I'd come across a team of murderers, and there'd certainly been a lot of planning involved to pull off this evening's spectacle, but something about the obsessive nature of the crime made me believe that I was only looking for one culprit. One totally batty suspect who clearly didn't like me much.

I was feeling both hard done by and somehow grateful that I'd been selected out of everyone in school for my very own tribute, when a far more significant thought occurred to me that I should have considered as soon as I found the messages. Energised by the discovery, I ran from the room.

"Come on you three," I shouted to my current posse of assistants – I operate a rotating door policy.

Nurse Crouch looked particularly excited about whatever task she would have to tackle next. "Let's do this!" she grunted and wrapped one meaty fist in the palm of her hand as she thundered after me.

"Coming!" Danny rose to his feet before having to sit back down again. "Or perhaps I should have a little sleep."

Shandy was there to look after him, but our illustrious nurse could see that her work was not done and returned to take one of his arms. "No man left behind!" she said, and I wondered whether she'd started her career as an army medic.

The three of them hobbled after me like a three-person entry in a four-legged race, which certainly slowed me down somewhat. It took ages to get back to the hall, especially as we had to leave Danny in the nurse's office, where I was confident Mum and Dad would watch over him and, should there be an emergency, call my mobile.

So then Shandy and Nurse Crouch followed me into the drunken party, and I took out Pete's phones to dial G.G.'s number. The throng of dancers had thinned out a bit – not only because there were now four people dead, but also as, the more alcohol people consumed, the more they needed to pass out at the side of the room or, in the case of the teachers, wander about the school looking for dark spaces to smush in.

In an appropriate if unintended mark of respect to poor, dead Pete Boon, the song at that moment was 'November Rain' by Guns 'n' Roses, which certainly wasn't the most danceable song. Several men had their phone flashlights in the air in place of lighters, and far more were playing air guitar as wives, girlfriends and women in general looked on unimpressed. The loud rock ballad made it difficult to hear a phone going off, and I couldn't see anyone answering a call. I walked into the centre of the hall and, just as I was about to hang up, I caught the strain of a high-pitched trill. Shandy had worked out what I was doing and heard the noise too – Nurse Crouch had got distracted and started dancing with Mr Cody by now – and we followed the notes of a retro ringtone through the huddled dancers.

"There," she said, pointing at Robert Mitchell, who looked more than a little worse for wear. "It's coming from him."

Chapter Twenty

Robert Mitchell; everyone's sweetheart. He'd been the most beloved boy in school from the time we started there. Not only had Becky and Verity been madly in love with the sports star, there were a couple of younger teachers who flirted like crazy with him on trips to the theatre/parents' evening. He had curly red hair which might normally have marked him out for special treatment from the bullies, yet it was so thick and luscious that we all looked at it with envy. He was the fastest runner, the dirtiest dancer, the cheekiest joker and the hunkiest guy that West Wickham High had ever produced.

Now it turned out that he was also involved in a string of murders. *Huh. Who'd a thunk it?*

I was trying to get my head around this possibility when Shandy went for him.

"Robert, what have you got in your pocket?"

He laughed and swayed towards her. "I dunno, a magical ring?"

I certainly wasn't expecting a Lord of the Rings joke from him, and neither was Shandy, who upped her anger. "We're not messing around, Mitchell. Take out the phone."

He was at the stage of drunkenness when compliance seems like the only option. He reached into his inside pocket and removed his top-of-the-range iPhone as nearby dancers noticed the commotion and gathered round. "This phone?"

I could still hear the ringtone, but it wasn't any louder than before. I went over to frisk him and found something in the breast pocket of his smart blue blazer. "Nope, this one." I looked at the cheap yet solid device that was still chirping out 'Für Elise'. It wasn't difficult to imagine why he had two phones.

"Did you buy a burner so that you could message girls while you were still married?"

Wait. That doesn't make sense. If he's G.G., it wasn't girls he was messaging.

"Or rather boys. You were in the toilet with Pete before he died."

This sobered him up somewhat. "Wait, Pete's dead? How did he die? He was here dancing twenty minutes ago." I didn't answer him as nothing was fitting together as it should have. "Sorry, are you saying that this is Pete's phone?"

He was evidently just as confused by the situation as I was. "Maybe... I don't know."

"Don't believe him, Izzy." Shandy was almost as fired up as our nurse had been and wouldn't let him off the hook so easily. "He went to the toilet with Pete and stabbed him to death. That's the only thing that makes sense."

"Is it?" Robert blinked a few times to make things clearer. I don't think it worked.

"He's been here the whole time." An unexpected voice spoke up, and Robert's ex-wife pushed through to us. "I've been watching him make a fool of himself. If someone's dead, Robert isn't to blame."

He became a bit emotional at this and put his hand to his chest. "Oh... Becky-boos. That's so sweet of you. Does this mean you forgive me for sleeping with Sprinklez3000?"

"No, it does not." This was as much as Becky would say on the matter and spun on her heel to return to her table of solace.

"Wait a moment, tall girl." Rich boy Michael Andersen still couldn't remember my name. I mean, how was that even possible? He'd met my mum on countless occasions. He'd seen me naked. He'd heard me sing a song which the British public voted as the best track to play at a funeral!

"Are you saying there's a killer here?" His loud, slightly nasal voice cut through the 'November Rain' guitar solo, and the news spread about the hall. No one was dancing now; the whole party had been cut down in its prime. A miserable crowd had gathered with me in the centre and the people wanted answers.

"This is your fault, Izzy Palmer!" a boy that I'd once let copy my maths homework screeched from the back of the group.

"Yeah, who invited the murder magnet?" a skinny girl yelled.

It was not the perfect moment for little Lorna to come by, but she pulled on my arm to get my attention. "Izzy," she hamstered. "I need to talk to you. Mrs Davies—"

I didn't hear what she said after this as the crowd started baying for blood.

"Tell us what happened. Who's been murdered?"

"Are we going to be next?"

"Why would anyone do such a thing?"

I glanced from angry face to angry face. I didn't know what to tell them. I wasn't a people person. My idea of socialising was slowly building up a group of similarly quirky friends over a period of years without ever having to step foot in a bar or club. This was all too public, too loud. I considered rolling up in a ball on the floor or running away, but the person I needed most in the world squeezed through the melee at that moment to make things better.

"Ladies and gentlemen," Ramesh declared with his hands aloft. "My colleague Izzy Palmer will take questions in a civil manner. Now, everyone, take three steps back and calm down." He pressed a button on his phone and the music stopped, leaving an odd hush that our ears were not prepared for. It was almost as if the new calm that descended was louder than that epic rock song. "Thank you very much."

I heard Michael Andersen mumbling to Robert that, "Ramesh is here now. He'll sort out this mess." Which sparked the question: how the heck did he recognise Ramesh but not me?

Less helpfully, my public liaison officer/bestie wheeled over a stage block from the side of the room to provide a literal and metaphorical platform. I climbed on top of it and was happy that several of my friends did the same. Shandy, Mr Cody, Crouchy, and Ramesh(y) all had my back, and I can't tell you what a difference it made as I embarked upon my second speech of the evening.

"Soon after we arrived this evening, there was a technical malfunction in the school security system which cut us off from the outside world. Being a bunch of meddlers and nosy parkers, my friends and I set out to solve the problem. We soon came across the bodies of two of our former classmates. Tommy Hathaway and Clara Higson died doing what they loved best—"

Luckily someone interrupted me before I could say any more. "Who were Tommy Hathaway and Clara Higson?" Actually, quite a few people posed this question, but they were soon drowned out by the wailing of the dead couple's friends.

"Not Tommy and Clara!" Barry lamented. "They were going to be the godparents to our children if we ever had any."

"Sadly, that wasn't all," I continued, not so much because there was any pressure to reveal the truth, but because I couldn't bear to leave a story half told. "I had assumed that the first deaths were an accident, as the poor folks were crushed to death by falling computer equipment."

"Is there no justice in this world?" Samantha, the husband swapper, bemoaned.

I continued as though she hadn't said anything. "But shortly after that, I discovered another body. Our be…be…" I struggled over this word for some reason. "Our *beloved* P.E. teacher, Mr Bath, suffered a similar fate in Mrs Davies's office when several hundred volts passed through him from an electric car battery rigged up to a phone. However, it was not just office equipment that the murderer has been making use of for his or her wicked schemes. Mere minutes ago, in the West Block toilets, Pete Boon was murdered with a chisel from the technology lab."

I think this was the detail that really shocked them. Everyone knew Pete. He was one of those larger-than-life characters who you couldn't help but have an opinion on. Some people loved him, a lot really didn't, but we all felt something for him. And now he was dead.

"Why didn't you let anyone know what's been going on?" Robert asked, to break the fragile silence.

"Yeah, why didn't you tell us?" Michael barked in support.

"What else are you hiding from us?" Mandy Johnson bellowed above all other voices. "Were you even telling the truth when you implied that you'd come and see my spare bedroom?"

There were questions coming at me from all sides, and I wanted to run away again. I could no longer remember why it had seemed like a good idea to keep everything secret. I wished that Mrs Davies had been there to get her former students under control, but she was probably lying dead somewhere – the next victim of the sick killer's game. I looked at Lorna and her face was wracked with fear. I was sure that as soon as I came down from that really far too small stage, she would break the bad news, and this made it even more difficult to concentrate on the crowd's demands.

It was just like in the recurring nightmares I'd had over the years. I was back at school, and everyone was calling my name, but I hadn't a clue what they wanted. I felt like a fool who had been elevated (again both literally and metaphorically) to the centre of attention, only for everyone to criticise and complain at me.

"Alright, enough of that," my hero Shandy stepped forward to use her teacher's voice. "This isn't Izzy's fault. She has been looking out for our interests all night while you lot enjoyed the punch and a good long dance."

There were a few half-hearted jeers, but Ramesh stepped forward to nip them in the bud.

"Don't be like that, Anthony! Or you Kim. I thought we had something special here tonight. I thought we'd formed a bond that a few murders couldn't break." The room had fallen silent, and he peered around a sea of guilty faces. "To be perfectly honest, I'm disappointed in you, and I think you should say sorry to Izzy for your bad manners."

Their heads bowed, and a murmur of apology struck up.

"I can't hear you," Shandy rebuked them.

"We're sorry, Izzy," they said as one, like they were back in a primary school assembly.

"That's better." Ramesh shook his head and pursed his lips.

How is it that everyone but us has developed an authoritative voice for addressing wayward crowds? Perhaps Ramesh was born to be a teacher.

I was about to address the room again when Nurse Crouch stepped forward to do it for me. She rolled her sleeves up ever so slowly, to give us a peek at her impressive biceps, before delivering her instructions. "The police are aware of the situation but, until they break through the barriers, you will report anything you know about the murders or why they might have happened to Izzy Palmer. Is that understood?"

"Yes, Miss. Course, Miss," a few of the naughtier children replied. Such a response surely becomes involuntary when you've been sent to the headmistress's office so many times in your life.

She kept watching them for a few moments as they began to disperse, then nodded and turned to her former colleague. "Come on, Cody, we haven't finished our dance."

Chapter Twenty-One

The atmosphere in the room was a little more sedate after that. I wanted to talk to Lorna or grill Shandy on exactly what she'd seen as the killer escaped from the toilets, but Nurse Crouch's entreaty had worked a little too well and I was inundated with *leads*.

"I always thought that there was something funny about the old technology teacher, Mrs Pearson," Michael Andersen informed me. "Are you going to look into her?"

"No."

"Why on Earth not? I'm bringing you a solid piece of evidence here and you're ignoring it." He sounded typically put out.

"I'm not going to waste time considering the possibility that Mrs Pearson was responsible for any of the murders, as I know for a fact that Mrs Pearson is dead."

His jaw dropped. "You mean the killer got her too?"

"No, I mean she was killed in a hit and run outside the school about five years ago."

He bit his lip and had a good think. "Still, just because she's dead, that doesn't mean she wasn't involved."

"Yes, it does."

He shook his head in that special way that only rich people who don't think they're getting their due service can. "You're not listening. I'm not saying Mrs Pearson wielded the chisel or what have you. I'm saying that whatever went on between her and Mr Bath back when she was teaching us could explain what's happened tonight."

I let out an extremely weary breath and asked the inevitable question. "Did something go on between Mr Bath and Mrs Pearson?"

"You tell me; you're the detective!"

This was the seventh of many such conversations that I would have to endure before people lost interest. The one thing this afforded me was a chance to observe the party-goers as the fallout from the revelations continued. It was clear now who was really drunk, and who'd been sobered up by the twist in the evening. Some of the lads from my class were so far gone that they either couldn't remember that there was a killer on the loose or they were past caring. Even without any music, a few of them returned to the dance floor.

Led by some of the main protagonists of the night, there was another group who was evidently taking the news badly. Robert Mitchell really lost it and went out to the foyer to bang on the shutters and demand that the police let him out. There were any number of people there to reassure him, but the news of our incarceration had unsettled the crowd. A small posse of MacGyver types made it their goal to set us free and fruitlessly wandered off to look for a window that was somehow unsecured or a device that could penetrate plate metal.

The group of likely suspects was becoming more settled in my head. I could cross Pete Boon off the list, which was a good thing as the motive *he was an inherently evil psychopath* has never been my favourite. It overrides all cleverness and proof and is quite the antithesis of the classic murder mystery conclusion. The Pete Boons of this world (or the next, for that matter) are not the types to lock everyone in a school or set up traps. If Pete was the killer, he'd have punched everyone to death or hit them with a bit of wood.

Izzy, you snob!

Focussing on potential killers who were still breathing, Verity could have been the one to speed off to the toilet and kill Pete. She clearly had a few screws loose and, as the reunion-organiser, she also had access to the school to plant the first two traps. It struck me that she was even smart enough to do it. Back when we were in year ten, Lorna and Shandy had only won the technology prize because Verity was eliminated. She'd unfairly used a Solidscape benchMark 3D printer that her father had bought her from the States, but her design for a torch powered by kinetic energy was miles ahead of every other entry.

Her brother wasn't off the hook either. There was nothing to say they weren't working together, and I noticed that Gary was now sitting silently in a chair in a corner of the room, as though plotting his next move (or getting a bit sleepy). The Mitchells could have been involved, too. Becky was the girl every boy desired, so perhaps she'd lured her ex-husband's best friend to the toilets for a bit of payback, then planted the burner phone on Robert.

The good thing about Pete's death – if that doesn't sound too callous – was that it made me feel more confident that the teachers weren't involved. Up until now, this could all have been an argument between warring members of staff, but Pete's murder made that less likely. He wasn't the nicest kid when we were at school, but he was more of a lackey than a gang leader. He trailed along behind Robert Mitchell and Martin Thompson, fulfilling their demands. He was a hard person to like, but not the kind to all-out hate, at least not for teachers who are used to that sort of thing.

It was perhaps a bit ridiculous trying to narrow the names down in a group of over a hundred suspects. Who was to say that Samantha and Barry weren't using the whole chain of events to cover the fact they'd murdered their supposed best friends, Tommy and Clara? Perhaps there are internal rivalries in swingers' groups that I didn't know about.

I also couldn't rule out the possibility that someone I hadn't even spoken to that night was to blame. It would have been easier for a shy kid I barely remembered to have carried out the crimes than a character like Becky, who everyone knew. Navigating the school without being spotted would be as hard for the Mitchells as it is for a famous actor strolling around L.A.

So, what did all this leave us with? Four dead bodies (that we knew about), a few possible suspects, because they happened to have been the people I'd spoken to, a trail of clever traps and a near miss with the killer which apparently didn't get us any closer to catching her... or him.

Oh, and the world's most boring woman, offering me her interpretation of the case. "The way I see it, anybody could be the killer. I really don't have anything to say that could help you catch him, but I felt I just had to come and tell you that." Mandy's eyebrows rose as though she'd said something really very illuminating. "I don't see how you'll be able to tell who did it when there are so many people here who could be guilty. I mean, what's to say that the boy who used to sit behind me in history, isn't the one? What do we even know about Toby Garson?"

"I see what you're saying," I began, already feeling like I wanted to jump through the window next to me, even though I knew I'd hit a metal barrier on the other side. "But I don't think it—"

"Wait just a second." She put her hands to her temples as though receiving a message from the afterlife. "Now that I think about it,

I did always find Toby a bit of a weirdo. He used to smell my hair sometimes. And I heard a rumour that his dad went to prison for tax evasion." Over the course of this short speech, the blood drained from her face, and she turned quite pale. "OMG, it's him, isn't it? It's Toby Garson. I knew he was a psycho ever since he told Debbie Jones that she looked like a My Little Pony. I mean, who says things like that?"

I really didn't know how to respond to such mindlessness. "I don't think that Toby is to blame. For one thing, he's been trying to dance with you half the night. I also know for a fact that he had a crush on you throughout high school but never found the courage to admit it. And he told Debbie Jones that she looked like a My Little Pony because she did. She came to every mufti day with dyed pink hair that she tied on top of her head in a ponytail, and she's got a face like a horse."

Mandy looked truly dumbstruck. "Wait, are you seriously telling me that Toby Garson fancies me?" She waited for a response that I would not provide and finally melted. "Wow, I always thought he was cute. Perhaps, if I wasn't married…"

I can only imagine that she considered a different life for herself at that moment, united with the formerly weird, now apparently cute, Toby Garson. Having stood in silence for a few seconds, she shook the thoughts away and wandered back to her friends.

"Thanks, Izzy," she shouted over her shoulder. "You always know just what to say to make me feel better."

Thankfully, she was the last idiot I would have to put up with… for a while at least. Lorna had apparently got tired of waiting for me, but I finally had a chance to talk to Shandy, who was back making out with my ex.

"Excuse me. Could I…?" I began, but they showed no sign of hearing me as Danny's hands worked their way up and down Shandy's pretty back – yes, even her back was pretty!

Damn her!

Where was I? Right, Danny's hands. So, they were working up and down Shandy's back like a couple of window cleaners scaling ladders.

"Sorry to interrupt, it's just that…"

There was no response, and I knew I'd have to take drastic measures.

"If I could just…" I shoved my two hands into the body pile to put a bit of light between them. It didn't work. "Guys, stop!"

Even my yelled imperative didn't quite do the trick. One of Danny's busy hands shot out with the *one second* gesture and, approximately a minute later, they came up for air. I wasn't sure what sort of response I would get from them as they were drunk on love (and spiked punch).

"Hi, Izzy!" Danny said as though I'd just arrived.

"Wait, aren't you supposed to be in the nurse's office?" I had to ask the invalid, who had been doing an impressive job of kissing, considering the tight bandage around his jaw.

"It's fine," he said, ignoring his medical training. "A little head wound never hurt anyone. Besides, your mother gave me the all-clear."

He really must be drunk if he's taking medical advice from Bu-Bu La Mer.

"Whatever you say." I was past caring what my friends got up to by now. "It's Shandy I want to talk to anyway."

Danny stood up to give us some privacy and immediately felt dizzy again. "Perhaps I should get Nurse Crouch to check me for a concussion. I'll be in the surprisingly well-stocked first-aid room if anyone needs me."

"Shandy," I said once he'd tottered over to see the nurse who was throwing Mr Cody around like a rag-doll – a sexy, high-necked-jumper-wearing rag-doll. "Listen, I need you to take me through what happened when you arrived in the West Block one more time."

She nodded and cast her mind back. "It's like I said, Verity was some way ahead of us and, by the time we walked through that tunnel bit and turned right into the corridor where the toilets are, there was no sign of her. We both figured she'd gone into the toilet, but it was dark in that whole block and, when I looked inside, there was no noise of any kind. I walked all the way through the toilets and, as I got to the cubicles, someone jumped out of the door and pushed past me. I fell backwards into the cubicle behind me and couldn't get up until I'd recovered my balance. By the time I was on my feet, the killer had gone. I picked myself up and, when I got outside, I found Danny knocked out on the floor. I did what I could for him, but I knew I didn't have the knowledge to help much, so I went looking for someone. It's lucky the big scary nurse was here tonight."

Her concern for the, let's be honest, probable future love of her life, was touching, but there were more important elements of her story that I still hadn't grasped.

"So you didn't get a good look at the person who pushed you?"

She didn't need to think long. "No, it was too dark. I wish I'd looked harder for the light switch now, but it wasn't in an obvious place."

"Do you think that whoever it was had time to run from the toilet, knock Danny over and get all the way back here without you seeing them?"

She nodded. "I wondered that myself. I thought perhaps they escaped into the room next door and messed up the table to make it look as though some young – or not so young – lovers had been messing around in there before escaping through the far door. By the time I'd got Danny some wet paper towels and finished checking on him, the killer had had plenty of time to escape entirely. Perhaps I should have given chase sooner, but I couldn't bear the thought of Danny being hurt."

Her eyes cast towards the doorway where our still clearly worse-for-wear friend was being helped from the room.

"Another dead end," I muttered under my breath, a touch too loudly for Shandy to miss.

She put one hand on my shoulder and spoke to me in her most sympathetic nursery-teacher voice. "It'll be alright, Izzy. You'll get there in the end. I know you will. You've worked so hard, and it won't be long before all the pieces fit together. I really don't know who could be behind all this, but I bet you have a pretty good idea."

Her smile was so reassuring, and I thought about asking for a hug, but managed to control myself.

I totally see what Danny likes about her. You know, if we'd been born with a Y chromosome...

"Thanks, Shandy. I'll do my best."

So then she left to check on Danny. Her version of events had changed slightly in the retelling, but that tends to be the case with witnesses, and I didn't hold it against her. Imagining lovely Shandy as a killer is like watching the Nightmare on Elm Street films and thinking, *hmmm, that Freddy Kruger would make a good doctor.*

I needed to find Dean and Lorna, but they weren't in the hall and no one I asked had seen them – or, in fact, knew who they were. Ramesh had abandoned his role as a party guru and was busy entertaining the crowd in a different capacity. He was at the piano on the stage, singing some love songs. His version of Robbie Williams's 'Angels' was a hell of a lot better than mine.

"Play 'Streets of London'!" one of his fans requested, but I had to intervene.

"I'm sorry, ladies and gentlemen, but Ramesh will be taking a short break and will be back before long."

Ramesh raised his hands to say, *really, you're too kind!* And then there were some moans of disappointment, some rude comments at my expense and more calls of "'Streets of London'! Play Ralph McTell's 'Streets of London'!" from one determined spectator.

"Ra, I need your help," I told him.

He continued to tinkle the ivories in a jazzy style, like he was working in a piano bar and obliged to keep the music going. "Of course you do, Izzy. Of course you do." He played a few dramatic chords in a lower octave to underline this fact. "What's the problem now? Or are you here to point out that I told you so?"

"Fine, you predicted that the first victims were murdered, and you were probably right."

"Thank you!" The music became jollier again.

"I need to find Dean and Lorna, though. I haven't seen them since everyone here found out about the killings, and I'm starting to get worried."

He crashed all his fingers down on the keys and stopped playing. "Why did you let anyone go off on their own? There's a killer stalking the halls, and we'd all be a lot safer if we stayed together."

It was a rare moment that Ramesh got a chance to tell me off. Even less common was the fact he was right.

"Have you never watched a slasher film, Izzy? At this very moment, our friends are being hacked to death." His eyes were wild as they locked on to me. "Poor little Lorna has been turned into dog food and Dean – lovely, rich Dean – will be having his fingernails removed one by one with a… Oh, no. Actually, they're just over there." He pointed across the hall and, sure enough, Dean and Lorna had just walked into the room.

"Now…" He gave a musical flourish and raised his voice to the group of spectators who had remained on the stage. "Did I hear someone request a performance of Britney Spears's 'Lucky'?"

"No, 'Streets of London'!" that same tiresome bloke demanded, and Ramesh lost his cool.

"I don't know 'Streets of London'. In fact, the only songs I know are pop ballads released from 1994 to 2009, and Christmas hits. So would you like to hear Aerosmith's 'I Don't Want to Miss a Thing' or my take on 'Jingle Bell Rock'?"

I left his new fans to settle this conundrum while I went to talk to a couple of people who at least appeared to have brains.

"We're worried about Mrs Davies." For once, Dean's face communicated the level of emotion required. "Lorna's been looking for her since we finished the call in the nurse's office, but she's just vanished."

Lorna contributed a nod of support before Dean filled in more information.

"We've been round the whole school without any luck."

This was worrying and, though I really didn't need an extra person's murder to solve on top of the ones I was already dealing with, I decided I should help. "We should get the keys from the office and try the rooms that are locked."

I left the hall and walked through to reception, where – assuming nothing had changed in the last decade and a half – the office staff kept a bunch of keys on hooks above the telephone. They would occasionally dole them out to students who needed access to the games cupboard or lost property room. Sure enough, they were still there, and so I grabbed a line of keys for each block and handed them out among the three of us.

"What?" Dean snorted his derision at this plan. "You think we should split up and take a block each? We're bound to get murdered that way."

"No, genius. I think we should keep the different keys apart so that we know which is which."

"Oh." He pushed his hair back off his face and turned his head to the side. "That is a pretty good idea, actually."

I led us out of the office and down towards the South Block, which I'd yet to revisit. "You know, there are enough people doubting my abilities without you jumping on the bandwagon,"

Lorna released a soft hum, which I took to be a sign of most welcome sympathy.

We left the main building and travelled through another shuttered walkway to get to the furthest block. It was good to have a task to complete. I'd begun to feel as though we were just waiting for the killer to reveal themselves. Whenever I'd been sure of a fact – *the killer was definitely a girl!* – it was soon undermined – *perhaps Pete was gay!*

I'd been certain that G.G.'s phone would lead us to the culprit, but then we found it in Robert's pocket. Perhaps the swine realised his (or her) mistake in leaving Pete's phone behind and attempted to shift the blame by planting the burner on the curly sports star of West Wickham. Or perhaps Robert really was the killer, and his ex-wife was lying for him. I still couldn't say how any of it fit together, which is not the best conclusion for a famous detective to come to.

It was strange being back in the South Block where I'd spent so long as a kid. That was where the artsy students used to hang out. Me and my only friend Simon thought we were really cool because, at break times, we'd stand fairly near older kids who had piercings in unusual places and talked about bands we'd never heard of. Mr Cody's drama class was down there too, and he would let us come inside when it was raining. I've never felt so in with the in crowd as when he made us all cups of hot chocolate and talked about his favourite movies.

So that's why you're so obsessed with hot chocolate! I am learning so much about you tonight.

Weird thing for my brain to say, but okay.

"We had a quick look around here before, but the place is dead. If you stop and listen, you'll hear there's no one about." Dean did as he said and paused in the entrance to the building just as a faint drumming sound rumbled over from the music room.

"Good point, Dean. I should take your advice more often."

He raised one hand to respond but realised it was hopeless and gave up.

Lorna ran ahead, suddenly full of energy and made it to the room before us. Of course, running ahead in excitement and actually opening a door where a killer might be are two different things. She bravely stopped outside and waited for me to go first.

I experimentally tried the handle, and the door was locked. That wasn't a problem for us, of course, as we'd planned ahead. I extracted the first key but had to try a few more before I found the right one. And that was as far as I got, as I was actually just as scared as Lorna. We turned to Dean in the hope he might be brave on our behalf.

"What? Because I'm the man, I have to go in there?" He scrunched his face up in disgust. "That is out-and-out sexism. I thought better of you. I really did."

"Fine!" I whispered, just to shut him up. "We'll all go together. Ready?" I pushed gently against the door. "One… Two… Three." No one took the cue and so I kept counting. "Four… Five… Six… Oh, forget it. I'll go first."

I took a deep breath and poked my head inside. There was a standard lamp in the corner, and I remembered that our hippy music teacher, Mr Padfield, had tried to design a space there that he claimed would chill everyone out. How an Ikea uplighter achieved this was anyone's guess, but it probably wasn't the most important thing to think about at that moment as there was a man in a hoody running straight at me with a metal bar in his hand.

Chapter Twenty-Two

"Ahhhhhhhhhhhhhhhh!" the big chap yelled.

So I yelled back, "Ahhhhhhhhhhhhhhhh!" Well, you know the sort of thing.

Of course, it would have made more sense to just close the door and duck back out again but, instead, I screamed and waited for the killer to bash my head in. I suppose if I'm being nice to myself, I might say that I was frozen in fear, but stupidity certainly played a part too. That giant hurtled towards me, and I didn't know what else to do, so I yelled (as already noted) before closing my eyes to await death.

"Izzy?"

I peeped out through narrowed eyelids and discovered that the big guy had come to a stop a few feet away.

"Izzy, is that you?"

"I think so," I replied as, while I should have been more confident of such a fact, the situation was a little unnerving.

One thing I definitely didn't know was the identity of the large, violent man who had nearly attacked me. His hood was low over his eyes and, despite the tasteful lamp in the corner, the room was quite dark.

I asked him the only obvious question. "And who, may I ask, do I have the pleasure of addressing?"

Was that the obvious question? You sounded like a prince from a children's cartoon.

The, let's be honest, probably-not-killer pulled his hood back and there was the only boy I'd called a friend until I went to university. "Simon? What are you doing skulking in the music room?"

"I'm not skulking, Izzy." My childhood bestie sounded rather defensive. "I came down here to look around and then..." Whatever belief he'd had in this argument died away. "And then I lost my courage and decided not to go to the party after all. Skulking is just the word for it."

"You mean you've been here the whole time and not even had a drink of spiked punch?"

I hadn't seen him in over a decade, but Simon hadn't changed. He was still as shy as ever. Still looked like he should be hanging out with a bunch of goths in a supermarket carpark, and I was fairly sure he would still have had to call his mum to take him home early if he stayed at my house for a sleepover.

"I wanted to come. I wanted to see you more than anything – but I collected my nametag and freaked out." He sat down on one of the desks and looked into the middle distance to recall his ordeal. "I could see them all in there. You know, all those popular idiots who used to make fun of us. Pete Boon, Tim Cornish, Robert bloody Mitchell. I saw them there, and I just ran."

"Well, I can promise you one thing, they've been having a worse night tonight than you have."

I sat down beside him, then remembered there were two people standing on the other side of the door who were even bigger cowards than soft Simon. "Ummm, Dean, Lorna? Would you mind coming in here to check that I'm not being murdered?"

All thoughts of James Bond-ishness were forgotten as Dean gingerly peered around the door, saw Simon and immediately pulled back. I've met braver rabbits than him.

"Don't worry," I called. "It's just an old friend. No one's going to hurt you."

He peeked again and was slightly reassured to see me sitting safely next to the pale giant in the black hoody. To be fair to Simon, it was a very smart hoody and just the kind of thing to wear to a formal occasion. If you really love hoodies, that is.

Dean and Lorna stepped inside, both now pretending that they hadn't been too cowardly to enter before. They shrugged their shoulders and looked about the place in a casual manner as if to say, *what massive guy with a metal pipe in his hand? I hadn't noticed anyone.* It had taken me until this moment to realise just how much the pair had in common. Okay, Dean was a tech-millionaire and Lorna was a… a… well, I hadn't actually asked her what her job was. Judging from her old-fashioned clothes and the fact she was normally too shy to talk to herself, I could only imagine that she did a job which didn't require much human contact. But otherwise, they were identical.

"Simon was my best friend at school," I explained, and the boy I had told my darkest secrets to throughout our teenage years grinned a little and bowed his head. "He was just telling me how he ended up here in the music room."

"I came for a walk around and it brought back a lot of old memories, so I spent most of the evening gobbling Mr Padfield's chocolate Hobnobs and playing the drums." He held up the metal bar, and I recognised it as part of the mount from a tom-tom.

"I forgot that you played the drums. You used to be really good." Whenever two unrelated groups of friends brush up against one another, I have the irresistible urge to explain everything like a translator. "Simon was a bit of a music geek when we were here. Whereas I was… just a geek, I suppose."

"That doesn't explain why he ran at you with a deadly weapon," Lorna squeaked, then immediately hid behind her companion, who would most likely have hidden behind her if he could have.

"Someone locked me in here." Simon's expression was a mix of indignation and defeat. "I thought it was one of the idiots I'd seen in the hall. It reminded me of the nasty tricks they played on me back at school and, to be perfectly honest, I was glad to be trapped here. At least I didn't have to walk home with my tail between my legs. And Mr Padfield has a surprisingly large amount of food in his desk. I would probably have made it through the weekend."

Dean had a perplexed (or possibly constipated) look on his face. "No, sorry. That still doesn't explain why you would run at us with a metal bar. We could have been coming to help you. Scratch that; we were coming to help you."

Simon became more withdrawn again. He'd never coped well with confrontation. He was more of a *hide under the bed and refuse to go to school because Martin Thompson had told him that he would give him a wedgie* sort of person than a fighter. More a woodlouse than a lion.

"I didn't mean to scare you." He was softly spoken at the best of times but could hardly be heard over the sound of his nervous tapping on the shiny chrome bar. "But I thought you were the killer."

"How do you know about the killer?" Lorna was doing my job for me. I thought I wouldn't like it, but it was actually quite relaxing. It was like watching an interview on telly rather than having to go to the trouble myself.

"Mrs Davies told me."

Dean looked around the room and, in quiet wonder, replied, "Is she in here now?"

"No, she's next door." Simon stood up and walked over to a grate in the wall beside the musical instrument cupboard. "Mrs Davies, are you still there?"

There was a pause that was just long enough for us to conclude that Simon had lost his mind, but then a reply came back. "Of course I'm still, here, Simon. The killer locked me inside, as you well know."

"Thanks, Miss. Just checking." He walked back over in the usual round-backed, lurking manner that I remembered. "See, she's next door."

"Are you saying that the killer trapped you both in here?" I couldn't imagine how this made any sense.

"Yeah, something like that. Mrs Davies was looking around, and I didn't want her to find me, so I hid in the cupboard and didn't make a sound. Then, after a few seconds, I heard her fall over and a door slammed shut. Unfortunately for both of us, whoever pushed her must have decided to lock me in too. It was a while before I knew what happened because I stayed very quiet, and she did the same. If I hadn't gone to eat a Hobnob and made a rustling noise, she would never have known I was in here."

"Simon?" she called through the grate. "Who are you talking to? Please tell me you haven't gone mad already. We've only been in here a couple of hours."

"No, Miss. Nothing like that." He had a light-hearted attitude when not in abject fear. "It's Izzy and her friends. They're here to save us."

"Izzy, there might be—" Lorna began, but she was the type of person I sometimes find myself talking over without even meaning to.

"That's terrible. I can't imagine who would want to hurt Mrs Davies like that. Everyone likes our headmistress. Everyone."

"Thank you so much, Isobel," the far-off voice replied. "It really is a compliment to hear such comments from past students. It makes the hours that we teachers put in to planning classes and filling out endless forms all the more worth it."

"Izzy, there's a problem."

It was Dean's turn not to hear Lorna. He'd walked over to the ventilation grate and bent down to speak into it. "Don't worry,

Frances." How the hell did everyone know each other's names? "We'll have you out of there in no time."

"She's fine," Simon said (ha ha ha) with a nonchalant wave of the hand. "I've been posting her Hobnobs through the little holes. She's had as many as me."

"Everyone, listen!" Lorna finally raised her voice above a tremulous quaver. I was quite proud of her. "We can't save Mrs Davies because I closed the door after us. We're locked in."

Chapter Twenty-Three

Every face turned to stone… for about three seconds until my brain kicked in.

Izzy, check your bag.

I did just that and found a solution to the world's shortest, least dramatic cliffhanger.

"Don't worry, I've got a key." I held the pretty little miracle up in my hand and there were some cheers as I tried it in the lock. It didn't actually fit as that was the wrong one, but a couple of minutes later (it's always the last one you try, right?) I managed to get the door open.

"Freedom!" Dean yelled, and I was unsure whether he was doing a truly apathetic Braveheart impression, or he really had suffered during his one hundred and eighty seconds of imprisonment.

After a deep breath of that sweet, fresh air, we walked to the neighbouring room to rescue the fair maiden.

"You're next, Miss," I shouted, hoping that this would set her mind at ease before remembering that there was a killer on the loose and rephrasing my sentence. "I mean, we'll have you out in a jiffy."

"I believe I've heard that expression before, Izzy," her voice came back through the door. "And I cannot say that it is the most reassuring one you could choose."

It had been a long time since we'd heard anything from D.I. Irons and her non-wrecking crew. Unlike the clowns in the police, it only took me a couple of minutes to release Mrs Davies from her prison within a prison (always the last key you try).

Hey, go easy on the police, you clown! They work tirelessly for the Britain with very little thanks. Just because they're not master locksmiths capable of cracking a high-tech anti-theft system in a timeframe that suits you, that's no excuse to speak so rudely of them.

Yes, brain. Sorry, brain. It won't happen again.

Things must have been tough for my former headmistress; she'd removed her neckerchief and undone a button on her blouse. I didn't think I'd ever see her resort to such extreme measures.

"Thank you," she said as though receiving a commendation in a teachers' awards ceremony, if such a thing exists.

They probably don't. It's not just the police who go underappreciated in today's society. Teachers, nurses, doctors, binmen: none of them get the thanks they deserve. But I say, God Bless 'em one and all! And God Bless the King!

My brain becomes very patriotic for some reason when considering the plight of civil servants.

Mrs Davies was still talking. "Thank you, all of you. It's wonderful to be relatively free."

"I don't understand why someone would have pushed you in there?" As I said this, I noticed a nasty bruise on her forehead where she must have hit the floor.

She let out a brief, polite laugh. "It was rather a shock to me too. I came down here as I remembered the people who installed the security system saying something about a power point or an override or some such thing being in the South Block. When I was halfway along this corridor, someone rushed me from behind and pushed me into the drama studio. I tripped and banged my head on the way down. My first thought, much like Simon's, was that one of my ex-pupils was playing a joke on me, but there was no laughter, no sign that it was meant in jest. I could only conclude, therefore, that the killer wanted to get me out of the way. It's as simple as that."

This provoked another question, to which I couldn't imagine the answer. "But if that's the case, why did they decide to spare you? They clearly don't mind subjecting others in the school to violence, and a bump on the head is a bit of a let off if you ask me."

I was hoping one of them might actually have an answer to my question. Instead, they all looked a bit gormless, and Simon shrugged.

Don't do it unless Simon says "shrug"!

I think I've already made that joke, thank you.

You know, like in the game "Simon Says"?

If you have to explain a joke, then it probably isn't funny. And to be honest, this one wasn't that great in the first place.

"Come on then, let's get back to the hall," I said with a sigh. "Who knows, someone else might be dead by now."

"Oooooh!" Simon sounded a little too excited by this. "Who's copped it so far?"

"Well, I guess you know about Tommy Hathaway and his wife Clara Higson?"

"Yep, and Mr Bath." He wore a guilty grin just then. "Mrs Davies filled me in on all the gory details."

Our headmistress looked disapprovingly at us but said nothing.

"Since you were both locked away," I replied, "Pete Boon took a knife to the chest, and the killer knocked out my friend Danny."

"Oh, no, poor Danny?" Mrs Davies cooed. "Is he going to be alright?"

She clearly didn't think much of poor Pete Boon. And I'm once more amazed that I could summon so much sympathy for a boy who tormented me for seven years.

Go easy, Izzy. The man had a cat. A CAT!

My three fellow misfits chatted serenely as they walked ahead of us, and so I took the opportunity to have a word with Mrs Davies.

"Frances…" Nope, too weird. "I mean, Mrs Davies. Is it possible that a member of staff could be behind what's happening here?" Instead of just letting her answer my first question, I kept on blathering. "I hoped I could rule out the idea when Pete was killed, especially as I thought that you were the real target of the first two killings, but is there anything you know that might implicate one of your colleagues?"

She looked alarmed as she considered the possibility. "I don't think so. After all, what could link Pete Boon, Ernie Bath and that libidinous couple?"

"I really can't say, but seeing how the killer spared your life, I'm left wondering whether any of my conclusions are accurate. If you weren't the target in the security room and then in your office, perhaps those seemingly unconnected people were." I paused, as I wasn't sure whether to share everything that had happened that evening. "There's something else too. At each crime scene, the killer left a memento. They're almost like trophies in reverse. Instead of taking something from the victims, the culprit left a reference to someone from my year at school. Becky Mitchell's lipstick, her ex-husband's sweat band and an Agatha Christie novel, which presumably stands in for me."

Mrs Davies seemed unconcerned with exactly what this could mean and returned to my previous point. "Doesn't that prove one of your classmates is responsible? A member of staff wouldn't be so fixated on such things. If you ask me, the killer is in the hall, hiding in the crowd and popping out whenever he feels like doing something nasty. It's surely the best way to go undetected."

I flicked through the case notes that I stored in my brain and looked for the other questions I'd been hoping to put to her. "Then what about the security system? Why did you install something so impenetrable? And how could you even afford it?"

She looked a little cagey again and tucked her chin into the neck of her blouse. "We had a string of thefts a few years back. There's a lot of petty theft these days and you can't be too careful."

"That might explain the metal detectors, but not the military-strength shutters. You're keeping something from me, now what is it?"

She looked along the corridor to where my companions were disappearing from sight. "The system really was designed to protect against burglary. A local company offered to pay for the system, so long as they could try out some new technological developments that they were working on. One of the owners used to go to the school."

"That might explain the financing, but it's so extreme. Did you really agree to all this?" I glanced at the metal walls on either side of us as we descended the tunnel again.

"It wouldn't have been my first choice." She swallowed then, as though recalling how she had given in to the plan. "But then things deteriorated, and I said they could do whatever they wanted." She paused again and took a deep breath. "I didn't tell you before because I don't like to think about it, but there were several bomb scares in the years just after you left. Packages with suspicious powders were sent to the school, and there were anonymous messages left on my phone in the middle of the night saying that someone planned to wipe this place off the face of the earth. The police were sure that it was just a student playing a prank, but it went on for a long time, and I thought it was better to be safe than sorry."

"Then why did you lie?"

She evidently didn't appreciate my choice of words and took a step away before replying. "We've kept it a secret to avoid copycats. That's all there is to it. The fact is, all that business stopped five years ago, and I've tried to push it from my mind."

With her piece said, she nodded to herself in that businesslike manner of hers and marched off after my little helpers. I was about to do the same when my bag started buzzing. Well, the phone inside it did.

"This is Izzy. Talk to me!"

"Hi, Iz. Irons here." The D.I. did a little heavy breathing down the line. She would have made a great stalker if her career hadn't taken her in another direction. "We're still waiting on that industrial-strength blowtorch or what have you, but the fire brigade has brought a couple of very large hammers, and we're trying to break in through a shuttered skylight in the gym. Just thought I'd give you a heads-up."

I just so happened to be passing the building where I'd suffered so much indignity as a teenager. I stopped to check that the door was locked before giving her the go-ahead. "You're fine. Do your worst."

"Go for it, girls," she said with some glee, and I could hear the blows go raining down on the poor unsuspecting Teflon-coated armour which covered the roof of the gymnasium. "Nope, no good," Irons soon concluded. "To be honest, I didn't hold out much hope. I just thought it would be cool to climb up here with a couple of sledgehammers. Any more violence at your end?"

"A bit," I confirmed. "One of my bullies was murdered. But considering how many unlikeable targets there are here, I think we're lucky that the death toll has remained relatively low."

"That's great." Her voice was almost merry.

"I don't suppose you've considered looking into the criminal records of everyone here?"

I could hear her bristling. "Watch it, you. Just because my team isn't made up of Poirot-esque geniuses, that doesn't mean we haven't been working our butts off." I loved the fact she referenced Christie. I swear she'd never read a whodunit until she met me!

Congratulations. That really is some achievement.

"So you've found out something useful?" I was probably a bit too optimistic.

"Now I didn't say that, did I? All I know is that, of everyone who was in your year at school, only Lorna Inglis, Becky Mitchell and Michael Andersen have been prosecuted for crimes.

"Lorna has a criminal record?" This blew my mind for a moment.

"Yes, but only for speeding about a decade ago. In fact, all three of the prosecutions were car-related, and Michael Andersen's was overturned. Must have had a good lawyer."

This fitted with everything I knew about Richie Rich.

I could hear some papers rustling as Irons consulted her notes. "There was a teacher who was arrested for public indecency, but he retired and moved to Thailand."

"Pervy Peterson!" I said with far too much cheer in my voice. "He was actually much nicer than his extra-curricular activities might suggest."

Irons sighed. "They always are, Izzy. The weird ones always are."

"Alright, buddy." Perhaps I was overstepping the mark calling her by any such name, but I was beginning to feel like Bruce Willis in 'Die Hard' and she was my cop pal on the outside. "I've got some investigating of my own to do. Let me know if you come up with anything."

"Sure thing, Iz." I thought she would hang up then, but she hadn't quite finished. "Oh, and Iz? Hang in there, man. Hang in there, do you hear me?"

Whoa! That was so cool. I wish you could talk like that and not sound like an idiot.

"Sure thing, pardner."

As I said, I wish you could talk like that and not sound like an idiot.

I hung up before I could pretend to be American again and then ran after my friends. Standing outside the hall, Simon didn't look nearly as afraid as I might have expected. I had to conclude that having the even more socially awkward Lorna at his side helped relax him.

You know, Lorna should have come to the reunion with Simon instead of practically already married Dean. Even though they look like a before and after picture demonstrating the use of shrink-ray technology, I think they go really well together.

Nooooo! Please tell me we won't be the only ones leaving this place alone tonight. Danny and Shandy, Lorna and Simon, Nurse Crouch and Mr Cody, Frau Schmidt and Mr Roberts. This whole reunion is basically a singles night, and we've got no one.

We have each other.

That's not much comfort, but thanks.

Inside the hall, the atmosphere had changed once more, and I could tell that people were going stir-crazy. There was no one left on the dancefloor, Ramesh's jazzy piano stylings were no longer soothing the masses, and several people were fighting over the small provision of furniture, as though playing a particularly violent version of musical chairs.

"I knew we couldn't expect everyone to just mingle," Mrs Davies muttered to herself as two women had a tug-of-war over a lab stool from the Science Block. "I told Verity we'd need more places to sit, but she wouldn't listen."

She strode away to assess the situation, and, with my friends already dispersed, I was left alone as West Wickham High's angry ex-alumni shot judgemental looks in my direction.

I heard their mumbled comments of, "Some detective!" and, "I bet she never even found that missing squirrel. She probably just fobbed that old lady off with any old squirrel from the park." I saw their disgruntled faces and somehow heard every doubting thought that entered their tiny minds in one endless barrage of public opprobrium.

"I'm sorry," I found myself whispering before realising that I wanted them all to hear it and so raising my voice. "I said, I'm sorry, but I'm a detective, not a magician. It's not my job to find a murderer before the girl in the fish tank runs out of air. I'm here to follow clues and come to the right conclusion."

I turned around slowly to address as many of them as possible. Some were faceless in the shadows, others brightly illuminated by the now static shards of light that bounced off the disco ball. "I'm sorry I haven't found the killer yet, but very few murder investigations are sewn up in a few hours, and I'll need more time."

Far from winning them over, this triggered more disgruntled murmuring, and so I accepted defeat. "Whatever you think of me, the safest thing now is for you to stay together. If you have to go anywhere, go in a big group. That's the best chance that any of us have of surviving the night."

It was hardly the most cheerful message, but then we West-Wickhamites have never been fans of the naked truth. The grim mood would have remained for some time if one of the suspects hadn't burst into the room to interrupt my thoughts. It was something of a shock when the party's organiser crashed through the door, looking really very different from her usual prim and proper self. Verity's deep red lipstick was smeared. She had an ecstatic smile on her face and was clearly as drunk as anyone else there. I was about to go in search of my friends, but she grabbed me by the arm before I could get away.

"Isn't this the most wonderful party, Izzy? I don't know why I was so worried. Everything has worked out exactly as I planned." Her face curled up then and a realisation struck me.

"It was you, wasn't it?" I pulled her fingers off me, one at a time, and people in the crowd noticed the commotion and craned their necks to see.

"I don't know what you mean." She still wore that duplicitous expression, this time with a dirty smile on her face to match. I knew she was taunting me. She'd killed those poor people for... some reason, and now she was rubbing it in my face.

She raised one finger to her lip and said, "Shhh! It's a secret. No one must know." She even winked this time, and her smile grew.

"Why did you do it?" I couldn't control my voice and my yells brought more attention from the former revellers. "Was this whole thing your way of getting revenge for something I did when I was a kid? Revenge for Gary? Did you want to show everyone that I'm not such a great detective after all?"

She looked a little confused and rocked back and forth on her heels. "Gary? What's my brother got to do with anything? I've been having a splendid time with—"

Before she could say another word, the lights turned off, Verity seemed to collapse forward onto me, and I heard the pluck of a string. It sounded like the noise a homemade musical instrument might make, and it wouldn't be long before I discovered what had caused it. The lights turned back on and there, sliding across the glossy floor towards me, was an archer's bow.

"Oh dear," Verity muttered as she stared down at the arrow sticking out of her stomach. "That's not very nice."

Chapter Twenty-Four

Panic ripped through the room as people caught sight of the stain that was turning Verity's pink dress red. The centre of the room cleared entirely, and those lucky enough to have a chair or table instantly hid behind them.

"Call Danny!" I yelled as Verity placed all her weight onto me. "Get Nurse Crouch and Danny from the first-aid room and tell them what's happened."

I didn't know whether to hold her or not, as any movement could surely make her lose blood faster. I scanned the room for someone who could help and noticed that every last one of my suspects was there. Any of them could have shot her and thrown the bow in our direction. I had no idea how they would have made the lights turn off, but then I'd leave that for Dean to work out.

"I won't let you die, Verity. I promise."

There was something serene about her expression as I lay her down on her side on the wooden floor. "Of course not, dear." She spoke in that rather old-ladyish voice of hers, as though she was fifty years my senior. "But just in case I do, I want to say thank you."

There was a tear in my eye, but I couldn't really say why. I'm not a crier and, just a few seconds before this, I thought she was a mass murderer. "Thank me? Why would you want to thank me?"

I don't know whether it was the drink or the blood loss, but it took her a moment to respond. "For being here, Izzy. If it weren't for you, none of this would have been possible. He'd never have come."

I stood up as Danny and his assistant arrived. They were carrying towels, compresses, scissors and hopefully some slightly more high-tech medical equipment that could save her life.

"Clear the way, Izzy," he said, apparently back to his normal self, or at least shocked into a higher state of functionality by the circumstances. "Nurse, we'll need to stem the bleeding."

"Yes, Doctor." Crouchy grabbed something from her bag and handed it to her temporary boss before turning to smile at me. "My whole life has been building up to this moment. This is amazing."

"Wait," I said, stepping around her shoulder to get Verity's attention.

"Who wouldn't have come tonight if I hadn't shown up? What were you talking about?"

The patient turned her head back in my direction, but she had no words for me and displayed that weak smile once more. I could hardly shove the two people who might actually save her life out of the way, and so I stood back to let them work.

I hadn't felt so nervous all night, but something about the way Verity had been attacked was so reckless that I couldn't breathe comfortably and had to take huge gulps of air to calm myself down.

"Are you alright?" Dean asked and rubbed his hand across my back to soothe me as I bent at the waist.

"No. No, I'm not. It's all too much. This isn't a whodunit, it's a horror film."

Simon and Lorna arrived next, and I felt quite loved as they gathered around me in a little comfort circle.

"Did you see who did it, Iz?" they appeared to ask as one.

"No. From the position it must have been fired from, it could have been half the people in the room. Did any of you spot anything?"

That really wasn't their job, and so they all looked furtive and hoped someone else would respond.

"It was too dark," Dean eventually answered. "The lights were off just long enough for the killer to have retrieved the weapon, taken the shot and moved to stand out of sight before the back-up system kicked in."

Feeling more settled, I straightened up and cast my eyes about the troubled scene. No one had approached the weapon that was still lying a short distance from where Verity was receiving treatment.

Shandy had arrived to admire the dishy doctor's handiwork, but her eyes had become fixed on the bow, and she eventually walked over to see it. "It's another token, isn't it? Another reference to one of us. That could be Verity's bow from our archery class when she almost hit Becky. Do you remember all the fuss that people made?"

I went to inspect it and, at first, it looked like any bow that any child might use in archery classes in schools across the country.

Wait, do schools actually teach archery these days? Or is that just a weird West Wickham thing?

"It's the same one," I accepted, remembering the uproar that had roared up when Verity's arrow had strayed towards Becky's target. It was a lot of fuss over nothing, of course, but Queen Becky had already mentioned it once that evening and so clearly some people hadn't forgotten what happened. "The letters V and F are scratched into the riser on the upper limb. It fits with the rest of the items we found."

"Verity's lucky that the arrow didn't kill her outright." Shandy spoke rather sombrely.

I wasn't sure how lucky she really was at this stage. At least there were people on hand with the right skills to help her, but without being able to get her to a hospital, what did this mean for her chances of making it out alive? I mean, what was Danny going to do? Just leave the arrow in to plug the wound and keep pressure on around it?

"We're going to leave the arrow in to plug the wound and keep pressure on around it," he explained in a loud, authoritative voice, and I thought, *Oh, right. That is what he's going to do.*

I also realised that, no matter how impressive he looked, – especially now that he'd removed his dinner jacket to reveal his trademark black V-neck T-shirt, which stuck to his muscly chest like paint – I wasn't in love with him. Even in full action-man mode, he seemed like a brother and nothing more, and I was right to break off our relationship when I did. He was better off with Shandy, and I was better off with my future husband, wherever and whoever he might be.

"Of course, what I really need is something to remove the arrow, cauterise the wound and suture her back up again. But we're not going to find such equipment in a school."

"The best day of my life!" Nurse Crouch bellowed into the air like a werewolf and then calmed herself down in order to explain. "I stocked my nurse's office for just such an eventuality. We've got everything we need in there. An electrocauter, laughing gas, scalpels and scrubs."

The initially hesitant spectators had closed in around us and watched Dr Danny as he issued orders. "Excellent work, nurse. Go ahead of us and prepare the room. I'll follow just behind with the patient."

Nurse Crouch couldn't believe her luck. She jumped to her feet to thunder across the hall – which was a pretty impressive feat for a fifty-year-old with a bad back.

"Izzy, Shandy, help me move her." Danny was already lifting

Verity, who hadn't said anything for some time.

I took her other arm and Shandy cleared the way through the onlookers and then rushed off to open doors. By the time we got to the nurse's office, the operating theatre had been prepared and, except for the fact that my mother, father, stepfather and a host of their entourage were watching the scene nervously on a projection on the wall, it looked just like a real hospital. Nurse Crouch had even found her old medical hat and gown and was putting them on.

"This is the stuff!" She was, to say the least, very eager. "I knew this stuff would come in handy one day."

I couldn't decide whether to stay and watch or give them some privacy. My family, of course, had no such dilemma. Dad had brought out a fresh box of homemade butterfly cakes and was passing them around the audience as they kept their eyes fixed on whatever screen they were watching.

After a few minutes of tense investigation under an angled lamp with an extra strong bulb, Danny made his first prognosis. "We have to cross our fingers that the arrow hasn't punctured a major organ. I need to remove it without doing any further damage and then sew her up like I said."

A bottle of alcohol was produced, the wound was sterilised, Danny cut one end of the arrow and I decided I'd seen enough. Hey, I'm tough, but I'm not *spurting-vein-because-the-doctor-just-removed-a-projectile-lodged-in-a-woman's-gut* tough.

It came as no surprise whatsoever that, back in the hall, my old schoolmates looked at me as though I was the one who'd fired the arrow, stabbed a bully, electrocuted a teacher and squashed a loving couple.

"Are you sure you're not the killer, Izzy?" Ramesh suggested when I went to find our posse of outcasts. Even he couldn't entertain the crowd now, and he'd decided to hang up his white gloves for the night. "I mean, we all know you hated Mr Bath and Pete Boon. And you were arguing with Verity as the lights went out. Isn't it possible that you're to blame for—"

"Don't." This was all I said, and it was enough to make him stop speaking for once. I rarely told the chattiest man in London to be quiet. I loved every ridiculous opinion he wished to share, but this was not the time.

"It'll be fine, Iz." Dean was a slightly better judge of when to change the tone and did so accordingly. "Danny's looking after her. She couldn't be in safer hands."

Lorna whispered an equally comforting phrase as she patted my shoulder, and Simon didn't have to say anything. His drooping frown said it all.

"We need to find the killer," I stated as I crashed down at their table. How they'd managed to get such a prime spot at the edge of the hall and reserve me a seat too, was beyond me, but there were more important mysteries to solve.

"You'll find him, Izzy." I could tell that Dean really believed this. In fact, the whole lot of them seemed to believe in me and my ability to stop anyone else from suffering. Perhaps it was the pressure I felt not to disappoint them, but I finally came up with a plan.

"There'll be clues as to what happened tonight scattered throughout the school. We just have to follow them. We'll start back at the beginning and take our time. We'll catch the evidence that we didn't spot before and get to the killer before anyone else has to die."

Dean managed a smile. "The electricity is running off the back-up generators now. The killer won't be able to pull the trick with the lights a third time. That should mean that everyone here is safe, at least."

"We'll all go with you this time, Izzy." Ramesh rose from his seat and held out his hand to help me up. "You're right; we'll find the clues we need. And when the police break through the shutters, we'll be able to hand over the culprit."

He stroked the back of my hand with his thumb in little circles and it was enough to force me back to my feet and out of that hall. I was there with three of my best friends from different stages of my life (and Lorna) and, for the first time that night, I felt we really could put an end to the killings.

It certainly didn't hurt that, as we passed the nurse's office, Danny stuck his head out and said, "The internal bleeding is manageable. It will take me some time to operate, but Verity's chances are good."

Shandy had been sitting outside like a Year Seven kid with a bloody nose, waiting for the doctor to see her. Now that he was there, she rushed forward to embrace him. Smiles spread around our little clique of Scooby Doo-ish heroes, but I wasn't about to celebrate just yet.

I had to remind myself that soldiers in the First World War had been patched up with shrapnel wounds as bombs exploded all around them, yet still lived to be a hundred. I had to believe that Verity would survive, at the very least because five dead bodies are more than most whodunits can handle. Five bodies in the space of a few hours would see us leave behind the world of old lady detectives and gentlemen geniuses and approach serial killer territory. I did not want the evening to turn into 'And Then There Were None', and so I kept walking.

Chapter Twenty-Five

"Let's start back at the beginning," Dean was the most technically minded member of our party and would be setting the agenda for the next half an hour. "We didn't look closely enough at how the first trap was set. It could tell us something that we should have questioned when we first went into the security room."

We trailed after him in single file, just like when I was at school. No one spoke, and I think we all had a lot on our minds just then. We were calculating the likelihood of the police carting off each suspect to prison if they ever breached the shutters.

The others stood back when we got to our destination, though. They stood back and let me lead, after all. We inspected the room, no longer worried about disrupting a crime scene and concerned only with finding the culprit.

"Behind the case!" Dean declared in a frustrated tone. "I should have noticed it before."

I had to step over the still relatively fresh bodies to see what he meant. There wasn't much space behind the door, but he pointed to the wall where the server cabinet had once been screwed in place.

"I don't see anything."

He waved his finger as if that would explain. "The screws have been loosened and there's a pile of bricks on the floor. Someone definitely set the cabinet up to fall when the door was opened, then closed again." He looked behind us and quickly found what he was looking for. "There's even a thin metal wire leading from the top of the door. When that snapped, the cabinet collapsed, and Tommy and Clara were crushed."

"How could you not have noticed all that the first time we were here?" I tried to conceal the irritation in my voice. Well, I didn't try very hard, actually, and he didn't either.

"Oh, I'm sorry, Izzy. I came here tonight expecting bad music and dull conversation, not a couple of swingers crushed to death."

"Always expect dead bodies, Dean. Always!"

"But we already knew how they died." Lorna had to throw her tiny voice to interrupt our bickering. It sounded as though she was very far away indeed. "What good does it do us?"

"Because we guessed the first time, but now we know for sure," I replied, as any certainty at that moment was a good thing. "It tells us the killer knew how to rig up such a trap, if that was ever in doubt."

Dean passed judgement on the matter. "The killer is definitely smart and, from what I've seen, has significant technological knowledge."

"What do you do, Simon?" Ramesh asked a little suspiciously.

He answered in all innocence with an impressive smile shaping his face. "I trained as an electrical engineer."

"Oopsie!" Ramesh took a few steps away from my childhood friend, just to be on the safe side.

"But you were in the music room all night, right?" I felt I had to point out. "Mrs Davies can vouch for that?"

Simon didn't seem upset by this line of questioning. "Absolutely! Except for the few times when she went quiet for half an hour or so. She was either sleeping or tired of talking to me. I do tend to go on about my job in excruciating details when I'm nervous. There's only so much tech talk that most people can take."

"See," I said to his millionaire counterpart. "Nothing to worry about. Simon has an alibi for large parts of the evening."

"What about the sweatband?" Dean said to change the topic. "Is there anything we should consider there?"

Over the course of the evening, I noticed that Lorna had become increasingly talkative and actually seemed quite comfortable sharing her thoughts with us by now. "Fluorescent green with a Slazenger logo; it's definitely the same one that Robert Mitchell wore on sports day back in 2006. It was the day he broke the eight-hundred-metre record."

I couldn't fault her memory. I bet I wasn't the only one who watched Robert zooming around that running track, wishing I was one of the beads of sweat on his brow.

I bet you were.

"Do you mean it looks just like it, or it's the same one?" Ramesh asked and moved over to the bank of computers where the famous piece of school sporting history still lay.

"It's the same one," I replied with some confidence.

Without touching it, Ramesh bent over and had a good sniff. "I'm getting... historic sweat... a touch of Vidal Sassoon conditioner and... yep, Lynx Africa – a deodorant worn almost exclusively by sixteen-year-old boys. It's the real deal, people!"

"And?" Dean did not seem impressed by Ramesh's almost supernatural olfactory ability.

I personally thought he made some dogs look like talentless try-hards. "And it shows that the killer was already obsessed with Robert way back then."

"Totally!" Lorna was excited now. Perhaps she would become just as addicted to solving crimes as I was.

Poor girl! Don't wish that on her.

"You mean the killer took this from Robert all that time ago?" The man who had just sniffed out ancient traces of sweat was slightly repulsed by this idea and shivered melodramatically.

"It looks like it. Now let's see what the second crime scene can tell us." I don't know about the boys, but Lorna and I were dead set on solving this case. I even gave her a little high-five in celebration, as I'd apparently exorcised such demons by this stage in the evening. Admittedly, she didn't quite catch what I was doing and simply held her hand up near mine like she was waving, but it was close enough.

When we got to the headmistress's office, there wasn't enough space for us all to fit inside, and so Ramesh and Simon volunteered to wait in the corridor.

"Wait a second," Ramesh held one arm across the door to bar the way. "Are you certain that there will be nothing in there that requires careful smelling?"

"I'm pretty sure we'll be okay," I told him. "But we'll call you if we need your services."

He frowned like a reluctant security guard and moved aside for us to pass. We didn't need Ramesh, as the smell of the old P.E. teacher's frazzled hair and zapped flesh was so strong that even my puny nostrils could detect it. Mr Ernie Bath was still dead, still fried, and still huddled over our headmistress's desk with his hands on two phones.

"It's hard to say whether he was the target, but it does seem more likely now that we know the killer had another chance to murder Mrs Davies and didn't take it."

"Unless the person who pushed her into the drama studio wasn't the killer?" Dean suggested, and it was a good point that I was happy to ignore.

"If only we could access his phone," Lorna warbled and pointed to the mobile in his hand. "Perhaps we could work out what he was doing here."

"Allow me, ladies." Dean licked the ends of his fingers and smoothed his eyebrows – yuck – then rolled up his sleeves.

"Gloves!" I said before he did too much damage. I held out another pair from my bag and he carefully put them on. He didn't look so cool after that; it turns out that forensic equipment doesn't go brilliantly with Armani suits.

He leant in towards the body in order to extract the phone from the dead man's grip, using the tips of two sheathed fingers. "Voila."

"Alright, Mr Smug," I foolishly responded. "But you still have to unlock the—" He fiddled around on the screen for ten seconds, then held it up to show me what he'd done. "You've already cracked the code, haven't you?"

"Yes, I indeedy do have." He coughed and cleared his throat. "Urmmm, yeah. It's unlocked."

The three of us gathered around to look at the six-inch screen. The background photo held an image of Mr Bath with about twenty-seven grandchildren. It was one of those slideshow thingies, so the first picture was soon replaced by one of him receiving a medal from the Queen and then another of him presenting a cheque to Shelter UK for one point five million pounds. The man was a saint!

I opened his social media, which it he'd apparently never signed in to, and then his messaging app, which was mainly loving messages from his family thanking him for being such a great guy, before I finally opened the text messages as I should have done at the beginning.

Go to the headmistress's office and ring this number if you don't want anyone to know your little secret. 07527850132

I checked it against the number on Pete's phone and, sure enough, they matched.

"G.G.," I said, as though that really was the killer's name.

"I wonder what his little secret was," Dean mused, but Lorna was a bright spark and came up with an answer before I could.

"The killer didn't need to know. It was enough just to suggest that they were holding something over him. We all have secrets, and so he did as instructed. It's not as though he was asked to shoot someone in the street. He only had to make a phone call."

"Yeah," I said, trying to hide my modicum of jealousy. "That's exactly what I was going to say."

Lorna smiled at me but, instead of being nice and telling her how well she'd done, I moved us swiftly on to the next point.

Mean!

"And now we know that Mrs Davies wasn't the target here."

Dean scratched his head. "Yeah, but that might be because she was meant to die in the security room. Suppose that the power was set to turn off at a certain time, and Tommy and Clara had already wandered in there and been crushed to death. That would mean your headmistress missed her date with death. The killer had already set the second trap in motion, so Mr Bath was the next to go."

I let the ramifications of his theory play out in my brain. "I guess it's lucky she had a mobile with her or she might have ended up being the wrong target of this one. In fact, if you're right, plenty of stuff went wrong for the killer tonight. First Mrs Davies lived, then Pete failed to stick to the plan."

"How do you mean?" Just occasionally, Dean is a bit slow, and it makes me feel smart... for a few minutes until he says something clever, and I instantly feel dumb again.

"The text messages on Pete's phone." Lorna nudged him for not keeping up with us.

"That's right." I liked her again now and smiled as I spoke. "Pete was supposed to meet his phantom date 'G.G.' in Mrs Long's history room, but he changed the plan and told her to go to the toilets instead. He messed everything up and G.G. almost got caught by Danny and Shandy."

Dean folded and unfolded his arms, and then refolded them for good measure. "Huh, I didn't think of that before. It does seem like a foolish plan to kill someone somewhere so public. Anyone from the party could have gone to the toilets just then."

"The thing is, if G.G. hadn't previously intended to kill Pete in such a manner..." There wasn't much space in that office with Mr Bath and the three of us in there, but Lorna was determined to pace around it. "...perhaps there's another trap in the history class that hasn't been triggered. It would fit better with the rest of the killer's schemes. G.G. did everything by phone or at arm's length. Why suddenly change and kill Pete Boon with a chisel?"

Dean pulled his neck in and looked at Lorna. "Wow, you're good at this."

"Oh, is she?" I definitely failed to hide my modicum of jealousy. "You never say nice stuff like that about me."

Dean would not show me the sympathy I deserved. "It's literally your job. Have you ever complimented me on my computer skills or the microchip I helped develop that is now used in spyware across the globe?"

"No, but in my defence, I have no idea what any of that means."

Lorna laughed at the pair of us and dashed off to check out the history room on the way to the scene of Pete's death.

Chapter Twenty-Six

Shandy had joined us by now and, with Ramesh and Simon back in the fold, it felt like a fun family outing.

What sort of family goes on outings to crime scenes?

My kind of family!

The only thing that made the experience a little less comfortable was my lingering fear that one of my friends was responsible for all those nasty murders.

"Dean," I whispered, and pulled on his arm to hold him back from the rest of the group.

"What is it?" he practically shouted, so that the others glanced back, and I had to whistle a little tune to show that nothing suspicious was happening.

"Keep it down, would you?" I gave him the evil eye. "I need to ask you something."

"Well, go on then." He still sounded grumpy, but at least he was quieter this time.

"I need to know whether you were standing with Simon when Verity was shot."

He went through a couple of his favourite thinking poses before finding the answer. "No, sorry. I was off in the bathroom. I wouldn't have drunk so much punch if you had bothered to tell me it was full of vodka. I don't think I've ever been this drunk before."

"You seem exactly the same as normal."

"Yep, that's what I'm like when I'm drunk. It's both a blessing and a curse."

It was my turn to scratch my head as, not only could I not work out how this was a problem for him, I was worried that Simon was involved in the killings. There was no time to worry about that, as we soon reached the history class where I'd spent so many hours of my teenage life studying... well, history obviously.

Of course, no one was desperate to walk into a potentially booby-trapped room and so we went through another negotiation to decide who would kick the door open.

"You have the biggest feet," Ramesh kindly pointed out.

"You have the biggest ego," I countered.

"I'll do it." Simon was just as lovely as I remembered – so the thought of him being the killer was faintly horrific. We'd stayed friends and seen each other during the holidays for a few years when we finished school, and I really don't know why we lost touch in our twenties.

No one was about to argue with him, and Dean and Lorna quickly stood clear. In fact, we made a line on either side of the door for him to run through as though he were a champion athlete – which was not something that you could accuse me of.

"Go for it, Simon," Dean said from some way off.

"Try not to get blown up or shot or anything," I added. "Danny's busy enough with Verity as it is."

Simon took a deep breath, psyched himself up a little and, commenced his short run up.

"Wait!" I shouted when he was mere feet away from danger. "There's a better solution. Why don't we just use a broom or something to push it open?"

"A broom!" Ramesh declared. "The woman's a genius."

Simon once again volunteered to seek out the required implement in a neighbouring cupboard. With his heroic task achieved, we all remained at a safe distance, and he pushed down the handle and shoved the door wide. Sure enough, there were several angry thuds, and we witnessed a whole barrage of glass embed itself in the wood.

"I think Pete got off lightly," Lorna said with a frightened gulp.

"Was this meant for him, then?" Shandy asked. With so many assistants on hand that night, I sometimes forgot who knew what.

"That's right." I shuddered at the thought of it. "I reckon that a chisel to the heart was a happier outcome."

"Are we going inside?" Simon asked, full of innocence or perhaps guile. It really was hard to know which.

I stood in front of the door to block the way. "Noooooo. Definitely not. The police can work out how the trap was set when they eventually get in there. It's probably a good thing we checked this out. Another poor, horny couple might have set it off otherwise. I'm sure that their fear of a serial killer isn't enough to stop some drunken idiots wandering from the hall." With my judgemental commentary concluded, I had a question for Dean. "Just out of interest, how do you think the killer set the trap?"

He shrugged as though it was really very obvious. "When the door flung open, it pulled a trigger that fired the shrapnel, possibly using high-pressure hydraulics or a small explosion. Would you like me to be any more technical than that?"

"Nope, that was perfect. I understood almost every word." I pointed ahead of us down the corridor. "On to the toilets we go."

Shandy led us off, once more taking us through her story of what happened. "Danny and I were tasked with keeping an eye on Verity, and then she got a phone call and left the hall, so we tailed her."

"You didn't tell me that she got a phone call before." I was reminded once more that she was by far our least reliable witness.

"Didn't I?" She shook her curly hair to remind us all how ditzy she could be when not in teacher mode. "Sorry, I've got a brain like a sieve sometimes. But that's why we followed her. She got a phone call and acted all coy, so me and Danny sped after her – at a discreet distance."

"So that means Verity probably wasn't the killer." Ramesh didn't sound very sure of himself. "I mean, aside from the fact that she was just shot with an arrow, it seems unlikely she was meeting Pete in the toilets as he'd already received the text from G.G. and, I'm guessing that there was no call received on his phone or Izzy would have told us."

"That's right," I confirmed. Considering the state she was in, I'd dismissed the possibility that Verity was involved, but Ramesh's comment made me reconsider. "Unless, of course, she was working with someone else."

"And they shot her?" Dean's scepticism was plain for all to hear.

"Exactly. She was working with G.G., who told her that they were meeting Pete in the toilets to kill him. So Verity ran along to help or what have you, before noticing Danny and Shandy on her trail and hiding in another room and warning G.G. that she was being followed. G.G. finished up with Pete, escaped from the toilets, and knocked Danny out with the nearest weapon that came to hand."

"The trophy outside the toilets," Shandy reminded everyone.

"That's the one. And then, for whatever reason, G.G. decided that

Verity was no longer useful and shot her with her own bow."

Dean stroked his chin, once more relying on very literal human gestures. "That might make sense, actually. This whole plot would have been easier to carry out with two people."

"What good would Verity be?" Now part of the gang, Lorna even felt confident enough to disagree with us. "She might have organised the reunion, but I doubt she has any technical skills."

We'd come to a stop near the toilets, right next to the bloodstained trophy that had made contact with Danny's poor head. I wonder if other surgeons had carried out an operation with a head wound of their own before. It was lucky that Nurse Crouch was on hand to shout at him when needed.

"Verity had access to the school before the party, for one thing. She could have brought the equipment in, like that massive car battery in Mrs Davies office, when she delivered the drinks and decorations. If the killer knew how to set all the traps, it wasn't necessary for them both to know." I was thinking on the go, but this sounded as though it made sense. "Verity could have been the one to keep an eye on everything in the hall while the killer was occupied with the serious business of murder." I had no idea whether this was close to the truth, but I was willing to run with the hypothesis and remembered the scene when Verity was shot. "She told me that none of this would have been possible if I hadn't been here. She said that 'he'd never have come.'"

"The killer?" Simon asked.

"Maybe. Maybe this whole thing was about me. Perhaps the killer wanted to see how good I was and so planned out these crimes to test me. It would explain why there was so little connection between the victims."

"I suppose there's some logic to that." Dean gave a loud sniff before explaining his thinking. "Perhaps Pete thought he was texting Verity Gresham. G.G. could be Gresham Girl, or Gary's Girl." I'm not so insecure that I had to tell everyone that I'd had this thought first. Fine, maybe I am, but I decided to let him have his moment.

"That doesn't add up." Lorna had found a flaw in the argument. "Why would Verity go along with a killing spree? I think that the murderer was working alone. We've got no evidence that two people were involved."

We let her words sink in for a moment before Ramesh found something scary to say. "And there's always the possibility that the arrow was meant for you, Iz."

"For me? Why would anyone want to murder me?"

"To stop you solving the case?" Shandy suggested.

"I'll have you know that I'm nowhere near solving this case and haven't been all evening." I thought this was something of a boast until I said the words aloud and realised otherwise.

"You were arguing with Verity at the time," Dean reminded me. "It's more than possible that, in the dark and with limited bow skills, the killer hit the wrong target."

It had been a couple of years since anyone had tried to murder me, and I had torn feelings on the matter.

"Don't worry, Izzy." Lorna of all people felt sorry for me. "I don't think anyone would want to murder you."

"Hmmm, I don't know," three other people said at the exact same moment, and I glared at Dean, Ramesh and Shandy in turn.

Dean didn't take the hint. "Don't forget that, at each of the killings, the murderer left behind artefacts connected to a third party. With Verity, the artefact was her own. If you'd died, the bow would have made more sense."

I really lost it then. "No, you're all wrong – except Lorna... and Simon who hasn't said much on the matter. I'm the detective, not a potential victim. No one tries to murder Miss Marple, and I am very much a young, attractive, above-average-height Miss Marple!"

There was an awkward hush as my friends glanced at one another and made *ooh-er, Izzy is a bit sensitive* expressions. I could see what they were doing, but this didn't put them off.

It fell to Simon to smooth things over. "Perhaps we should look at the penultimate crime scene?"

"Good idea." I glared at the others once more and they got the message this time and stopped being so cheeky.

"This is all very exciting to me as I don't know much of the story so far," Simon... uttered as we approached the toilets. "It's like going for a ride-along in a police car, or binge watching a whole season of a TV show to catch up."

"Have you ever seen a dead body before tonight?" Ramesh asked in a macabre tone, only for Simon to shake his head in mute excitement. "Ahh, you get used to them after a while. It's really no big thing."

I decided not to point out that Ramesh was the most squeamish person I'd ever taken for a ride-along on one of my cases. "Right, it's time you saw another one. No touching anything. And Shandy, take us through what happened."

"Will do!" My friend was an interesting combination of ultra-organised in her professional life but a hot mess away from school. This meant I never felt completely useless in her presence, but she was a less-than-perfect sidekick for a murder investigation. "Wait, where did I get to?"

"You followed Verity when she received a phone call?" Simon said…

Ha! You said it! You said "Simon said!"

Quiet!

"Okay!" Shandy cued up the rest of her account as we all filed into the toilet. "We lost Verity when she turned into the corridor outside. So she either came in here or went into the art room next door. As there was no sign of her, I came for a look around." She paused then, as though she had to relive the fear she'd previously experienced. "It was dark, and I used the screen on my phone to see what was going on. There was no noise, so I wandered past the sinks to the cubicles. When I got there, he burst out of the second cubicle, and I fell backwards through the opposite door."

"And you didn't get a look at what the killer was wearing or how tall he was?" Lorna *was* good at this. She'd homed in on the exact details we needed to know.

Shandy wrinkled her nose. "No, sorry. I was so surprised by the fall that I didn't get a second to take in what was happening."

"He?" Simon pointed out. "You said, 'he'. Are you sure it was a man?"

It took her a few moments to answer. "No, not at all. It's just what people say, isn't it? We assume that every killer is a man until proven otherwise."

"Yeah, just like every dog is a boy," Ramesh helped her out. "And everything that Taylor Swift records is amazing." He held his hand up for a high-five, but there were no takers. "No? No Swifties in the house? Hmmm, you don't know what you're missing. I could talk for hours about why 'Folklore' is the greatest album ever written."

"Please don't... again." This was me, obviously. "Can we please get back to all the dead people?"

Shandy found some of her magic teacher-energy to push through the tale. "So, the male or female killer left the toilet, saw Danny out in the hall and picked up a heavy trophy to bash him on the head. Then they must have escaped, either through the art room next door – which Izzy found signs that people had been in tonight – or back the way we'd come."

We'd reached the cubicle where Pete's body lay (not quite) rotting (just yet). I still had my gloves on and slowly pushed the door open for us to inspect the scene of the crime. We really didn't need that many people in there, and I had no idea how I'd attracted such an entourage.

We work best alone!

That's not true, but it's an ambition we can strive for.

"Is it your book, Izzy?" Simon asked, pointing at the floor. "I mean, is that your exact copy? Because it seems that the other artefacts the killer left belonged to each person."

I turned my head to look at the paperback in a plastic sleeve. "No, I have several copies of each Christie book at home. I have my own editions that I was given as a child, first editions that my mum's cousin left me in her—"

"And you wanted me to hurry up?" Ramesh sounded offended again. It was one of his three main states of being. "If you're going to talk about your Agatha Christie library, I'm going to talk about Tay Tay. Born in West Reading, Pennsylvania, young Taylor Alison Swift discovered a love of—"

"Fine, it's not my copy!" I shouted to make it stop. "But it's possible that I read it when I was at school."

"In the library at lunchtime." Simon clicked his fingers as he remembered another one of our regular hangouts. "I went there to read my drumming magazines, and you demanded that the school librarian stock up on murder mysteries. You used to check them out just to prove to her that it was a wise investment."

"Yeah, her name was Miss Radish! Ahh, unhappy days!" I said with something approaching nostalgia for the most miserable period of my teenage existence. "It was either that or find ourselves tormented by idiots in the playground."

"So it's not your book, then?" Ramesh only likes it when *he* prattles on about nonsense. He's oddly intolerant of the same trait in other people.

"It's close enough." Lorna bent down to look at the phone that I'd put back in Pete's jacket pocket. "If Robert Mitchell isn't to blame, then that means the killer must have planted G.G.'s phone on him."

"Definitely," I agreed. "We know that Pete was meant to die in the history room, so perhaps the killer ran out of time after killing him. The culprit heard Shandy enter and didn't think of taking Pete's phone before running away. When they got back to the hall, they realised they needed to ditch their own phone so as not to be caught."

"Then why wouldn't they have done the same thing after Mr Bath was killed?" Dean was always so smart and clever, picking holes in my theories and spoiling all the fun.

"Mr Bath was sitting down in the headmistress's office to use the school landline. There was no reason to suspect his mobile of being important." I love Lorna. Have I ever mentioned that I love Lorna?

"Can we go now?" Ramesh interrupted. He'd already departed from our huddle and was walking up and down in front of the sinks. "I know I said you get used to being around dead bodies, but not for this length of time. It's becoming gross."

"Yes! Let us voyage forth to the final crime scene." I pointed to the door and said this far too dramatically, so it was always going to be an anti-climax when they slowly filed out ahead of me.

Philistines! They don't know anything about building tension.

Chapter Twenty-Seven

When we returned to the hall from our little excursion, there was none of the anger or excitement that we'd previously witnessed. I had the feeling that everyone there was resigned to the pathetic situation in which we found ourselves. This was the comedown – the start of the hangover – and there was a lot of hugging and crying going on.

Robert Mitchell's friendship group was no longer as large as it had been at school, but he still had Michael Andersen to console him. The two of them had their arms around one another and were getting a lot of stuff off their chest as we passed.

"I'm sorry I kissed your little sister, Robby!" Michael wailed.

"I'm sorry I kissed your mum, Mike."

"You did what?"

I would have loved to hang around to eavesdrop, but we hurried onwards. From the next table, I caught a snatch of Becky Mitchell's woeful lament as she sat beside Mandy Johnson.

"I could bake cakes if I wanted to, but I don't. I mean, who has time to make their own food these days? That's why we employ a cook!"

"I know, babe. I know. You're so much better than Sprinklez3000."

Becky looked up to the ceiling and felt sorry for herself... well, sorrier for herself. "And now I'm going to die in this miserable hall. You know, I always thought that, if I ever got murdered, it would at least happen somewhere pretty."

"The killer might not go for you," Mandy attempted to reassure her, much to Becky's chagrin.

"Please, don't say that." She looked offended by her friend's thoughtless words. "If he doesn't go for me, that means I'm no longer the most popular woman here."

Good old Mandy could always be trusted to say the first thing that popped into her head. "Exactly. There's no need to worry. Izzy Palmer's much more popular than you these days. People are mad about her. Just think of that speech she gave this evening. She's like a geek princess."

Becky's jaw fell open. She could muster no other response than to burst into tears. Admittedly, I had stopped to enjoy this exchange but, now that it was over (and I felt pretty amazing about my new identity as the geek princess of West Wickham), I followed the others to the killer's approximate position when Verity was shot.

"This is it," Simon... confirmed. "From the angle that the arrow pierced Verity's gut, I reckon it was fired from here."

Dean stepped forward with a frankly ludicrous thought. "The question is, where would the killer get a bow from, and how would they hide it?"

Lorna responded in a diplomatic tone. "West Wickham High is well known for the fine crop of archers it has produced over the decades. In fact, we've made it to the British youth archery finals for the last five years running."

"And it's normal to give children deadly weapons?" Perhaps understandably, Dean was confused.

"It's a weird school. Don't worry about it." I tried to get us back on track. "More importantly, I think the killer must have stashed the bow somewhere for the moment when it was needed. Perhaps if we look about, we'll find more arrows or a bag that's been—"

"Found it!" Simon was beaming. He'd gone off to the nearest window and pulled back the heavy curtain. "There's a bunch of helical-fletched arrows here in a detachable bow-mounted quiver." Sorry for all the archery jargon. If you'd been to a school whose only claim to fame was being moderately good at archery, then you'd know all this stuff too.

"I've been thinking." Dean didn't scratch his head to demonstrate this for once. "Surely our list of suspects is greatly reduced by the fact that most people couldn't easily shoot an arrow across a room at such a distance."

I'm happy to say that I wasn't the first person to laugh at him. I believe that was Simon, followed by Shandy, followed by every other person in the room who'd been to West Wickham High. His words travelled around the hall, and people were soon in floods of laughter as they tried to make sense of his frankly unbelievable ignorance.

"Where'd you go to school, buddy?" one woman heckled. "Bromley High?"

Dean couldn't understand the reaction and spat back. "As a matter of fact, yes, I did. Now what's so funny?"

It was Lorna who kindly set him straight again. "It's just that…" She clearly felt sorry for the poor little millionaire. "You see, Izzy was the absolute worst archer in our year, and even she had a handicap of twenty-three."

I felt I should provide some context. "Hey, I may have been the worst, but by the time we left school, I was also the most improved."

"Wait." Dean still couldn't make sense of any of this. "Is twenty-three bad?"

Shandy put her hand on his shoulder out of pity. "No, hon. Twenty-three is actually pretty good… by most amateur standards." She couldn't resist a laugh of her own then. "But this is West Wickham High. Mrs Davies cancelled morning break so that we could spend more time doing something that really mattered."

"You mean archery practice?" Dean's whole face had crumpled in stark confusion. "Where are we? The Middle Ages?"

"The point everyone is failing to come to is that there are tons of people in this room who could have made a shot like that even in the dark." I was starting to feel a little sorry for him.

"Well… whatever." Dean went to sit down in a huff, and so I pressed on with the story.

"No matter who shot her, they stashed the bow and arrows behind that curtain and, when the lights went out, they knew that they'd have about ten seconds to grab the weapon and shoot Verity before the generator came back on."

"Is that why the lights went out earlier too?" Simon suggested.

"No, that was to trigger the security system and trap us all in here. But it would have told the killer how long they would have to carry out the last attack."

Shandy walked over to examine a smeared trace of blood where Verity had fallen. "It doesn't make any sense. All night long, the killer did everything they could to avoid being near when the victims were killed. So why shoot Verity in such a risky manner?"

It was not an easy question to answer, but it had already been running through my head for some time. "Perhaps they felt empowered after killing Pete without anyone catching them. Perhaps they thought they could get away with anything by this point."

"Or…" Lorna's unmistakable trill fired up, and I knew she would come up with something better than my unsubstantiated guess. "Maybe the killer wanted to be caught. Maybe the list of targets was ticked off, and this was supposed to be the last kill."

"Then why hide when it was over?"

She hesitated, and I knew she didn't have an answer. Her tongue clicked in her mouth as she considered various explanations but, in the end, she gave up.

"Thanks for your help, everyone, but this is as far as we go." I didn't wait for their kindly responses and words of support. I wandered over to Dean's table and plopped myself down to sulk.

It was hard not to conclude that we knew just as little about our killer as when we'd entered the building. I looked at my friends in the hope that one of them might shed some light on the case. It felt ridiculous that we'd found so much evidence – revisited every crime scene and discussed countless motives – without landing on a concrete solution.

Our investigation in the hall had not gone unnoticed either and not just because of the clueless comment that Dean had made. All the likely suspects were there watching us, waiting to see if – depending on whether they liked me or not – that old phoney Izzy Palmer would crash and burn, or the "geek princess" would earn her crown. Robert Mitchell, now with a shiny black eye from the ex-friend who was still sitting beside him, was gritting his teeth as he watched. I've no doubt he wanted me to fall flat on my face. His ex-wife wore a similar expression, whereas Mandy gave me a wave and a "Cooee, Izzy!"

It's her! She's the killer. No one ever suspects the idiot!

I noticed that Mrs Davies had given up her role as the reunion's supervisor and was sitting alone in the corner, sipping punch. She looked thoroughly broken by the events of the night, and I didn't like to imagine all that she'd been through. Knowing that someone wants to kill you is never much fun (unless you're Becky Mitchell), but there was something in her expression which was so distant that I felt a rush of sympathy for her.

It should have been easy to work out who had the biggest chip on their shoulder. But the two kids who'd got into trouble most often when we were at school were already dead. The real dropouts hadn't bothered coming to the reunion, and I'd failed to uncover any secret grudges. The Mitchells, Mandy Johnson, Tim Cornish and Michael Anderson were the only popular kids remaining; I'd wasted most of my time thinking about them, but had I really uncovered anything that would single one of them out as a killer?

I thought about who else I'd crossed paths with that night. The culprit clearly knew the layout of the school extremely well, which didn't narrow the field down too much, but could suggest a teacher was involved. Those frisky educators, Mr Roberts and Frau Schmidt, might have been using their dalliances around the school as cover for a whole other kind of extracurricular activity. Or perhaps dreamy Mr Cody used his down-right handsomeness to elude detection.

Impossible! No man that good looking would bother being a killer.

I think you might have made such claims before. Now stop interrupting.

Coming up with imagined motives was easy enough, but where was that final piece of evidence that would tie everything together?

"You know what?" I said out loud after a weirdly long silence. "I need my mum."

Chapter Twenty-Eight

"Let us know if we're disturbing you," I shouted to Danny, who was hidden behind a green medical curtain and could be heard issuing brief commands like "scalpel," "electrocauter" and "suture!" I was kind of hoping he'd say "stat" at some point, but it didn't happen.

Mother was disappointed that she was missing out on the surgery because she had to talk to me. "It's just like watching an episode of 'Grey's Anatomy'. Only the doctor is even dishier."

"I'm terribly sorry, but I need your help." What with the lifesaving surgery taking place, I'd slimmed down my group of helpers to just my regulars. Shandy, Simon and Lorna had to wait in the hall.

"We just have to tie up a few loose ends." Ramesh was taking the case seriously for once. Perhaps he wanted it to be over so he could stage another dance off.

"Well, get on with it." Even Greg was upset that his viewing had been interrupted. "Let's solve the case quickly, and then we can get back to the real drama."

"All we need to know is who the killer is and what their motive could be." Ra managed to make this sound simple but, of the five or so people still huddled around a screen in my old bedroom, four of them sighed in disappointment.

"That mean girl you always thought was so wonderful." Dad was clearly trying to hurry things along. "Becky Mitchell. She's your killer. She's angry at you about the divorce, and she's trying to show you up."

"But she was in the hall when Pete was killed." I had to reconsider this then as, though she'd provided her ex with an alibi, perhaps she'd only done it to make me think she'd been there herself. Was Becky really that clever?

"So then it must be her ex-husband for the same reason," Mother tried. "Case closed. Now turn the other channel back on."

"I've always preferred medical dramas to crime shows," Brian from the supermarket explained. "I can't be doing with all that violence."

I considered telling him that my cases weren't normally too gory, but Dean moved the conversation along. "I think we should go through

191

the possible killers one by one. As Izzy said, Becky has an alibi."

"Pete's dead," Ramesh added ever so helpfully. "I'd assumed that he was the only one cruel enough to go electrocuting your teachers and squashing old classmates with cabinets, but he's off our list now." He looked at me then just to check I wasn't going to spring a surprise and reveal that Pete hadn't been murdered after all.

"That's right. And from that same group of friends, Mandy Johnson is dimmer than a one-watt bulb, and Michael Andersen still doesn't remember who I am. He wouldn't have left a copy of an Agatha Christie book beside Pete's body without reason."

"Unless he's only saying he doesn't know you in order to hide his true intentions." Dad had found something to get excited about. "That's a rather clever stratagem, don't you think? He carried out a series of murders for you to solve and insulted your fragile ego by denying that he even knows you."

"Hey! My ego isn't that fragile." I sounded a little hurt then because… well, I was a little hurt. "Besides, Michael Andersen is so rich he'd probably pay someone to kill his enemies rather than go to all the trouble himself."

My meticulous stepfather stood up from his seat to look over the list of suspects on his pad. "Gary Flint, isn't he a possible culprit?"

No one responded then. I think we were all mulling over the same question until I said it out loud. "Would he really try to kill his own sister? I have to admit, I've dismissed the possibility."

Dean hadn't. "You have to admit that she might not have been his target. Perhaps he saw the two of you arguing and shot the wrong person. They've both been acting weird tonight. It's quite possible they were in it together."

"You really are clever, aren't you, Dean?" Ramesh was impressed. "From what I understand, whilst I was making friends, influencing people and conducting a truly successful dance-off, Verity made something of a scene."

I reopened a chapter that I thought had been read to death but looked at it with fresh eyes. "That was my very first theory. I was convinced that this whole thing was set up to exact revenge upon me, and the only thing that changed my mind was the arrow."

"There you go," Mum was in a hurry. "Mystery solved."

I thought about what Verity had said as she lay bleeding. "No, it doesn't fit. She did have an ulterior motive for setting up this reunion. And she was desperate for me to come, but it had nothing to do with me."

"What then?" Unlike my parents, Auntie Val looked like she wanted to climb through the screen to help us investigate.

"She thanked me for being here and said that, without me, 'he'd never have come'." I had to hit myself around the back of the head then as punishment for being thick. "Ahhh! It's so obvious. She practically told me why she'd planned this whole thing. It wasn't for me, or Gary. She was just trying to hook up with Robert Mitchell."

"Scandal!" Ramesh loves a scandal. "She was in love with Robert Mitchell and spent months organising this reunion just to get him alone here."

"Then why did she need you?" Dean seemed to doubt just how big a booking I was.

"Because Robert Mitchell has a true crime/baking podcast which he runs with his former lover/current business partner Sprinklez3000."

"Oh yeah! Cakez 'n' Crimez!" Unsurprisingly, it was Ramesh who knew about such things. "They're so goofy. I love them."

"Verity knew that, if I came to the reunion, the boy she'd had a massive crush on since we were eleven was bound to come too. That's why she made such a big deal about getting me here."

"So they aren't the killers then?" Mother clicked her fingers in frustration.

There was one thing that needed more thought before I could agree. "Gary might still be. On the one hand, he's smart, technical, and he has a grudge against me. He was one of the best archers in our year too, second only to Robert Mitchell. But the killings don't fit. Why would he have killed Tommy and Clara, or Mr Bath for that matter? He was sporty and popular when we were kids. Everyone loved him."

"Yeah, and the texts to Pete wouldn't make any sense either." Dean was on my side for once.

There wasn't much room, what with half of the space being taken up by the impromptu surgery, but I had a brief walk about, nonetheless. "Something I haven't told anyone is that Pete recorded his own death. There's no video of any use, but there's the very muffled sound of him and the killer kissing before he's killed."

"Wait, why did he record it?" My poor innocent father was baffled.

"Because he was a weirdo, I guess. Why does anyone do anything in the modern world?" I left this unanswerable question hanging in mid-air. "The point is that I still think that Pete was there with a girl."

"Or a boy!" Ramesh finally had the chance to make such a supposition. "Perhaps it was your ex-boyfriend that Pete went to meet!" The more he said, the more excited he got. "That has to be it. G.G. is Gay Gary!"

He clapped his hands together as if to say, *there you are, my good woman. I've solved the case for you.* Worst of all, I couldn't think of anything to prove him wrong.

"Not every case has a secret homosexual relationship, Ra."

"Yes, but one of them did!" He was a giant ball of burning joy. "And if it can happen once, I will continue to predict it every single time."

"I know you will, buddy." I went over to pat him on the shoulder. "I know you will, and I'll continue to deny it."

"Leaving aside Gary and Pete's illicit love," Dean began, "what about Shandy's ex? He can't be very happy to see her hooking up with Dr Muscly Chest."

"I can hear you, you know?" Danny reminded us. "And I love that name!"

"You're very welcome," Dean responded, and the surgeon returned to his task.

There was only one flaw in his idea, and I was happy to point it out. "It's a bit of a stretch thinking that Tim Cornish planned a series of murderous traps on the off-chance that his ex-wife hooked up with a hunky medical practitioner this evening. And it's hardly the most obvious way to bring his family back together."

There was some silent pondering before my stepdad said something clever. "All this uncertainty, Izzy – and your lack of confidence to call even one person a likely suspect – I think it means we've been missing someone from the very beginning."

"How do you mean?" Auntie Val's eyes widened with excitement on the projection wall– I knew she could be trusted to stay invested in the investigation.

My stepfather had fallen silent again, and so Dean answered. "I think what Greg means is that we've done all this work, uncovered so many twists and turns and yet we still don't have a real hunch about who done it." This wasn't my friend's attempt at making a classic detective fiction reference. He just didn't speak very correct English. "It seems to me—"

I cut him off then, as I'd been thinking much the same thing, and I was the important one. "It seems there's someone we've dismissed out of hand who could just as easily be the killer."

"That's right." Greg had been looking at his pad and spun back around to stare into the camera. "It has to be Shandy."

"Shandy?" I repeated with a little more incredulity than he'd used.

"Well, Shandy or Simon." He no longer sounded so confident. "Or the school caretaker, or Lorna, or in fact, Mrs Dav—"

"So it could be anyone?" I sat down in a free chair, feeling thoroughly drained of optimism, once more. I was like the Duracell Bunny, powered with supermarket-brand batteries. "You guys were my last hope. I thought that, away from the action, you might have seen things more clearly."

"This lot? See clearly?" Mum started laughing, then realised it wasn't the moment and cut herself short. "Or rather, I'm sorry you feel that way, darling. I'm sure that all you need is a little quiet reflection, and you'll soon nab your man, or woman or…" She was babbling, and I had a sneaking suspicion that she was considering the possibility that an animal was to blame.

Dean and Ramesh were apparently more attuned to my feelings than my family and gave me a sympathetic glance and a squeeze of the shoulder in turn.

"We're here for you if you need anything, Iz." Ramesh breathed in deep as though suffering with me. "But maybe your mum's right and you should have a little peace and quiet. I'll go back to the hall and keep everyone entertained to stop them wandering off."

"And I'll…" Dean began. "Urmmm…. Watch him, I suppose." He shrugged and opened the door for the pair of them to leave.

After a little time had passed, my mother spoke again in a softer voice this time. "Izzy, my love, I can't tell you how sympathetic I feel. But do you think you might turn the camera back around and ask

Danny to open the curtain?"

Chapter Twenty-Nine

Something had felt off since we'd arrived at school. I don't just mean the nasty traps and ridiculously high death toll; I mean that there was something not quite right with me. This was my first full murder investigation since I'd got a grip on my life and started acting like an adult, so why did everything seem so difficult?

I hadn't doubted myself so much in years… well, *a year*, at the very least.

Perhaps it was the setting. Most of my murders took place in quaint, pretty places (or Croydon), and here I was back at the site of so many teenage dilemmas and embarrassments. I'd never wanted to go back there and yet, returning to that squat, unfriendly building and finding myself trapped inside felt like a rite of passage I had to live through.

I sat in the nurse's office while Danny worked away at Verity's insides with Nurse Crouch eagerly assisting him. There was the odd squelching noise, but I tried not to look. My friends and family half a mile away in my childhood bedroom did quite the opposite; my stepfather had even made popcorn to accompany the viewing party.

The whole thing made me feel quite useless. I'd always thought of my success as a shield I could hide behind. I'd been on TV and in the press. People were simply amazed at how I'd managed to solve unsolvable crimes and/or tracked down one particular squirrel, but none of that mattered now. Was my ego really so fragile as my father had suggested? Could I only judge myself against my latest case?

I would have cried if I knew why I felt so bad. And that's the funny thing about the jobs we do. Whether you're a cleaner or a county court judge, your work becomes a second life with all of its own stresses and excitements, rewards and failures. It's nice to believe that we can keep the two entirely separate and switch off when the bell for home time rings (if you happen to be a teacher, that is) but it's not always that easy. Sometimes one bleeds into the other, and the emotions from each become entwined.

I'd gone to the school that night expecting to be treated as either a great detective or a nerdy teenager. The truth was that I was neither and both of those things; I was a mixture – somewhere between the two. I wasn't the only one who defied categorisation, either. All those kids who I'd expected to stay the same had changed. They'd grown up, and perhaps I'd held on to my fears and prejudices more than most.

Becky Mitchell was no longer the world dominating superstar she'd been in high school. She was frustrated by her career, disappointed by family, and clearly quite infuriated by her social life. The bullies I'd spent my life cursing had walked sad paths and met sticky ends. And all the cliques that had seemed indestructible when we were sixteen had drifted apart. I'd really believed that everyone else's lives and loves would be perfect and that we'd step back into the past when we crossed the threshold to the school for the first time in fifteen years.

And that was my big mistake.

Wait, I'm confused. Are you saying that you went in with preconceptions about everyone we knew back then and so you approached the case all wrong?

Yeah.

Got it, carry on!

It didn't matter who was a bully and who was nice at school, none of that would help me find a killer. What counted was how we all fit together now. Ramesh was right. I was the prime suspect because I'd held on to the past so tightly and refused to accept that anything had changed. But don't worry, there isn't some out-of-body solution to this case. I wasn't planting traps and piercing chests in a fugue state. But there was someone in that building who, just like me, had never let go, and that was who I needed to find.

I went back through the names that we'd thrown about a few minutes earlier. The people we'd overlooked or simply assumed were on our side because they'd been good sorts when we were kids. I thought about all the teachers and students I'd interacted with, and the ones I'd seen lurking about but hadn't talked to. Admittedly, that would be a rubbish twist if the killer turned out to be nice, tall Andy Trinidad, who I'd walked past on the way to the toilets and not even mentioned at the time, but I wasn't ruling anyone out anymore.

To my surprise, I discovered that there were several narratives already constructed in my head. I found four potential names there, and it wasn't that I knew for sure who the killer must be, but I was convinced that it couldn't be anyone else.

"I've got it!" I yelled a little too wildly, and the people on the wall shushed me.

"Not now, Izzy." Brian from the supermarket was particularly put out. "Danny is just tying off a blood vessel."

"Yes, Izzy, not now." Mother leaned to one side as though this would help her see better. "This is the good bit."

I would not be put off by my ever-unsupportive family – or their random acquaintances – and so I hurried from the room. I hate to say that the truth had been staring me in the face for hours, but that's pretty much it. I'd not only bought into my own adolescent beliefs, but those of everyone around me. That was in the past now. I was awake to the possibilities as I ran from the mini-hospital and along the staff corridor.

They had always been there, ever since I stepped foot on the grounds when I was eleven years old. Between the coin-operated coffee machine and an architect's model of the school dating back to the 1960s, there were several rows of photographs on the wall.

At the bottom were the junior members of staff – newly qualified teachers who might make it through the first year if they were lucky but would probably buckle under the constant pressure from teachers, parents, ungrateful government ministers and the angry English press and give up teaching altogether. And then there were the old timers. Mr Cody was now head of the arts department, Mr Roberts led humanities and Frau Schmidt was one of only two language teachers but had been promoted to deputy head. And there, sitting pretty at the top of the pyramid, was Mrs Davies herself, peering down at me with neckerchief and steel-rimmed glasses neatly in place. She had a smile on her face that was mirrored on mine. I'd found just what I was looking for.

"Thanks, Miss," I whispered. "I'll see you in the hall."

Chapter Thirty

This was supposed to be the part I was good at; threading together the strands of a case, tying them up in a neat bow and revealing to an attentive audience how the pieces of this elaborate puzzle fitted together. The only problem was that I knew the names of almost everyone there and (except for Michael Anderson) they all knew me.

For some stupid reason, I'd decided to get up on stage to address them and was back behind the wrought-iron lectern that made our headmistress look like an evil genius, set on world domination.

"I'm here to speak to you this evening," I began in a truly pathetic mumble, like a nervous health visitor who'd come to teach schoolchildren about the dangers of not washing your hands carefully enough.

Why don't you picture everyone naked?

We tried that last time; it didn't work!

"I'm here to talk about..." I tried again. "...murder." This one word sent a ripple across the room. It was hard to know whether this dramatic proclamation had hooked them, or they were saying, "Well, obvs." Either way, it helped settle my nerves, and I forced myself to keep going. "Murder and hatred, shame and frustration. But mainly murder."

I don't know whether it was unconscious or planned, but the audience had divided itself up into tribes. Standing at the side of the stage to watch their wayward former pupils, the teachers had formed a line. Davies, Cody, Schmidt, Roberts and my history teacher Mrs Long (who I'd admittedly failed to spot until then) wore their serious, professional expressions just as they had in every assembly ever. An amalgamation of popular and popular-adjacent personalities had formed around the nucleus of Becky Mitchell and, on the other side of the hall, the misfits and inbetweeners were waiting to discover the truth.

"The killer's plan must have been sketched out well in advance, and several lethal traps were set up before most of us even arrived this evening. The order in which the victims died was perhaps irrelevant, but the first thing that had to happen for everything else to work was the power cut that caused the anti-theft shutters to close and trapped us in the building. Without that, we could have escaped, which would have ruined the killer's evening. Sadly for us, the police aren't very good at hacking through excessively secure security systems and apparently the fire brigade aren't too *hot* at it either." I thought this was a half-decent pun, but no one laughed.

"The first to die were Tommy Hathaway and Clara Higson. You might not remember them from when we were at school, as they spent most of their free time in the dark room developing photographs."

"That's not all we did," their friend Barry said with a wink and a leer. His girlfriend delivered an elbow to the ribs to make him shut up, which saved me having to get down from the stage to do it.

"I spent the evening assuming that they were unlucky, and the killer was really after someone else, but I'm not so sure anymore. I thought that the trap in the security room was meant for our beloved Headmistress Mrs Davies, who, as the member of staff in charge this evening, was bound to go there to reset the security system when the shutters came down. But what if someone had given them a tip for a cool new part of the school to take a look at?" I was trying to avoid mentioning the fact that they'd gone there to have sex.

"Either way, they died before we knew there was a killer on the premises and, at first, I concluded that their deaths were an accident. Perhaps the killer wished to conceal what had really happened, but it wouldn't be long before the truth came out. Whilst Ramesh conducted his dance off, I was alerted to a scream that came from Mrs Davies's office, where I discovered the dead body of a man that we all knew."

"She's talking about Mr Bath!" a few voices whispered, and I have no idea why I was being so cryptic considering the fact that I'd already told them this part of the story.

"Ramesh, Ramesh, Ramesh!" others hollered.

"Mr Bath was killed by a telephone handset connected up to the battery from a Nissan Leaf. The added voltage of an electric car battery was needed in order to ensure that whoever picked up that phone would touch an exposed wire and be truly fried. As an experienced educator, Mrs Davies hasn't given up imparting wisdom wherever she goes, and she was the one who taught me this significant fact. It also proved once more that the killer had substantial knowledge of electronics and technology or, at the very least, access to the internet."

I should have kept talking instead of pausing to allow everyone to mutter how great the internet is. "Finally convinced that a murderer was at large here in West Wickham High, my investigation began. Next to die was Pete Boon. He managed to avoid the trap that had been set for him in Mrs Long's history class but suffered a chisel to the chest in the girls' toilets instead. The killer might have been caught at that moment, had there not been a large trophy with a marble base on hand for them to swing at my friend, Danny, who had come to investigate."

Inevitably, there was some swooning from a few of the single ladies present at the mention of my hunky ex.

"In Pete's pocket was the telephone that the killer had forgotten to retrieve after the attack and, on it, were a number of text messages from someone saved in the phone as 'G.G.' Ringing that number here in the hall, I discovered a spare phone in Robert Mitchell's pocket, but he had an alibi for the time when Pete was killed, and I can only assume that the killer had planted it on him. The final attack happened here before your eyes when the kind-hearted organiser of this evening's reunion was shot with an arrow by the heartless attacker. Luckily for Verity, we had a surgeon standing by and a surprising amount of medical equipment with which to extract the projectile. On last check, her prognosis was good."

There were some whoops of applause at this, and a few more chants of "Ramesh, Ramesh, Ramesh!" for good measure. Everyone loves Ramesh. It should probably be jealous, but I admit he's just so darn hard not to like.

"And there we have it. Four dead bodies and an injured woman in the course of a single evening is a record for me, and I have done everything I can to find a connection between the victims. But except for the fact we all spent years of our lives here at West Wickham High, there was no obvious common link."

The problem with talking into a microphone on a stand is that it's very static. Normally, I'd have liked to move about a bit, perhaps even get down off the stage and look people in the eyes, but I was stuck there like a lemon in a bowl and, unless someone presented me with a cordless microphone, I'd—

"Oh thank you, Mr Cody, for this cordless microphone." He'd evidently spied my predicament and looked around backstage to find what I needed. He even gave me a sexy wink and a smile. "I considered every last person I could remember from our year and even the teachers. I thought about Robert and Becky Mitchell and their very public breakup. Becky told me that she blamed me for the end of her marriage, and I wondered whether the lady was protesting too much. It crossed my mind that, if the two Mitchells had really wanted to, they could have worked together to bring me down, using their supposed animosity towards one another as a smokescreen."

I allowed the possibility that the school's golden couple had turned into savage murderers to sit there for a few seconds. "Well, that didn't make much sense. If they were willing to work together, they couldn't be so angry that they would have needed to plot against me in the first place. It would also be quite illogical to kill a bunch of unconnected people in order to exact their revenge on me. So I moved on to other suspects.

"Michael Anderson claims not to remember me. That would be a good way to hide the real motive for a series of murders."

Michael had been looking at me with his head tilted at a funny angle throughout my speech, and he finally broke his silence. "Wait, were you the one who sang 'Angels' by Robbie Williams at my sixteenth birthday party? I do remember now."

I shrugged and took a step down off the stage. "So much for that theory!" As I reached the floor, people shuffled out of my way as though I were a stand-up comedian, and they were afraid I might involve them in my act – or accuse them of murder. "Tim Cornish would do anything to get back with the wife that he cheated on. Not that killing a bunch of practical strangers would help win Shandy back. And Mandy Johnson's father—" I was about to reveal a scandal that it wasn't my place to discuss and so I did my best to cover my slip. "Mandy's father always said to me, I doubt that my daughter will ever murder anyone."

Dim little Mandy produced a handkerchief and dabbed at her eyes. "What a stirring tribute to my dad. I had no idea you even knew one another. That's just the sort of thing he liked to say."

I was beginning to ramble, and my audience's attention had

become equally unfocussed, so I decided to get to the point. "All the usual suspects were ruled out, and it would take some effort to find the killer. I had to put aside my pre-conceptions about this place and everyone here. I had to forget about which kids had been nice to me and which of you treated me like a piece of old chewing gum stuck to the soles of your shoes. I had to forget the past to focus on the present. And by doing that, I could finally single out the people here who had something to kill for."

Pause for effect, one, two, three. "I made a new list of suspects and, at the top of it were Shandy Duchamps, Simon Barnes and Mrs Frances Davies."

Chapter Thirty-One

This caused a whirlwind of chatter before I realised that the tone was more confused than impressed, and I had to add. "Frances is our headmistress's first name." This admittedly robbed some of the drama from my big moment, and the resultant "Ohhhh, I see!" from the four corners of the room didn't help either. I pretended that I hadn't noticed and continued in a smooth, mysterious tone.

"You see, Shandy never fit into any one group when we were at school. She was too nice to be lumped in with the in-crowd, too pretty to be a misfit and too clever to just fade into the background, as so many of us were happy to do. She worked hard, got excellent grades without stepping on anyone's toes, and I think it's fair to say that it's really very difficult not to like her. But then I remembered just how good she'd been at technology at school, and it made me wonder whether she'd have had the knowledge required to set up the various deadly traps this evening. After all, she and Lorna Inglis won the under-sixteen Greater London Environmental Technology Prize for a device that sorted different types of recycling."

I was weaving around between the loose groupings of old friends and forgotten faces, searching for the girl who'd convinced me to go to the reunion. "When we left sixth form, Shandy trained to be a science teacher and went to work at a nearby school. That would make her familiar with educational settings and perhaps even security systems such as the excessively efficient one here. She also provided herself with a clever alibi this evening, as she spent most of the time sucking the face of a rather handsome doctor who may or may not be my ex-boyfriend." I thought about telling them how Danny and I had mutually decided to separate as we realised that we felt more like siblings, but I thought that would sound like I was trying to hide how jealous I was. I mean, I really wasn't (by this stage), but they weren't to know that.

"Of course, most of what the killer did here this evening was achieved with remote controls and unattended mantraps. Shandy could have been snogging Danny's lips off when Tommy and Clara got squashed and Mr Bath was electrocuted. It doesn't prove for a second that she wasn't involved." As I said these words, I emerged in a small clearing and caught sight of the woman I was accusing,

She didn't look particularly happy and had a response ready to fire at me. "What about Pete? I found his body when Danny was with me."

"Yes, but we only have your word for what went on in the toilets. For all we know, Pete was already dead when you arrived. You could have smashed Danny over the head in order to give yourself an alibi." I was only a few feet away now and held her gaze. "No one would think that you were guilty after you came face to face with the killer."

No one but you, Izzy Palmer. No one but you.

She had nothing to say to this and so I kept talking. "You followed Verity out of the hall to suggest that she was the culprit – that she had pushed you over and knocked out Danny. When, in reality, she was in the art room making out with Robert Mitchell."

My arm shot out and I pointed to the table against the back wall where Robert was still feeling sorry for himself. At the neighbouring table, Becky's eyes grew as big as a Disney Princess's and her lower lip trembled.

"That's not..." he responded before giving up on even this feeble rejoinder. "Fine, I met Verity in the art room. She's always been into me and, I have to say, she is kind of sexy, in a really intense way."

"Robby, you dog!" some idiot lad celebrated in the gang of cool (no longer) kids, and Becky began to sob. She would probably have charged from the room but, well, you know... killer on the loose, military-grade shutters, etc.

Meanwhile, I kept my focus on Shandy. "Maybe the G.G. on Pete's phone was *gorgeous girl*. Pete and his oily friends were all mad about you at school. Did you flirt with him in order to get him alone and murder him?"

"No," Shandy said, but there was a waver in her voice, and I think even she doubted that this was true. "I didn't kill anyone."

I maintained my silence for a few seconds before speaking again. "No, of course you didn't. You're one of the nicest people who's ever attended this school, but I still had to consider such unrealistic possibilities to get to the truth."

She breathed a huge sigh of relief. Shandy was so nice that she even forgave me for war-gaming the idea she was a crazed killer.

"Another of these far-fetched theories was the idea that my own best friend from my time here, shy, big-hearted Simon Barnes, was actually a psychopathic murderer."

I didn't have to look far this time. Simon was standing a few feet away, flanked by my friends, and I actually got quite emotional when I noticed that he and Lorna were standing really close and looked ever so sweet together. He gave me a smile as if to say, *Go on, Iz. Do your worst, I don't mind.*

"I didn't even know that Simon was here for half the evening because he didn't walk into the hall like everyone else. He claims that he took one look at all his old foes and headed off to the South Block to hang out in the music room like we used to when we were kids. He says he got locked in there by the killer, who also pushed Mrs Davies into the room next door. However, there were long periods of silence between the two of them. Long periods that might well have coincided with Pete's stabbing in the toilets and the killer shooting Verity with an arrow when the lights went out for a second time.

"When we were at school, Simon worked hard at not being noticed. He learnt the best ways to blend in, even though he was one of the tallest kids here. He could have easily slunk through the shadows to kill Pete or slipped in and out of the hall as everyone fussed over Verity. The traps wouldn't be hard to set for…" Admittedly, this pause was far too hammy for its own good. "…an electrical engineer!"

Despite my over-the-top delivery, there was a genuine gasp from my audience at this. I imagine it was easier for them to believe that one of us weirdos was responsible for the massacre than good-looking airheads like Robert Mitchell. I tried not to get too upset at this injustice, as I built towards the big finish.

"But then, Simon hasn't stepped foot in this school since we left and would have been unlikely to know about the anti-theft system that was supposed to keep thieves out but ended up trapping—"

"Sorry, Izzy," he interrupted. "I'm not just an electrical engineer. It was my company who did the work here."

I shot him an exasperated look, as he really wasn't helping. "Oh, well then he did know about the security system, but he isn't the killer because…"

"In actual fact," he continued, just to make my job a bit more difficult, "I was the one who put forward West Wickham High as a tax-deductible test site for my company. I thought I could give something back to the school which got me interested in technology in the first place."

"Right, yes…" I tried to think up a piece of evidence that would directly rule out his involvement, but… well, I didn't have one. "Anyway, Simon isn't the killer because… someone else did it."

"And I really was locked in the music room eating chocolate Hobnobs and playing the drums." He had such a noble soul and deserved to be back at our old school, enjoying a few moments in the spotlight without anyone making fun of his weight or screaming names at him. "Besides, I'm just a manager these days and wouldn't know the first thing about these modern burglar prevention systems."

"There you go. He was locked in the music room by the real killer. But if Simon could have used his supposed incarceration as an alibi, couldn't the same also be true for the woman who was roughly pushed into the drama studio next door? We only have Mrs Davies's word that she was locked in there and Simon – who, to recap, is not the killer – told me that there were long periods when our devoted headmistress was oddly quiet. Couldn't she have ducked out of her hiding place to despatch the victims?"

I spun round on the ball of my feet at this moment to glare across the room at Mrs Davies. The only problem was that there were about fifty people between us. I couldn't see her, and she couldn't see me, so that wasn't nearly as effective as I'd been hoping. I let out a little huff. Summing up the facts of a case is exhausting, and I really didn't have the energy to trek back across the room but was about to start on my circuitous route through the audience when she popped out of the crowd.

"Oh, there you are. Thanks for coming." This made things a lot easier. In fact, I was tempted to pull up a chair and have everyone sit down on the floor like when we were in primary school, but I wasn't a headmistress and didn't have the organisational skills to wrangle everyone at that moment.

Such breaks really do make me lose my train of thought. I was trying to…

You were about to build the case against Mrs Davies.

Right! I was about to build the case against Mrs Davies.
Starting with the first three victims.
Exactly! The first three victims. Thanks for that.

"The way in which the first three victims died made me believe that it was Mrs Davies who was the real target. The killer might have known that our headmistress would have to reset the security system after the first power cut, and she would also have been the likely person to pick up the phone in her own office. But what if that was what the killer wanted us to think? What if it was Frances herself who had set those traps and was killing off the people who she really didn't like?"

There was a bit of mumbling, and I realised that many of them had forgotten Mrs Davies's Christian name. I wasn't about to dumb down my big finale and explain everything to the slower members of the audience and kept walking, ever closer to my target.

"Being a headmistress of a school like this one must be a thankless task, and judging from the insane security system, the place has gone downhill in the years since we left. Are you tired of the way that people treat you here, Miss? The way they take you for granted?"

I was expecting a denial, or at least stern silence, but when has anyone gone along with one of my plans?

"Yes, that's just it." Mrs Davies looked quite heartened by my comments.

"You claimed that you couldn't remember any of the names of the students from our year and had to look them up on the school computer to match them with our faces, but I don't think that's true." I glanced at the crowd that had morphed as I walked around the room and had now formed a large circle with me in the centre. "We all knew that we were the worst year in school. We had the most thugs and bullies, the most thoughtless imbeciles, the most prissy, needy drama queens and wannabe superstars. We were awful and every other teacher I've spoken to this evening remembers us well."

"Fine." Mrs Davies crossed her arms over her chest. "You caught me. I did remember Martin Thompson and Pete Boon. I remembered the self-entitled brats like Becky Mitchell and Mandy Johnson. I even remember the hard-done-by sorts like you, Izzy Palmer."

This was going better than I expected, and I admit that I enjoyed a brief peek at bawling Becky as she endured this insult. Poor thing.

"If our stalwart headmistress lied to me about that, I had to wonder what else could she be hiding?" I allowed my words to ping about from head to head. I could see Robert Mitchell and his posse of identi-clad followers. My own friends were eagerly enjoying my big moment, and I noticed that Tim Cornish was feigning boredom near the stage as though he wasn't desperate to find out who'd offed his friend. The only person I couldn't see was Gary Flint, but then he'd been on the outside of things all night, hanging back from the action and watching from afar.

"Let's be clear about one thing; the killer had to know the school well to carry out their plans this evening. There would be ways to achieve this without working here, but it certainly helped. And if we accept that the killer is a member of staff, then everything is simpler. It would have given them time to smuggle all the necessary equipment into school and set the traps without being discovered. They could have learnt about the security system and its weaknesses. They could even spike the vast vat of punch that we've all been imbibing this evening to keep us subdued."

I don't think that the alcohol content of the refreshments was a surprise to many people by this point. It certainly didn't cause much alarm.

"With Mrs Davies as the killer's target, I had no reason to suspect her of being the culprit, and it took me a long time to even consider the possibility. I admit, I was hung up on past rivalries. I thought this whole thing was about me and my time at the school. I thought that Gary Flint was trying to get his own back after I told everyone that he had an incredibly small... I mean, after I wasn't very nice to him. I thought that Becky blamed me for her divorce."

"I do!" came the response.

"And that she was trying to show me up as a bad detective." I left a pause for her to respond again, just in case, but she kept shtum. "I even cast doubt on my own friends before I considered the more likely scenario that Mrs Davies had the opportunity and motivation to carry out the killings. I couldn't understand what would link Tommy and Clara to Mr Bath and Pete Boon, and I really wasn't sure where Verity fitted into any of this. But then the one person who is affected by everything that happens at a school is its director, its principal, its head."

I paused again as I felt this idea deserved a little time of its own to mature. I wanted my audience to ruminate on the possibility that Frances Davies was the missing piece of the puzzle. "Our beloved leader is at the centre of everything at this school, and if you'd been working here as long as she has, you'd have any number of grudges. Teachers are the doormat of parents, students and politicians alike. She told me that she agreed to install this insane security system because of regular burglaries and even bomb threats in the years after we left. Imagine driving to work each day, not knowing whether the building would be there because someone might have bombed it in the night. Imagine the people you're trying to guide through life, despising you for doing your job."

After a previously febrile environment, the mood had changed, and the hall had fallen silent. Mrs Davies remained with her arms folded and her gaze straight ahead. I thought she might say something more to refute or embellish my claims, but she was as quiet as a caterpillar, and I moved on to the final part of my accusation.

"Tommy and Clara were horny little devils who convinced the school to spend thousands on photographic equipment that probably hasn't been used since they left. Mr Bath was a P.E. teacher whose beer belly was so big he could no longer run and, though he may have raised money for charity and been a popular figure in his own family, many of us found his educational philosophy outdated and sadistic. As for Pete Boon, he was perhaps a little unlucky that his even more despicable gang leader had already been murdered at a children's birthday party, but there was no love lost between him and Mrs Davies, and so he was the next obvious victim. I'm sure that Verity would have been a pain to work with on the reunion, too. She was so obsessed with it going to plan so that she could win the man of her dreams that she drove you to one last murder."

The silence finally broke as people realised that the crazy idea I'd put forward was starting to make sense. Our dear old headmistress really did have a reason not to like each of the victims, and the case against her was strong.

If anything, this made her more resilient, and her expression hardened as I delivered my final salvo. "You had the opportunity, and you had the motive to kill five people." Standing inches away now, my eyes were locked on hers. "So are you going to confess, Miss? Did you plan this evening to settle some scores?"

Chapter Thirty-Two

"Well, ladies and gentlemen, I've had an interesting time with you all." Mrs Davies turned away from me, apparently unwilling to answer the questions. "Hopefully, the police will break through the barriers at any moment, and we'll all be free to get on with our lives."

"Did you do it?" a voice called from the back of the hall, and then Gary Flint broke into the circle. "Did you kill those poor people and shoot my sister?"

She stopped walking to look at him. "No, of course I didn't."

"Then why didn't you answer the question?"

I felt a bit guilty and stepped between them. "Sorry, that's my fault. I think I did a bit too good a job of setting her up as the killer. I was expecting her to say no so that I could move on to the big reveal."

To be honest, it is a bit weird that she didn't just deny it. Kind of makes you wonder whether she had a hand in things after all.

"I didn't deny Izzy's accusation, because it was almost all true." This really got the crowd going and there were jeers and whistles as the culprit (seemingly) revealed herself. "I feel just as she described about the victims, and I'm ashamed that I could have shared such emotions with a killer."

"Wait, I'm confused," Mandy Johnson announced, but this was nothing new.

"Did you murder them or not?" Gary persisted.

"I've already told you. Teachers may think of killing their pupils on a daily basis, but I've never heard of one who went through with it. Sadly, the reverse has happened any number of times." Her lips pursed together, and she looked terribly moved by the experience. "I also didn't wish to embarrass Izzy by telling her she was wrong if that was what she truly believed. She has worked tirelessly this evening to bring the killer to justice, and I had no wish to show her up in front of everyone."

"Ahh, thanks, Miss."

She bowed her head obligingly. "It was really a very good effort, Isobel, and you deserve my commendation." I was kind of hoping she might give me a sticky gold star for the good work I'd done, but

I suppose that's not something teachers do when you haven't been in school for the last decade and a half.

"You do have someone else in mind, don't you?" There was a note of worry in her voice, as though she would have to put my work down a grade if this was all I'd managed to produce.

I was happy to set her mind at ease. "Yes, Miss. I have someone else in mind." She halted her retreat, and the circle re-formed around me. "You see, I went through the obvious names from our days here and drew a blank. I calculated the least probable options, and those didn't get me any closer either, but there had to be someone here who had murdered those people and I felt that, if they'd wanted to get away with it, they'd have kept a careful eye on everything that happened."

I returned to the spot under the disco ball that was still shooting out fragments of light across the room. "Mrs Davies might have ticked certain boxes, but she'd been missing for a long time when Pete was killed and would have needed to go into the hall to plant the killer's phone on Robert Mitchell without being seen. That would be difficult even for the most anonymous person here, but for our headmistress, I felt it would be impossible."

I stopped to scan every face. I wanted them to know that they were all suspects – that I'd considered each and every last one of them as potential killers. "The truth is that, if Mrs Davies wasn't to blame, I was stumped as to who could be. I was looking for someone with a knowledge of the school, an advanced understanding of electronics and a grudge against the lot of us. You see, each of the traps could have killed quite discriminately. Pete avoided a fistful of glass to the face by arranging to meet the killer in the girls' toilet, but any one of us could have walked into Mrs Long's classroom and triggered that savage trap. The killer didn't care. All they wanted was revenge and the attention they felt they deserved."

I don't think I'd like to work in a circus. I'd constantly feel guilty for having my back to half the audience. I kept turning and turning and was starting to get dizzy. "What I was looking for was someone with a teacher's knowledge of the school, but a student's anger against the place. I interviewed all the teachers who were here."

"Except for me, Izzy!" my former history teacher sang.

"Except for Mrs Long, who we all know is a sweetheart."

Quick thinking there. Bravo!

"And ruled out each of them. Time has passed since we were here, and in those fifteen years, I'm sure they've found new students to hate. Kids these days are much tougher than we ever were, and so it's hard to imagine that Mr Cody would have held onto such distaste for long-forgotten students, or that Mr Roberts kept a photograph of us all on his dartboard at home."

I could see the way that each of the (at least moderately intelligent) members of the audience were sifting through the evidence just as I had. They were coming to small conclusions with each twist of the tale. "So that meant one of us must be responsible." I turned from group to group, from Mandy to Robert, to Shandy and on to Gary Flint. "Someone who felt so mistreated by their time here and so abused by their bullies that people had to die."

My eyes were still on Gary as I spoke and, for a moment, I remembered the feeling I'd had when he left me at home on the night of the school dance. Every muscle in my body stung with the memory, but he showed no emotion, and I turned to the person next to him instead.

"There is someone in this room who believes they are the victim, even now. Someone who should have been treasured and adored but found herself an outcast." Becky held my focus, and the same nervous energy that had run through her all night was plain to see in her twitching nerves and batted eyelashes. I dropped my gaze to the floor so as not to have to see any of those familiar faces, and when I peered back up again, I was looking at my friends.

"I'm sorry, Lorna," I said to the shy creature who had done so much to help me investigate. "I'm sorry for the way the world has treated you. I'm sorry that no one here remembered your name, and that I didn't even ask what your job was when I met you for the first time in fifteen years."

His expression no longer full of its usual glee, Simon took hold of Lorna's hand. I saw his grip tighten, and the pale-faced phantom standing next to him shook.

"I remember Shandy saying that you were on the same course at university together, but it wasn't until I saw your photo on the wall outside the staff room that I realised you worked here. Head of technology ever since Mrs Pearson was killed in an unfortunate hit and run? Your parents must be very proud."

"You don't know anything about me," she whispered, but this was the only retort she could summon.

"I know that you plotted to kill Mrs Davies, Mr Bath and Pete Boon. Three people who you felt deserved to die for the way they treated you. Mr Bath bullied everyone; he thought that was the best way to get results from weaker kids like you and me. Pete Boon was a moron who took pleasure in tormenting us, just like his vicious friends. Mrs Davies is the one I can't understand. Surely she was your real target, but why?"

Lorna's ghostlike blue eyes glistened in the light of the mirror ball. "Because I thought she would have put a stop to everything else. I thought that, if anyone here could have got in the way, it was her. But I couldn't do it. She's nicer than the others and so—"

"And so you told Tommy and Clara that there would be no one in the server room if they fancied some sexy time. Clara was a school inspector, like her friend Samantha. I've no doubt you had run-ins with her and decided that she was just as bad as all the others; so she and her boyfriend were the first to die. And, later, when you got the chance to follow Mrs Davies and lock her in the drama studio, it was as good as killing her off."

"G.G.!" Shandy said, jumping ahead of the story, just as everyone always does. "It was her, wasn't it? She'd been texting Pete and met him in the toilets. She's the one who pushed me over and knocked out my poor Danny!"

"G.G." I repeated. "The name that was saved in Pete Boon's phone. The name he used to refer to the girl who he'd been chatting to for weeks. The cruel nickname he'd had for Lorna when we were kids. G.G. or Ghost Girl. Was it you who called in bomb threats to the school after we left? Are you the reason that this place is locked down like a viral laboratory after a leak?"

A crisp whisper spread out from where I stood, like the shockwave from an earthquake. Lorna had long since bowed her head. She was a limp, spectral figure and might have collapsed altogether if Simon hadn't been holding her.

As she wasn't saying anything, I thought it was time to make this about me. "I might have taken a while to get over what happened at high school – I might have felt sorry for myself and hoped that all the idiots we had to tolerate ended up with bad jobs and worse families – but I managed to move on with my life." I really wanted Lorna to look up at me then, but she was as still as an unmanned puppet. "You held onto every bitter memory. You kept mementoes from all of us that you scattered around the crime scenes. You are obsessed with a place that you hate."

My words wouldn't kick her into life, and so it was time to lay the evidence out against her. "I should have realised it was you as soon as those first bodies fell. You ran to the security room to check on Mrs Davies, but there was no security room here when we were at school, and you shouldn't have known where it was. You were the one who destroyed the computer that controlled the security cameras. I left you in there to guard the bodies, and you made sure that the rest of your activities tonight went unrecorded."

She lifted her head to respond, but it fell back again before she could muster a word.

"Whenever our headmistress gave us instructions, your name came to her lips, not because she remembered you from all that time ago, but because you've been working with her for years. I ruled out all the old teachers who were here tonight, but there was one more I didn't know about. And that makes me wonder just how long you've been planning this. Did you take a job here to relive your torment or get even?"

A whimper floated over to me which finally turned into a word. "No…" She breathed in loudly and finally found the strength to hold her head up. "I came here in the hope that I could make things better for kids like me… for kids like us, Izzy. I wanted to treat my students fairly, unlike most of the teachers we had back then. Mr Bath and Mrs Drake. Mr Coleman and Mrs Pearson. Think about the impact all those heartless disciplinarians had on us. I came here to put things right, but it's not only the teachers who need changing, the kids are just as cruel. No matter what I tried, I couldn't get through to them – they barely even heard my voice. I'm a defective product of this place; I'm as much a problem as anyone else."

"And so you decided that murdering a bunch of people would make things better?" As I asked this, a faint sound that had been purring in the background grew louder, and I realised that it was coming from somewhere overhead.

Lorna's voice was stronger now, and she shouted back at me. "No, I thought I might finally be noticed." She seemed to pant for breath before continuing. "You were always such a sad kid at school, Izzy, but at least people knew who you were. I was a ghost, just like Pete always said. I barely existed. And it was the same tonight. You didn't talk to me, not really. No one asked me what I do now or what I've achieved. I saw it in Tommy Hathaway's eyes when I spoke to him. I was just the ghost girl. That was all he could remember about me."

I was almost too sickened by this rationalisation to go on listening. Almost. "That's not an excuse, Lorna. Whatever you think of me, I didn't have it easy. I bet even Becky Mitchell doesn't have the best memories of her time at school. We all have demons to fight and pain to resolve, but we'll never achieve that by harming others."

Things had got a bit personal by this point. The pair of us shouting our insecurities back and forth at one another wasn't supposed to be a part of my dramatic revelation. "You stayed close to me all night to make sure I didn't know it was you, but then something changed after you shot Verity. You said it yourself; the killer wanted to be caught."

She actually managed a smile then. "You're so clever, Izzy Palmer." The sarcasm dripping off her words me of the things I say to myself – the little voice that is never quite happy with what I do. I ignored them both and continued piling on the evidence.

"Everything you said over the last hour was true. You pulled me in the right direction, but I was still so hung up on the idea that one of my old foes must be responsible that I didn't stop to consider how you could know so much. You wanted to be caught because if no one knew you were the killer, no one would remember you."

"So smart, but there's one thing you got wrong." She turned from ghost to demon. "The arrow wasn't meant for Verity. It was supposed to be you bleeding to death on the floor of this hall. That was my finale. That was what I came here to do. The papers tomorrow would have had your face on them. 'Great Detective Izzy Palmer Slain in Massacre'! This was your Reichenbach Falls moment, and you ruined it for both of us."

Ooh, nice Sherlock Holmes reference. She's not all bad.

"Yeah, well, if you'd read enough detective fiction, you'd know that it's Moriarty who dies in that story, not Holmes."

Ummm, Izzy? Spoiler alert!

The faint scratching sound that I'd heard before had turned into an aggressive scrape and it was at this moment that plaster began to rain down from the ceiling and a chink of light broke through.

"Lorna, you are a…" I attempted to continue, but whoever was breaking us out of the place was really upstaging me.

The hole in the ceiling got bigger and Dean and Simon held on to the wriggling killer as first one police officer and then another abseiled down to us.

"Nothing to worry about, folks," the first called out, perhaps a little optimistically. "We'll get the shutters open in no time."

A third rope was dropped through the hole, and D.I. Irons was lowered down to us. "Izzy, I trust you've apprehended the killer by now?" She's never particularly impressed by my work these days and betrayed no emotion.

"Yep, you've just missed me wrapping up." I thumbed behind me at the diminutive culprit.

"Huh, she doesn't look the type."

"When do they ever?" Ramesh hollered before going to mingle with his new friends and admirers.

"They're sending a technician in now to repair the system and open the shutters from this side," Irons explained. "But it'll be a while before we can get everyone out of here. While we wait, you might as well run through that whole dramatic spectacle thingy that you do."

I was tired and hungry and frankly annoyed that no one had thought of providing hot chocolate at this so-called party.

Ain't no party like a hot chocolate party 'cos a hot chocolate party is delicious.

I sighed and reluctantly agreed to the inspector's request. "Oh, fine, Mum and Dads will want to know what happened anyway, but I'm going to do it sitting down."

Chapter Thirty-Three

Before I could fill in D.I. Irons (and the Hawes Lane Murder Appreciation Society) on everything that had happened, medics arrived to escort Verity to the hospital.

"Thank you so much, Danny," she said through an oxygen mask once the good doctor had sewn her up and she was loaded onto a gurney. "You saved my life."

"It was nothing," my dear friend replied. He really is one of the few people I know who could deliver such a line without any smugness.

"I'm going with her." Robert Mitchell rushed over and seized her hand. From the way he looked at her, I could only think she was more than just a sexy, intense fling. In fact, if it hadn't been for Becky claiming the school sports star as her property when we were fifteen, I always thought that Verity would've made a much better match for him. Verity or me, I mean. But then, I was just too clever for him.

We watched them rise through the air on ropes and then disappear through the now much wider hole in the ceiling – which Mrs Davies really wasn't happy about.

"What's the point of a security system to protect the windows if people can just blast through the walls?" she complained to my old friend, whose company had installed it. "I expect an upgrade for this, Simon. I really do."

I left them to thrash this out and fulfilled my promise to Irons in the nurse's office. By the time we came back out, they'd unlocked one section of shutters at the front of the building and the first party-goers were streaming out. My old classmates looked worse for wear, and it wasn't just the alcohol that had done it. When I'd told them that high school was torture, I hadn't realised I was speaking literally. We were lucky to get out alive.

Dean, Simon and I sat in the foyer watching our ex-schoolmates file out of the building to take their first gasp of sweet, fresh air.

"I have to say," Dean had to say, "it is pretty impressive all that Lorna achieved."

"I'm sorry, did you call a mass-murderer 'impressive'?"

"I mean, on a technical level. All those traps and knowing how to trigger the power cuts and the security system. If she'd come to me for a job, I'd definitely have found her one."

I held him in my gaze for a few moments and wondered what went on in that strange little head of his. "You have very unusual priorities, Dean."

"I'm not saying that I admire her violence. I just… well, you know, I—"

"Stop talking."

"I just—"

"Shh!" I turned to Simon as I was fairly sure he wasn't a murderer-admirer. "I'm sorry about Lorna," I told him. "I could tell you liked her, and it's a shame she turned out to be a psychopath."

"That's alright. I didn't like her like that." He smiled and let out a brief whistle. "I just had a weird feeling that something was not quite right and thought that I'd better keep an eye on her."

"Really?"

"Yeah. And besides, I've got a girlfriend." I was learning a lot about him.

"Really?" I tried not to sound surprised, which I really was.

"Yeah. We've been together for the best part of ten years. We're getting married this summer."

"Really?" my voice kept finding new tones of amazement.

"Yeah. You should come!"

To save me from another "Really?" Becky Mitchell appeared at this moment to have a word with me.

"…in private, if you don't mind." She marched off down the corridor and then glared at me until I joined her. "I just need to tell you how disappointed I am."

I can't say that this was much of a surprise, but before I could ask why, she unloaded her feelings on the matter.

"I barely featured in that whole narrative you told this evening. You made up perfectly good scenarios for everyone else's guilt, but what about mine? I could have been a killer. I could have hated every last one of you and wished to see your entrails decorating the school, but no." She had a bit of a sniff. "I don't mind telling you that I feel terribly left out."

Despite everything, I actually managed to feel a little sorry for the prettiest girl in school.

...after Shandy! Let's be honest, Becky is great as far as Barbie dolls go, but Shandy Duchamps is the kind of girl you'd introduce to your parents.

You're weird. Stop thinking.

"The thing is, Becky," I began in a more serious tone than I'd intended, "I wasn't sure you would want too much attention considering that you lied."

She seemed to pause like a video at this moment and, even as she replied, she hardly moved a muscle. "What do you mean?"

"You said that Robert was in the hall when he was actually off in the art room with Verity." I took a second to study her but she still hadn't reacted. "I know he had nothing to do with the murders now, but that doesn't explain why you gave him an alibi."

She breathed at last, and whatever she'd been holding in flowed out of her. "Oh, fine, I lied. The truth is that I might hate the cheating little toerag, but that doesn't stop me loving him. He's the father of my children and, as it happens, still the only man I've ever kissed. I didn't want him going to jail."

So then I felt really sorry for her and, no, I didn't start singing, but I did try to make her evening just that little bit brighter.

"Listen, why don't I come on your podcast or your Instagram – or whatever it is you do these days – to tell everyone the story of how vital you were to me solving the case?"

"That's the least you can do after you ruined my life." She sniffed and frowned and looked a tiny bit reassured. "I have no husband. My children's au pair despises me. I haven't signed a new corporate sponsor in months, and no one tried to kill me this evening. It's frankly demoralising."

"I'm sure it is." I gave her a sympathetic frown as I hoped this would get rid of her faster. "But you know, things could be worse. For a start, Gary Flint has always had a huge crush on you."

"Really? Gary?" The word acted as a giant handkerchief to absorb her tears. "I've always thought he was rather yummy."

"Oh, totally. And despite what you might have heard to the contrary, he actually has a massive—"

"Gary!" she shouted across the foyer as she caught sight of him queueing to leave. "Gary, wait for me."

"...penis," I whispered to myself, just to make sure that such a word still existed.

Danny and Shandy appeared at this moment with their arms around one another.

"Listen, Izzy," that beautiful curly-haired woman stopped by to say. "My parents are looking after my kids until the morning, and I'd rather like to spend the night pashing with this gorgeous man in the back of a limo. You don't mind us ditching you, do you?"

Danny kissed her on the top of the head. "That does sound great, Shandy, but perhaps we should park next to the hospital, just in case my bang to the head has any lingering effects."

I laughed and ushered them off. "Go for it. I hope it's the most romantic hospital car park you've ever visited." They wandered away, already smushing lips. "And remember to tell my dad to put up the privacy screen!"

Dean and Simon followed along after them, chatting away about a potential collaboration between their two companies, which just left me and Ramesh. He was standing beside the door, saying farewell to my former schoolmates.

"Timmy, mate!" he said and gave Tim Cornish a hug. "You should have won that second dance-off. You were robbed."

"Thanks, Ra." Shandy's ex looked rather emotional at the compliment. "That means a lot. And I have to say this whole experience has made me look differently at my life. I really feel I need to make a change for the better, and that's thanks to you."

They patted each other on the back, promised they'd hang out soon and, when Tim was about to leave, Ramesh had one last piece of advice for him. "Just remember, Tim, live every day like it's 1995."

The thuggish chap was clearly puzzled for a moment, but then a smile appeared on his lips, and he looked happier than he had all night. "That's it! I'll live every day like it's 1995. You're absolutely right!"

With a spring in his step, he jumped through the door, full of hope for the future.

"What on Earth did that mean?" I asked with mouth agape.

"I haven't a clue." Ramesh straightened his back and raised his chin proudly. "I am a channel for wisdom. I don't always have to understand what it is that I'm talking about. Can we go now? I've got a hankering for bacon and eggs from Fernando's Caff."

"Oh, go on then." I was about to turn to leave when the world's sexiest drama teacher appeared.

"Evening, Miss Palmer. I don't suppose you'd fancy a night cap somewhere after such a splendid performance?"

"What happened to Nurse Crouch?"

He smiled that smooth, confident smile of his, and my heart fluttered in my chest.

We should probably see a doctor about that. It could be an arrythmia.

"Nurse Crouch ended up making out with the caretaker in the South Block toilets. I'm flying solo, unless…"

I looked at Ramesh who was doing some kind of break dance on the terrace outside school and then back at the man I'd had to draw a picture of to put on my wall when I was twelve as I didn't have a photo of him.

"Sorry, sir, I've got plans for tonight."

"Ah… Very well. Maybe another time then," he smiled and walked off ahead of me through the door.

No, Izzy! Don't do it. Think about the little children you could have together with their little child-sized black turtlenecks.

Nah, let's keep that as a fantasy between the two of us. Besides, he's old enough to be my dad. There's grown up and there's far too grown up for my liking.

My brain didn't respond then, as it was busy making a filthy noise.

"Come on, Izzy," Ramesh called through the glass. "I want to show you my dance moves."

And with a smile on my face, I sailed out into the night.

The End

The next **Izzy Palmer Mystery** will be available in **2024** at **amazon**

BENEDICT BROWN

A CORPSE FROM THE PAST

Izzy's about to embark on her final case.

Find out how Izzy's adventure began...

"A CORPSE CALLED BOB" (BOOK ONE)

Izzy just found her horrible boss murdered in his office and all her dreams are about to come true! Miss Marple meets Bridget Jones in a fast and funny new detective series with a hilarious cast of characters and a wicked resolution you'll never see coming. Read now to discover why one Amazon reviewer called it, "**Sheer murder mystery bliss.**"

Lord Edgington Investigates...

Have you discovered my 1920s mystery series?
It's available now at **amazon**

Get your **Free** Izzy Palmer Novellas...

If you'd like to hear about forthcoming releases and download my free novellas, sign up to the Izzy Palmer readers' club via my website. I'll never spam you or inundate you with stuff you're not interested in, but I'd love to keep in contact.

www.benedictbrown.net

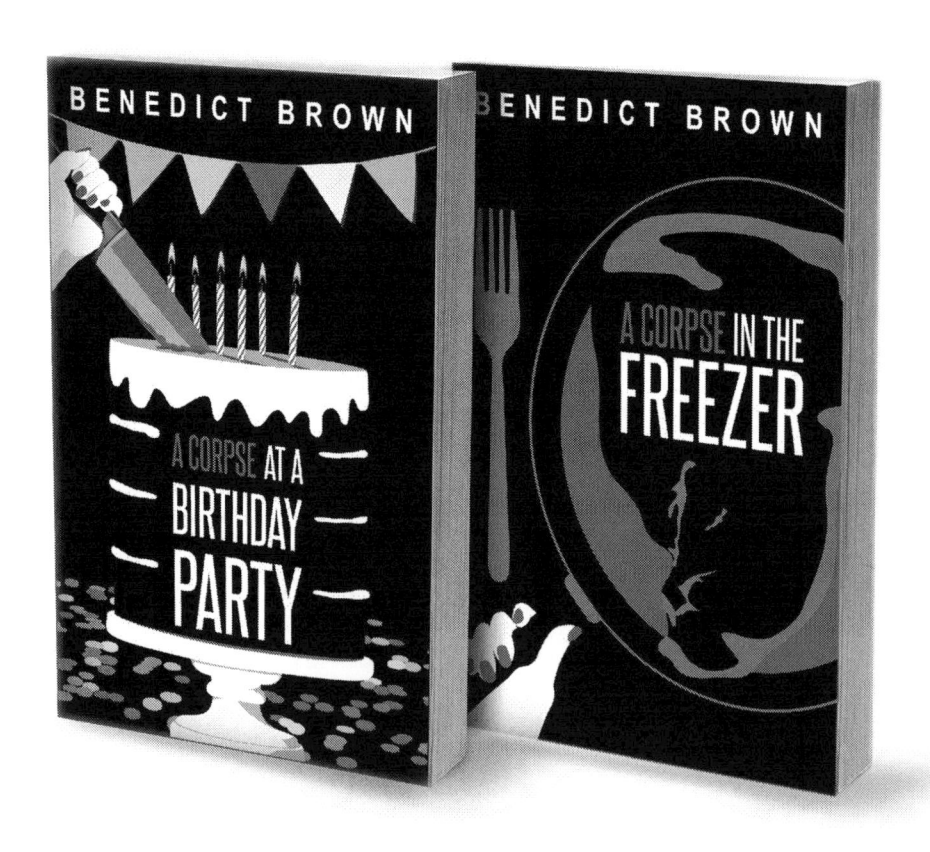

About This Book

I feel a bit emotional to be honest. There's a lot of me in this book, not least because the fictional West Wickham High School layout is modelled on my school in Surrey where I went from twelve to eighteen. It really feels as though I've spent a few weeks back there. I'm also a tiny bit moved as I finished reading this book, knowing it is the penultimate novel in the Izzy Palmer series. There will be one more for sure and, after that, I will only go back to visit the gang if I have enough money not to worry what I write, or the books were turned into TV shows and needed more #content.

People do occasionally ask me how I write from a woman's perspective, but – beyond Izzy's boy-mad mind – I don't think I make any massive changes to make her sound more feminine. I grew up wanting to believe that men and women aren't really so different. There are masculine women and feminine men, and wherever we are on that spectrum is absolutely fine. I'm not even really sure that, beyond the period language that I try hard to observe, there's a huge difference between Chrissy in the Lord Edgington books and Izzy in this series.

There's an actor called Jon Benjamin who voices various cartoon characters, from a suave spy to a middle-aged burger chef in a failing restaurant. He doesn't change his voice from one to the other, but he fits perfectly in each context. I don't think my narrators are quite as similar as that, but I do sometimes wonder.

Back to why I wrote this book in particular. When I planned out the Izzy Palmer series before writing **"A Corpse Called Bob"**, I came up with a long list of titles – I don't think that "A Corpse at a Music Festival", for example, will ever see the light of day. I remember enjoying the cheesy 90s movie "Romy and Michele's High School Reunion" – and no doubt, Ramesh did too – and I thought it would make the perfect setting for a murder mystery. I also had a mini-reunion last October at my friend Oliver's wedding where I got to see a few old school friends I hadn't seen since the day we got our exam results, twenty-two years ago. Unlike Izzy, I was really happy to see them, and we actually had a great time.

I've never even driven past my old school in all those years, let alone been inside, and yet that period of my and Izzy's life shaped us more than any other. Throughout the series, there have been references to Mr Bath, Gary Flint, Simon and the Mitchells. They are the ghosts that haunt Izzy and make her who she is. I'm not nearly so haunted by my adolescence as she is, but I was just as insecure and impressionable when I went to university and Izzy's propensity for escaping from high places was a feature of my later teenage years.

Ben, you weirdo!

Shhh!

So, yes, Izzy and I have quite a lot in common.

The difficulty with maintaining a series such as this one is that you have to show growth in your characters without resolving the plot too quickly. For Izzy, she couldn't end up with the right guy in the first book or become an uber-successful or confident detective too quickly. The nine novels and five novellas have shown her progression from geeky teenager in **"A Corpse in the Freezer"** – complete with window jumping scene! – to well-known crime-solving personality, and it wasn't just the missing squirrel that enabled that transition. If I had to put her story arc in one sentence, though, it might be "Young woman gets over high school", so this was a good way for her to lay some of those ghosts to rest. You'll be happy to know that my own experience wasn't nearly so traumatic as hers, and I never printed photos off the internet to get revenge on an ex.

With most of my books since the opening trilogy of Izzys, I've tried to write stories which a casual reader could jump into and not need to know much of what happened before to understand the plot. I think this just about holds true for this book, but there are a lot of in-jokes and self-referential moments. At this stage in the story, I've pretty much accepted that these will not be the books to make me a millionaire, though I can still dream of seeing Izzy and Ramesh's exploits turned into the funniest TV show since Father Ted. (Bearing in mind that I am an author, and we are renowned for our imaginations.)

Another element that is significant in this book is education. As

I'm sure anyone reading this knows by now, my mum was a teacher (just like Izzy's) for fifty years and I spent every afternoon until I was eleven, hanging around her/my primary school, waiting to go home. Half of the people in my family are teachers, and I have spent my life surrounded by Mum's teaching friends. So, I have a lot of sympathy for the realities of the job and, especially in Britain, it is an undervalued and under-supported profession.

There are teachers all over the UK who help their students way beyond the traditional expectations of that role. Especially after Covid and the cost-of-living crisis, it's often teachers who are plugging the gaps in social care and underfunding – for example, bringing food or clothes to students who don't have access to such necessities. To me, that sounds Victorian, and I pray that such issues will be resolved very soon. At the same time, it's teachers who are often accused of having cushy lifestyles with short hours and long holidays. I remember my mother once going three nights without sleep before a school inspection and her thinking she was useless as a teacher because of the pressures of her job. I remember her staying up until three, four, five o'clock in the morning to plan classes and mark work, and I remember the way that parents and bosses treated her, despite the fact she is an award-winning teacher who helped thousands of students – many of whom are still overjoyed when they bump into her in our town.

Hidden beneath the silliness, there is a serious point in this book about the way teachers are treated and the lack of respect our culture has for the people who do so much for our children. When I was working as an English teacher in a village in Spain, I was told by a parent whose five-year-old son had come to me to confess to scratching my car that I was lying and manipulating the child. The boy stood there in front of us and admitted what he'd done, but the father wouldn't accept it. It was one of the worst moments of my life, not because of the damage or expense, but the hatred that man showed towards me. I loved teaching, but that job in that particular school, made me even more desperate to write full time, and I'm very glad I didn't have to go back there the following year.

In this, the second book I've set in a school, I hope I've created some sympathetic teacher characters to balance out the former students

– though, of course, there are good and bad types of both. And finally, if anyone from my school in Banstead is reading this, I'd love to go to our school reunion. Terrifyingly, the 25th anniversary of our final day is coming up in just two years. Let's hope that, if anyone gets around to organising it, no one gets killed!

Acknowledgements

The people I have to say the biggest thank you to are all of you people who have read the whole series of Izzy Palmer books, sought out all her novellas, and emailed me to tell me that you've stayed up late laughing with her and her friends. I wouldn't have had the commitment to continue this series except for the love that some very passionate fans have shown her. I really want to know what happens in the next book, so thank you for that.

Special thanks are due to my crack team of experts – my cousin, Dr Heather Elliott (medicine), Paul Bickley (policing), Karen Baugh Menuhin (marketing) and Mar Pérez (dead people) for knowing far more than me. Thanks to all my fellow writers too, especially Pete, Suzanne, Rose and (the real Izzy Palmer) Lucy. I'm also very grateful to my Advanced Reading team who make such a massive difference to each new book. Please keep leaving positive **reviews on Amazon**. They really help!

Rebecca Brooks, Ferne Miller, Melinda Kimlinger, Emma James, Mindy Denkin, Namoi Lamont, Katharine Reibig, Linsey Neale, Karen Davis, Taylor Rain, Terri Roller, Margaret Liddle, Esther Lamin, Lori Willis, Anja Peerdeman, Kate Newnham, Marion Davis, Sarah Turner, Mary Nickell, Vanessa Rivington, Helena George, Anne Kavcic, Nancy Roberts, Pat Hathaway, Peggy Craddock, Sonya Elizabeth Richards, John Presler, Mary Harmon, Beth Weldon, Karen Quinn, Karen Alexander, Mindy Wygonik, Jacquie Erwin, Janet Rutherford, M.P. Smith, Robin Coots, Molly Bailey, Nancy Vieth, Ila Patlogan, Lisa Bjornstad, Randy Hartselle and Keryn De Maria.

About Me

Writing has always been my passion. It was my favourite half-an-hour a week at primary school, and I started on my first, truly abysmal book as a teenager. So it wasn't a difficult decision to study literature at university which led to a masters in Creative Writing.

I'm a Welsh-Irish-Englishman originally from **South London** but now living with my French/Spanish wife and presumably quite confused infant daughter in **Burgos**, a beautiful medieval city in the north of Spain. I write overlooking the Castilian countryside, trying not to be distracted by the vultures, hawks and red kites that fly past my window each day.

I previously spent years focussing on kids' books and wrote everything from fairy tales to environmental dystopian fantasies right through to issue-based teen fiction. My book **"The Princess and The Peach"** was long-listed for the Chicken House prize in The Times and an American producer even talked about adapting it into a film. I'll be slowly publishing those books over the next year on Amazon.

The final Izzy Palmer novel, **"A Corpse from the Past"** will be available at about this time next year. If you feel like telling me what you think about Izzy, my writing or the world at large, I'd love to hear from you, so feel free to get in touch via...

www.benedictbrown.net

Printed by Amazon Italia Logistica S.r.l.
Torrazza Piemonte (TO), Italy

48175773R00136